DEATH OF A SCIENTIST

DEATH OF A SCIENTIST

A TIME FOR WAR. A TIME TO DIE.
A TIME FOR JUSTICE?

MIKE WELHAM

Matador
9 Priory Business Park
Kibworth Beauchamp
Leicestershire LE8 0RX, UK
Tel: (+44) 116 279 2299
Fax: (+44) 116 279 2277
Email: books@troubador.co.uk
Web: www.troubador.co.uk/matador

ISBN 978 1780885 483

Cover picture design – Joe Welham

Typeset in Palatino by Troubador Publishing Ltd
Printed and bound in the UK by TJ International, Padstow, Cornwall

Matador is an imprint of Troubador Publishing Ltd

MIX
Paper from
responsible sources
FSC® C013056

This book is dedicated to victims of crime everywhere.

I

The French airforce Transall troop-carrying aircraft engines roared as it touched down, actioning the reverse thrust to bring it to a rapid stop. As soon as the wheels touched the ground the tail door began to lower, allowing the slight smell of Africa to drift into the vast open space of the aircraft's hold. It was always the same: east or west, north or south, no matter where in Africa, there was a distinctive smell. Not a nasty smell but one that told you that you were in Africa. It was in Africa, where the landscape differed but the same problems seemed to ensue wherever you went, there was poverty or war, and generally both. Whole peoples were ravaged because some tribal dictator wanted control, often over vast areas of bush scrub with little of real value. But people starving or sick meant overseas aid and that meant considerable amounts of money could be amassed by the corrupt. The country in which the aircraft had landed was no different. There were two opposing tribes, one in power and the other wanting power. To reach their objectives both sides were hell bent on destroying each other along with everything and anybody that stood in the way. In these conflicts it was always the innocent population who were exposed to brutality and extermination and, as in so many cases, outsiders got caught up in what were internal conflicts. They were generally white and providing some form of service to the population. That made them a

1

visible target for those bent on death and destruction. France had colonial links with Africa and was often in the forefront of sending military aid to help when law and order broke down. The military aid was not long term but focused on the extraction of the outsiders and not seen to be taking sides. For this operation France had deployed members of the elite 2ème Régiment Étranger de Parachutistes; more commonly known as the 2nd REP, the French Foreign Legion's parachute regiment. The Legionnaires had arrived tasked with a rescue mission that involved the extrication of some 20 French and other Europeans whose lives work had been to help the locals, but who had been caught up in a conflict with Government forces fighting a rebel force. The plan was to land by air, gather up those to be rescued and get out with minimum force and in the quickest time. The force comprised the 4th company of some 150 men, made up of 4 combat sections of 30 men. The 4th company specialized in behind-the-lines operations and provided the 'Tireur d' Elite', the snipers for the REP, trained for just such an operation. Other Legionnaires would be controlled from a tactical command post and be equipped with VPL armoured scout cars equipped with Milan anti-armour weapons and mortars as well as versatile P4 jeeps.

Among those waiting for the tail door to open and allow the Legionnaires to disembark was sergeant Dan Pierce. At slightly under 1.8 metres tall, he was powerfully built, a product of more than twelve years in the ongoing endurance-training regime which is an evolution of the Legion. Tanned from hours in the sun, his sandy-coloured-short cropped hair was topped with a green beret set at a rakish angle. It was adorned with the badge of the hand holding a winged dagger. His face had remained unscarred unlike other parts of his body that had been battered by years of harsh training and conflict. It was his life and with no other commitments, he thrived in

2

the military existence. It had taken him time to adapt to a life where the Legion controlled every hour of every day, but having attained the rank of sergeant, there was far more freedom when not on operations. When on operations he was responsible for the Regiments snipers and even trained snipers from other Legion Regiments as well as the regular French army. He had honed his skills at every opportunity with the result that he was a sniper second to none.

Darkness hung over the airport as he along with the others departed from the aircraft into the cool air. Leading his *groupe* of eight "tireurs d'elite" snipers and a radio operator, he headed towards the control tower that was just visible in the moonlight. Their ranger boots pounded the ground as they jogged past another C160 Transall that had stopped just behind theirs. They noted that its tail door was being lowered. The first task for the Legionnaires was to join up with their men who had been deployed prior to their arrival by a high altitude parachute drop. The *Commandos de Recherche et d'Action dans le Profondeur* was an elite platoon within the 2nd REP who were tasked with infiltrating covertly and carrying out a reconnaissance of the airport. Their role was to ensure that there would not be any unpleasant surprises waiting for the transport aircraft when they landed with their cargo of Legionnaires and equipment.

Some Legionnaires had moved out to secure the airport, a task that was accomplished with speed and without any opposition or shots being fired. Dan led the way as the team of snipers arrived at the control tower. Sweat had already begun to dampen shirts as they moved up the stairs, their normal small arms FAMAS rifles at the ready. Their sniper rifles were slung for carrying. Entering the tower in the tried and tested manner of 'move and cover', they quickly discovered that the place was deserted. Crossing the room Dan went out on to an open and exposed walkway. Although providing no protection, it gave a good panoramic view around the airport and he directed his men to split into their pairs and space themselves out to gain all-round cover. One from each pair scanned the ground with powerful night vision binoculars whilst the other prepared his sniper rifle. They were equipped with the Hecate II heavy sniper rifle.[1] Dan always carried the lighter FR F2 rifle, which is the standard sniper rifle of the French military.[2]

They were soon ready to engage any targets. Dan's spotter, a *caporal* (corporal) called Napoleon, had begun to get ranges for aiming purposes. The pair had become good friends as well as an effective two-man team. They acted in unison with minimum information flowing between them. Dan left the radio operator with Napoleon whilst he went down to the airport apron where officers and senior NCOs gathered at the makeshift HQ for an on-the-ground briefing.

On the runway, more Transalls had landed and disgorged more Legionnaires and their vehicles. Limited stores of food, ammunition and support equipment were held on the aircraft because this was a rapid intervention, and so the larger volumes of equipment would only be required if things went wrong or they were directed to stay. The overall plan had been

---

[1] *A bolt action rifle using a 12.7 mm round of which 7 rounds are contained in a magazine and its design is such that it has much less recoil than less powerful weapons. Fitted with a SCROME LTE J10 F1 10x telescopic sight it has a range of 1800 m. It was purpose-designed and has flexibility with a length of 138 cm that can be reduced to 114 cm with the removal of the stock. A bipod aids in the stability and an adjustable cheek rest means that it can be customized for each sniper. It weighs in at 16 kg, which is on the heavy side; it is not a weapon for general use but for taking out targets at long range with accuracy. The snipers may have a heavy load to carry, but once in action, the power of the weapon comes into its own and it is effective and deadly.]*

[2] *Also a bolt action rifle, chambered for 7.62 mm ammunition which is carried in a detachable box-shape magazine, holding 10 rounds. It is fitted with a SCROME J8 telescopic sight and has an effective range of 800 m. It is almost a third of the weight of the heavier weapon but has a length of 120 cm which makes it longer than the Hecate II when it does not have the stock fitted.]*

4

prepared before leaving camp Raffalli at Calvi in Corsica, but having arrived in the country there was a need to decide if any changes needed to be made. It had gone well so far, with everything on track to the original plan, and there had been no opposition. The Legionnaires, task was straightforward: take the airport and secure it; then rescue as many of the Europeans as possible, extract them and then extract themselves. Once the vehicles were ready, a fighting patrol departed to the town of Kanta some 15 kilometres along a tarmac road. It was estimated that up to 20 Europeans were holed up in the town and desperate to get out. The country was in turmoil as a rebel army had taken on the national government forces and were, according to intelligence, getting the upper hand. The rebels were well equipped and had made good progress in their advance. It was as in most conflicts in Africa, a situation in which the attacking force raped and murdered civilians as well as set fire to anything that would burn: it was an African nightmare, not the first and it would not be the last. The Legionnaires were only to engage the rebels as a matter of defence of themselves and those they were rescuing. They were not allowed to help local civilians and that included women or children. With no immediate change to the plan, Dan went back to his team at the tower. He watched vehicles with heavily-armed Legionnaires speed away from the airport toward the town. He checked each of the sniper pairs and then they waited for further orders.

Dan had joined the Legion having become disillusioned with the British army following the death of his brother by friendly fire in Maspamia. The impact on his family following the killing by US airforce aircraft had been devastating. He had decided to stay beyond his first five-year contract; he had been promoted to *caporal* and was doing what he wanted to do. He had always had a skill with weapons and it showed up in the Legion. Initial training had been tough, but so had that in the

5

British para's. He endured it and did well. He was assigned to the 2nd REP. His shooting skills had not gone unnoticed; he had been assigned to the 4th company and had trained to become a sniper. In a short time, his leadership skills and dedication were recognised and he was promoted to sergeant. He was now not only a sniper, but ran the sniper training courses for all comers. Being a sniper in the 4th company was hard work. Dan did not content himself with having the skill; but he took every opportunity to get his snipers out in the rugged landscape of Corsica. Legionnaire snipers found themselves in the desert, jungle, mountains and on all continents. It was a case of rehearsing for any assignment that they might be given. The training regime of the 2nd REP kept him fit. He planned to complete 15 years and then perhaps test the water in the outside world; but for now he was back in Africa, in a country that over the years tore itself apart.

Lt Clemmont, a young career officer in the French army, had volunteered for a two-year secondment with the Legion. If successful, it would look good on his record. As the officer in overall charge of the section, he joined them on the tower. He had immense respect for Dan, and allowed him virtually a free rein to command the snipers, leaving himself free to deal with the politics and the administration of the section. He also appreciated Dan's professionalism in weapon skills and the fact that he looked after his own weapons. No Legion sergeant ever cleaned his own weapon; that was left to the legionnaires to do it for them. He showed Dan a plan of the area and the road to the town. He identified a house set back from the road and pointed it out. Dan was to take his men to the house and set up sniper positions to cover the road and a track which ran alongside the house. The plan was for the civilians to be brought back on the vehicles, which would require a few trips; then once the civilians were safe, the Legionnaires would move back to the airport as fast as possible. Dan's task was to observe for any rebel troop movement and engage them if they could compromise the operation.

Dan briefed his men and they prepared to move. The long and heavy sniper rifles were slung whilst they had their FAMAS assault rifles held ready to use. The radio operator, carrying the radio as well as his own equipment, was confirming a communications link to company HQ. Legionnaires live by marching and this day was no different. They moved at a fast pace down the road that had been the route of the transport. They were spread out and had their rifles ready to use. They reached the junction where the track met the road. They were soon moving along the track, where vegetation gave them some cover. They all knew it was going to be a hot day and the water they each carried was all they would get. They had food jammed in their rucksacks and pockets, along with as much ammunition as they could carry.

The house was located, and the hand signal to move with care was passed to all the men. It was two stories high, but had an extra bit added to one end, and that gave it a third floor. Although it was set back from the road, it should give them a good view along both the road and track. Dan crouched behind a stone wall and observed the place for any signs of life. Intelligence had briefed him that it was the home of the airport manager. Having observed that nobody seemed to be in residence, Dan signalled to one of the Legionnaires to move forward with him, leaving Napoleon in charge of the remainder.

The pair moved towards the house in the classic method of covering each other until they reached the house. Once in the lee of the house, they edged to the porch and the front door. There was still no sound or sign of anything or anybody moving. Dan signalled to his cover, then bounded up the steps to stand alongside the front door. Covered by the other Legionnaire, he leant over and pushed the door handle down.

The door was not locked and began to open. Keeping back he pushed the door which slowly swung open. With his weapon at the ready he moved through the open door, his eyes scanning in all directions and the weapon following his eyes. He was aware that the Legionnaire had also entered the house behind him, his weapon also covering the area in front and up the open staircase. Everything looked in order and it appeared that the occupier had left in a hurry. Dan signalled to Napoleon, who with the others moved to the house. Leaving one Legionnaire to cover the front door entrance, the others moved quickly through the house, clearing each room as they went.

Dan moved up the stairs followed by his cover, and they checked each room. He then went to each of the upper floor windows and found that they gave a good view of the road and the track. He found the stairs to the higher part of the house and moved up them. At the top, he opened the door and carefully looked around. Nobody was at home. He called to one of the sniper pairs to join him. The open roof was edged with blocks of concrete with rails running between them creating a guard rail. There was an even better view of the road and the track. Dan told the pair to prepare a shooting position to cover the track. He did not want some rogue army unit sneaking along it.

The two men at the top prepared a position by dragging some heavy plant pots over, and whilst the shrubs did not offer any protection they did help to hide them. They also put on scrim nets to break up the shape of their heads. With four pairs available, Dan reviewed the views from two bedrooms before sending another pair to the upper roof. They would cover the main tarmac road but they also prepared a shooting position covering the track. That gave flexibility should they encounter the enemy. One pair occupied a bedroom that faced the track; they prepared a shooting position by moving furniture, allowing them to shoot well back from the open window. Dan,

Napoleon and the radio operator were in the bedroom that faced the tarmac road. The radio operator was tasked with covering the staircase.

Once ensconced in their fire positions, each sniper prepared his rifle, leaving the spotter to identify any noticeable objects and add them to the range cards they prepared. These identified objects that were readily visible, and the range was calculated. This meant that when the spotter saw something, he could use the range card to bring the sniper quickly onto target. Napoleon set about creating a shooting position and then producing a range card. Dan visited the others to make sure that they were OK. It was more of a formality than a need since these were professional soldiers: Legionnaires trained by him who needed little direction. Dan re-joined Napoleon and found the radio operator had set up his radio equipment and made contact with company HQ. He was able to pass on any orders from them, as well as keep the troops up to speed with what was happening. Equally, he could relay intelligence gained from their vantage point.

Whilst everybody was making final preparations, Dan moved down the stairs and checked each room looking for weak points that would allow the enemy to enter without making a noise. He was also looking for emergency evacuation routes should they have to abandon the house in a hurry. In a room to one side of the house he found French doors opening onto a patio. It was on the opposite side of the house to where they expected any enemy to approach. There was an open grassy area of about 10 metres to cross, and then they could enter bushy shrubs and trees. He decided that this route would give them the best option. He went into the kitchen and opened the fridge. Among the contents there was a pack of bottled water. He took eight bottles and placed them in a bag. He dug into a back pocket and found a 20€ note which he placed on top of the other bottles. His view was, that if he just took them it would be looting, and that was against Legion rules. He paid for the water; and that was his way. He then made his way back upstairs and gave out the water.

One of the observers on the upper level spotted vehicles moving down the road at speed. The sniper pulled the stock into his shoulder and put his eye to the scope. He zeroed in on them, made some adjustments and waited. The weapon's safety remained on. The prime target would be the drivers, and then anybody who appeared to be in-charge, as well as any radio operators. The spotter spoke as he stared through his binoculars. 'They're our vehicles, overloaded with civilians.' His voice was calm and calculated. The sniper relaxed and moved his finger from the trigger.

Dan responded through his personal radio, 'Got that,'

The signaller passed the information to HQ. At the airport, Legionnaires were ready to help get the civilians onto the aircraft, allowing the vehicles to speed off back to the town.

The spotter on the roof who scoured the track and countryside, looking for any sign of rebels, called out to Dan. 'Possible target out on the dirt road. Max distance.' He paused and observed. 'There's a civilian vehicle moving along the dirt road at speed.' He paused again, concentrating on the vehicle. 'It's a pick-up truck, looks like only a driver.'

The spotter's sniper raised his rifle and brought his eye to the scope. A minor adjustment, and he locked on to a vehicle that was in front of a dust cloud. He made another adjustment to the sight and then muttered, 'on it.' He slid a round into the breach and closed the bolt. Thumb on the safety catch, he readied himself for a shot. The vehicle was quite close, a cloud of dust billowing up behind it.

'Vehicle stopped,' said the spotter. 'Person out and gone to the front of the vehicle.' There was a pause. 'Lifting the bonnet and peering inside at the engine.' His voice as concentrated as his observation.

The dust cleared and the person became more visible. 'Shit,' he exclaimed. 'It's a white woman in civvy clothes.'

The sniper concentrated on looking through his scope. 'Confirmed,' he responded.

'Did you get that,' the spotter added.

'Yep, keep watching.' He then turned to Napoleon, 'keep an eye on the road; we can expect a second lot back from town anytime. I'm gonna have a looksee at what's going on with the woman.'

Without waiting for any response, he moved out of the room and went up onto the roof where the team were observing the woman. The spotter and sniper of the other pair had moved across to also cover the track. They then identified that in the distance, another vehicle was moving at speed along the track towards the stricken vehicle. The woman could not get the vehicle to start. Aware that she may have been followed she went round to the driver's door and leaned in. She came out holding an AK47 rifle along with a bag. She could see the cloud of dust moving closer and the spotter could just make out the vehicle piled high with people; and they were armed. Dan directed the snipers to prepare to fire in defence of the woman. He moved back to the door and told the radio operator sitting on the stairs below what the situation was, and for HQ to get some transport out quick to pick her up, as she was under threat from rebels. They would give covering fire. The radio operator was talking to HQ when Dan turned to look at his men targeting the suspected enemy force. The radio operator sent him word that transport was on its way to the woman, and to cover them going in.

The woman could see and hear the vehicle and she prepared herself. Taking careful aim she squeezed the trigger. The shot was well aimed and hit the windscreen in front of the rebel driver, causing the vehicle to swerve and roll in slow motion onto its side, throwing the rebels out. The Legionnaires were impressed with the woman's shooting as she selected another target and fired. She hit a rebel who, having been thrown out, was staggering about. Dan gave the order to select targets and engage the rebels. The spotters identified targets and the snipers fired when an opportunity arose. One spotter, whose sniper was engaging the rebels, looked beyond the damaged vehicle and spotted other vehicles moving along the track towards the woman. He passed the information to Dan, who had joined the pair in the room below. They joined in the action, bringing another heavy duty sniper rifle to good use. With the front rebel military vehicle crashed, others were coming into view; the snipers trained their weapons on these targets, and once in range they fired. Hitting a moving target is not as easy as a static one, but they achieved hits and sent the vehicles careering off the road either to crash or seek cover. The rebels who survived moved into the vegetation and took cover. The snipers searched them out and hit them when they showed themselves. More vehicles were observed in the distance; they were going to be more of a problem, because at least one was armoured and equipped with what appeared to be heavy machine guns.

Napoleon called Dan to announce that a vehicle flying a large French tricolour flag was speeding along the track towards the woman. Dan advised the pairs to keep shooting and observed that the woman with the rifle had fired only at confirmed targets and was aware of the fire support from the house. She then became aware of the vehicle speeding towards her and was relieved to see the flag. The rebels were not aware of the pending activity; when they realised, they began to fire at the woman and vehicle, but in doing so, they risked the sniper fire, which was accurate and effective. As the Legion vehicle slewed to a halt, sending up a cloud of dust, the woman ran over to it and was hauled onto it. With Legionnaires and the woman hanging on for dear life, it departed as quickly as it had arrived, sending up a cloud of dust providing some cover from the rebels.

The armoured vehicle was now in range and machine gun fire tore into the building; but it was poorly aimed. A spotter revealed that more vehicles had arrived behind the armour. The rebels dismounted and were infiltrating into the bush; they appeared to be heading in the direction of the house. The radio operator interjected and told Dan that HQ had ordered a rapid withdrawal to the airport. Dan told the pairs to get ready to move, but to take out the machine gunner first. No sooner said than two Hecate II sniper rifles were zeroed in on the man. Triggers squeezed. The rebel was no more and nobody rushed to take over his place on the machine gun. One sniper had what was considered to be the leader of the rebels in his sight and fired. He saw the body thrown back and no further movement. Dan gave orders to the team to withdraw. Snipers are well versed in the procedure as it is often the most riskiest part of the operation. They put the Hecates in their carry bags and slung them over their backs before moving down the stairs from the roof to the ground floor, their FAMAS assault weapons ready for close rapid fire when needed.

Napoleon had already gone down the stairs to make sure that the way was clear for the others. He caught sight of a rebel peering in through a broken window. The rebel fired a shot before he could swing his rifle into line of sight. In the exchange of fire the rebel died, but Napoleon took a hit to his side. Snipers piled down the stairs prepared to shoot anybody who got in the way. Dan saw Napoleon was down and noted the blood. Out of instinct he called out 'man down.' The radio operator relayed the information to HQ and one of the spotters joined Dan. He had medic training and began the

13

rapid process of wrapping a field dressing round the wound whilst Dan covered them. It was difficult to know how much damage was done to Napoleon, but they had to get him out; and it had to be achieved quickly. As the spotter applied dressings, Dan kept up a banter, telling Napoleon that he had to hang on because he owed him money, and that he was not going to get away with that. A sniper joined them, his rifle already slung over his back and his FAMAS ready to use. He said that some rebels were moving towards the house, and, they had to get out now. Dan had already made the decision; with help, he got Napoleon onto his shoulder and went out through the ground floor French doors of the pre-planned escape route. He ran, with Napoleon being jolted by the movement. The pain was not severe, as the powerful pain killer had been administered and was beginning to work. Dan crossed the open area of garden and straight into a large clump of bushes. They began the journey back to the airfield, moving as fast as possible. The snipers were moving forward, with their FAMAS rifles ready for covering fire. The spotters who were not burdened with the heavy sniper rifles provided rear guard cover. The radio operator was keeping HQ updated. As they progressed, Dan felt the weight of Napoleon on his back as he trudged as fast as he could through the undergrowth. Sweat poured from him. The radio operator who was behind Dan also struggled. He was weighed down with the radio, his own kit and some of Dan's. The remainder of Dan's kit was spread out between the others. They took the most direct route back to join the road; and then on towards the airport.

Napoleon was groaning with pain; but as far as Dan was concerned, he was alive and better medical help was not far away. He heard the radio operator talking on the radio, and gathered that Legionnaires from the company were moving rapidly towards them. He hoped that when they met, they would not be trigger-happy, thinking they were rebels. The meeting was instantaneous. They were moving along the edge of the tarmac road, when a Legionnaire came out from behind thick bushes. There was no reunion, just a hand indicating that they should continue to move along the road. About twenty steps further, and they met the medics with their vehicle. It was parked to one side of the road, hidden by the undergrowth. They lifted Napoleon off Dan's shoulder, and placed him on a stretcher that was fitted to the vehicle. Lt Clemmont appeared, and Dan briefed him as to the situation with the pursuing rebels. Once Napoleon was loaded onto the vehicle, a quick first aid job was administered; then he was taken to the airport and onto an aircraft, where he would be cared for by professional medics. As Dan's snipers joined the main group of Legionnaires, he watched two of their support vehicles, equipped with anti armour weapons and machine guns, moving cautiously down the road. Later, he heard the effects of their rounds, hopefully striking the rebel armour.

Lt Clemmont ordered Dan and his men back to the airport to take orders from the company commander. They jogged along the road, weighed down with weapons, and found the airport a hive of activity. One Transall full of those rescued had departed, and another was ready to go. The company commander told Dan to get his team to make their weapons safe and board the closest aircraft, adding that they were waiting to leave and to get a move on. The team needed no encouragement. They moved closer to the aircraft, turned and made their weapons safe, then jogged to the back of the aircraft and up the ramp. Dan was last up the ramp and even whilst still walking on it, it was being raised and the aircraft's engines were powered up. At full power, the brakes were released and the aircraft surged forward. Amidst the equipment and people, Dan found a seat; and even whilst finding his seat belt, the nose of the aircraft lifted as it left the ground. They were heading for Corsica.

The aircraft cabin was noisy from the engines but it was a smooth flight. When able, he unclipped himself and made his way forward through the kit and equipment, Legionnaires and a few civilians, to find two cots surrounded by medics. He could see that both men were alive and that one was Napoleon. When he got to the cot they exchanged a grin. One standing, with the other's blood smeared over his uniform, the other lying plumbed into an array of medical equipment and drips. It was too noisy to talk and Napoleon was very drowsy. With a 'thumbs up', Dan turned and made his way back to his seat. Moving carefully, he became aware that somebody was tugging on his trousers, and turned to see who it was. It took a few moments to realise that it was the civvy woman who was very handy with the gun. As he looked at her she mouthed something, but the noise of the aircraft drowned out the speech. He crouched down, turned his head and she shouted into his ear, 'Are you one of the snipers at the house?'

He nodded.

She again shouted in his ear, 'I was with the vehicle.'

Dan nodded.

'Thanks for your help, don't think I would have made it without,' she added.

Dan was mesmerized by her eyes, which seemed hypnotic. He shouted back into her ear:

'It's what we do.'

She looked towards the cots then back at Dan, again shouting in his ear, 'Your friend will be ok. It looks worse than it probably is.'

Dan just nodded.

She had seen the blood on Dan's uniform and she pointed at it. He shook his head and pointed at a cot.

'His', he mouthed.

She smiled and mouthed thanks again before he moved on to his seat. Next stop was Corsica and home; well, home as he knew it.

2

Camp Raffalli in Calvi had not changed in the few days of their absence, and they would automatically fit back into the general routine, alongside the rest of the Regiment. The following morning, Dan inspected his men and their weapons before allowing Lt Clemmont to undertake an inspection. The men knew that the weapons they used had to be cared for, as their lives depended upon them. Once the formalities were over, there was a debrief; and behind closed doors everybody had their say. Dan's view was that that was how they learnt; and so with constructive feed-back, they could improve for the next operation. The Legion had its established way of doing things, but that did not stop improvements at section level. He had just about wrapped up the briefing when a Legionnaire knocked on the door and entered to tell Dan that the CO wanted to see him in his office straight away. The Legionnaires were dismissed to the control of the corporals, and Dan made his way to the CO's office. The orderly told him to go straight in. He knocked; and at the response of 'enter', he opened the door and went in. The CO sat behind his desk, with the second-in-command standing by his side. His company commander was also present. He did not miss seeing the woman sitting opposite the CO. Dan stopped, stood to attention, saluted and gave out his name, rank and that he had been requested to attend the office. The CO told him to relax.

Dan was in the Legion and knew that when in the CO's office you did not relax.

The CO said, 'Good morning Sergeant Pierce. I have heard that Caporal Dubois, or Napoleon as he is known, is doing well in hospital. The bullet missed any vital organs and so he should be back with us soon. I have also been hearing about the actions of your team in saving this lady.' He nodded towards the woman when he said 'lady'.

'It was good work; but then you have the best snipers in the Legion, so it was to be expected.'

Dan, still not relaxed, just responded with a 'thank you, sir'.

The CO looked firm as he said,

'This lady has particular thanks to give as she had a special job to do in the country. She is American and employed by the US Government. She would certainly have been tortured and killed if the rebels had captured her.'

The woman, who was not introduced by name, had been looking at Dan; and when the CO stopped talking, she added her thanks. She had an American accent but looked of Arabic descent; but then America was a very diverse society. Dan looked at the woman and, as in the aircraft when she spoke to him, he was struck by her eyes. He could not reason why, but they were sort of hypnotic. Dan responded that he and his men were just doing their job. The CO thanked him again as did his company commander, who told Dan that he had been promoted to sergeant-chef, a senior sergeant. Dan showed no emotion, but thanked those present and departed the office. A short and to-the-point meeting which had again progressed his career in the Legion.

The Legionnaires who had been on the operation donned the appropriate uniform and departed to town for a night out. Uniforms were always worn by those undertaking their first five-year contract in the Legion. The tradition still survives.

The bars would be busy. Dan did not have to wear a uniform to go out; and so, dressed in slacks and a shirt, he made his way to the bars most frequented by the company. He found his snipers already engrossed in the art of downing beers and he joined them. He put some money up to buy a couple of rounds, finished his beer and left them to it. He walked along the street to a quieter bar. He sat outside in the warm evening air and ordered a beer. Having made the order, a car stopped close by and a woman got out. It was not any woman, but he recognised her as the attractive dark haired woman his team had supported in Africa. He had last seen her in the CO's office earlier in the day. She walked over to his table and greeted him. Formalities over, he invited her to join him for a drink. Accepting his offer, she sat and he called the waiter. She introduced herself as Rosie Portray, a name which Dan accepted. He had no idea if that was her real name; but that did not matter. The one thing he was certain of was that she was not an ordinary person. Attractive; and very handy with a weapon. With drinks, they toasted being out of a trouble-spot, and his promotion.

It was the first time that Dan had really looked at this unusual woman. In Africa she had been dressed in light brown bush clothes, and had been covered in dust. He could now see that she was, without doubt, a very beautiful woman. In fact he considered her to be absolutely stunning. He noted that she had piercing brown eyes, which made her very sexy and seductive, so that she always appeared to be flirting. When he asked her about being in Africa, she was very vague, but she told Dan that she was born in the Middle East. As she grew up, her family had moved to the USA, and so she became a US citizen. She was an interpreter for the American government, being fluent in Arabic, German and French. He considered that she was in some form of intelligence; but the woman in front of him didn't look as though she was in intelligence or a spy.

20

He was very wary of this type of flirtatious beautiful woman, because they could just sit down and chat; and then before you knew it, you'd given away all sorts of information.

Dan had asked what she was doing in Africa, especially in a country that had erupted into trouble; but she had avoided answering. Now she explained that the US Government had an interest in minerals that could be used in the process for manufacturing nasty weapons. She had gone to support a scientist who was trying to discover what countries, if any, had been supplied with any of the material. Dan had reasoned that she would have a false story, but was interested in the fact that she was open in talking about her role in Africa. He ventured to comment that her shooting skills were very good. She explained that interpreters in her particular line of business have to be adaptable and skilled in many things. Then she just smiled.

'What happened to your scientist, did he or she get out ok?' he enquired.

'It was a he, and I don't know,' she replied; then added, 'We were up country at a small township with an individual from the Middle East who spoke perfect English. Because they were going closer to where the rebels were, I was told to stay and wait for them in the town until they came back.' She sipped her drink. 'I hung around for a while and then heard shooting, so I hijacked the pick-up truck and got the hell out of the place.' She laughed and added, 'When I broke down and then saw the vehicle come down the road, I first thought it was people from the town, coming to get their pick-up back.'

Dan asked how long she was going to stay in Corsica. She told him that she had an early flight out from Bastia to Paris in the morning; then she expected to go back to the States. She asked Dan why he had joined the Legion. It was no secret, and he told her.

He explained, 'My brother joined the British army, an

21

armoured infantry regiment, so he got to go about in an armoured personnel carrier.' He paused then added, 'He enjoyed it, the travel and the comradeship.'

Looking directly at her, he continued, 'There had always been rivalry between my brother and me; so when I joined the army, it was not in an infantry regiment, but the paras. I was always winding my brother up about it. Then the first war in the Middle East changed everything.'

'How'? she asked.

'My brother was deployed because they used armoured units for the battle, and so he went in alongside the tanks.'

Dan grinned, 'The paras were not involved but were kept in the UK on stand-by, ready to go wherever required.'

'Bet that did not go down well,' she responded.

'Not with me,' he replied. 'I was at our base when I got called to see the company commander. He told me that my brother was dead.' He paused. 'It took a bit of time to sink in then I asked how it had happened,' 'They told me that it was friendly fire: an accident. I could not understand how you could get killed in an armoured vehicle by your own side.'

'Shit!' she exclaimed, 'I thought our vehicles were marked so they could be identified, especially by aircraft.'

'They were marked, and their location recorded; but it seems that the pilots were gung-ho, and any target would do,' he replied.

She tried to be positive, and replied, 'Well, those responsible could be identified and then interviewed, to find out why they fired on them.'

Dan, with a trace of anger in his voice, replied, 'The British military would or could not do anything; the Yanks refused to give out names or take any action, and the Brit Prime Minister at the time, a bloke called Proffitt, sided with the Americans and said that it was 'just an outcome of war'.'

He stared at his glass of beer, and continued: 'My father

wrote a number of letters to government ministers, and only got standard replies from some minion. That was the worst part: he lost a son, and got no acknowledgement from the man who sent him to war.' He added, 'My father continued to petition for information and help, to get those responsible to Britain to answer for their actions. Nothing happened, and in fact, in every instance, all the families were shunned. In my leave periods over the years, I went back to be with the family, but the toll on our father was immense and tragic to see.' He paused to gather his thoughts and said, 'That finished it for me: I wanted out of the army. It took about six months – but then I was out.' He looked at her again, 'I was then a lost civilian with a broken family. I needed something to take my mind off it, so I joined the Legion.'

'They say that being in the Legion is being a mercenary: how do you feel about that?' enquired Rosie.

'Well, we are all foreign fighters in an organisation that fights for France. They pay and equip us. But, as Legionnaires, we fight for the Legion and our comrades. It is a strange situation, but it works, and has worked for a long time. Am I a mercenary? Yes, I am, but not in the way that mercenaries are generally perceived. Outside, a mercenary fights for money as the main motivator. In the Legion, it is the Kepi Blanc and all that it stands for.'

Rosie quizzed further, 'Do you think that, when you leave the Legion, you will become a mercenary open to the highest bidder?'

'Who knows? That time has not come.'

There was a few moments of silence; then Rosie asked Dan about his job as a sniper.

'It's what I do best. We have a good team, and are skilled in the art. We have a lot of time for training – and so make the best of that time. Sniping is very personal. When you look through the sight, you see the face and body of the person. It's not like shooting a bunch of other soldiers, who you may or may not hit. When we fire a round, it is at an individual who can be identified. Not every soldier makes a good sniper.'

Rosie absorbed the information. She knew what it was like to face another individual, squeeze the trigger – and end a life.

Dan considered that these sorts of questions were a regular feature of meeting somebody new; but in this case, he felt that it was like an informal interview. To him, it became obvious that she worked for a US Government department; but he did not dig deeper. Then, as quickly as she had arrived, she looked at him, her eyes penetrating his, and said she had to go. 'I have to drive up to Bastia. I have a hotel reservation; and then I have to get up, to get to the airport to catch my flight.' Her parting words left Dan puzzled, 'We will meet and speak again,' then, smiling, 'Till then, *au revoir.*' She stood and walked to her car, not looking back. He felt that the 'interview' was over; whatever she had wanted to know must have been discovered; and he thought he had given nothing away. Anyway, the future was the future and he had not thought about it. In true Legion style, he ordered another beer and observed the women.

3

Chuck Cornell was born into an America where the 'land of opportunity and freedom' meant nothing to him, and he had spent his life in trouble with the authorities. He grew up in a rough neighbourhood, with a mother whose life comprised a series of men who abused both of them. He never knew who his father was: it was a case of "take your pick". His brother died when he was twelve: and the cops were not interested in finding out why. He took to the streets, and fought for his place in a gang. By nineteen, he had killed often, with severe violence: life was a matter of survival; and he feared nobody or anything. He had never been caught, and seemed to have a charmed life; but it was only a matter of time. That time had come, and he was sitting in the local jail, having been found guilty of assaulting and robbing a man with an iron bar. The man had not died, but was brain dead – and all for twenty-four dollars. The State had the death penalty; and many in authority hoped that the judge would invoke it, and that he would die. The man was not technically dead; but that was a technicality. The media were keen to get photographs of Cornell, in the short journey from the lock-up to the courtroom. He faced judge Archibald Deacon who, whilst fair in his dealings with criminals, did have a limit; and Cornell had crossed the line.

Cornell was brought into the courtroom, and it was noted

that there were more cops on hand than normal. When the judge entered the courtroom, everybody stood; but Cornell had to be dragged to his feet, a situation that did not go unnoticed by the judge. With everybody settled, he went through the formalities of defining the case and the guilty finding. He then glared at Cornell. 'You are a danger to society,' he began, 'and I'm gonna have to deal with you, so that you are no longer a danger.' He paused, 'I can't give a death sentence, although I would like to. I could bang you up in the state *pen* and throw away the key, but I am not allowed to. Our political masters have another idea that they want us judges to try out.'

The prosecutor became worried as to what hare brained scheme the judge was going to opt for. The *pen* was the only place for people like Cornell; and you did throw away the key.

'Mr Cornell, I have two choices. You can serve twenty years in the *pen*; or you can be sent to the US Marine Corps. If you opt for the Marines, you will do 10 years service. If, during that time, you commit a felony, you can be brought back to court where, without any debate you will automatically go to the *pen* and the twenty years would begin from then. Any time you may have done with the Marines would not count.'

Judge Deacon continued, 'In my mind, the Marines is the best option, because they know how to deal with problems like you; you would either come out as a good Marine, or in a wooden box. I don't mind which.'

Cornell sneered at the judge and shouted that he would go for the time in the *pen*.

Judge Deacon was not surprised-unlike others in the courtroom. He now relished the next bit. 'Chuck Cornell, you are sentenced to spend ten years in the US Marine Corps. The terms of this sentence are the following: if you commit a felony; break your service; or fail to meet the standards of the Marines, you will go to the *pen* and your twenty years, service will start at that time.' His gavel struck the block. The sentence was served, and Cornell had to be manhandled from the court by the cops. Judge Deacon reflected that it was good that he had, had additional officers brought in. He had served in the Marines and he had contacts. In Cornell's place he would have opted for the *pen*.

A police van conveyed Cornell to the Marine camp, where the cops unchained him and handed him over to the Marine police. Standing in his dirty clothes, he did not miss the immaculate uniforms of the Marines, who stood, saying nothing, but batting their batons into their free hands. He was aware that somebody was standing close to his back; and he did not like it. The person moved slowly round to face him up. Cornell was looking at the face of Drill Master Sergeant Cornelius Stamp. The two men stood staring at each other. Cornell spoke first. 'I don't like blacks telling me what to do…' Stamp interrupted, and in a quiet voice responded, 'Let me tell you something scum: I relish dealing with shit like you.' They were so close that they were almost nose to nose, 'Let me tell you something else: you are a nothing, a nobody. If you dropped dead right now, I would be angry, very angry, because you would have made a mess on my nice clean road.'

Cornell sneered; nobody ever spoke to him like that. In the *pen* he could fight for respect.

Cornell could never say how he ended up lying in the road, in pain. He looked up, and saw the immaculate Master Sergeant towering over him. Stamp told him to get up. Two MPs stepped forward and hauled him up. Cornell's brain assessed the information. He hadn't seen Stamp move. Well, that was one to him; but he wouldn't get another chance. He looked down and brushed his already dirty clothes. In fact, his clothes were dirtier than the road. 'Your road is full of crap, like you,' sneered Cornell. He didn't see Stamp move again, but he ended up on the ground just the same; and this time he could really feel the pain. That was not normal, because he could usually put pain out of his mind. He was hauled to his feet again.

'Cornell,' said Stamp, 'we can continue doing this for as long as you want – but you listen to me. You are in the US Marine Corps, and I am Master Sergeant Cornelius Stamp. You will address me as Master Sergeant. It's, sir, Master Sergeant, sir. You got that?' Cornell ended up on the ground three more times because he did not get it. When he did get it, he was marched off to the stores, and given basic kit. He did not go to the new recruits' accommodation, but to the military cell block. The cell contained a wash basin, a toilet, a wooden bench bed built in, two blankets and a small pillow. He was taken for a shower, his civvy clothes taken away, and dressed in fatigues. He was taken to a large room where the inmates ate. All furniture was bolted to the floor or to the walls.

Once he was fed, he was taken out to stand in the road. Master Sergeant Stamp was waiting. Cornell slouched as Stamp spoke to him. 'You said that my road is full of crap.' He looked up and down the road, 'Well, the only crap I can see is you; but I am an understanding person, and you may be right. So: you will scrub the road so it is clean by your standards.' Cornell looked left and right, then at a Marine holding a bucket of water and a scrubbing brush. Before he could speak, Stamp grinned and said, 'Please tell me you aint gonna do it.' Cornell began the task. Judge Deacon chuckled when he received a phone call describing Cornell's first day. Only nine years, three hundred and sixty four days to go.

If Cornell was bitter and twisted when he entered Marine Corps training, he was worse when he left; but he had learnt how to control the anger and aggression. He realised that to survive, he had to play the game. He could not beat them. He actually shone in this new job where he could kill people legitimately, and he enjoyed it. In fact, he fitted in so well that he was soon selected to join Marine Recon. This was even better, because you were first in and got instant action. In a remarkable twist, he was offered promotion – but turned it down because it would mean responsibility for others; he preferred to be an action man. Kill or be killed. Judge Deacon had taken a course of action because he thought it might solve a problem. In fact, he had perfected the development of a monster.

Cornell was a powerful well-built individual who had seen plenty of time in the gym. His face had a permanent scowl, crowned by a shorn head. He had amassed a chest full of medals, and saw action whenever he could. Whilst into his last year of service to meet the requirements of the court, he was approached by a man in a suit. He was offering him a job that would fit his capabilities. He gave little details, other than to say that if he decided to leave, there was a very lucrative job waiting. He gave Cornell a card which displayed the business name of Worldwide Executive Management. It had a Washington address. He was to give a call once he was out and they would make arrangements to get him interviewed and hopefully employed.

Cornell phoned a buddy who did some freelance work on the outside. They chatted, and he mentioned the meeting and the card. His buddy told him, 'They say that Sam Crompton, the US Vice President, is involved with the organisation. One of the bosses they say. They also say that the company does security stuff that no official organisation could do.'

'Who are the *they*?' enquired Cornell.

'Word on the street, just people talking; you know what I mean.'

'So what stuff do they do? asked Cornell.

'Well, you have a problem someplace, or an individual who is causing a problem and needs to be removed. Well, they send their people in to deal with it. They are a serious bunch,

29

said to stop at nothing to get the job done. I have heard that you have to be invited to join that part of the company.'

Cornell grinned, and said that that was the sort of job he wanted.

Cornell telephoned the number on the card. A woman answered, 'Worldwide Executive Management, how can I help?' She had a soft voice, and it was off-putting to macho Cornell. He was expecting somebody like Stamp to be at the end of the phone.

'Is this Worldwide Executive Management?' he enquired.

'Yes, it is,' cooed the woman.

Cornell gathered himself. 'I was given a business card and told to call if I was seeking some employment.'

'That's fine, sir; can you give me the identity number on the card, and your name?'

He gave both.

'Thank you, sir, do you have a pen and paper handy?' she enquired.

He did. She gave him a name, address and telephone number. He had to repeat it back to her. She then gave a date and a time, and asked if he could make it. He knew that he did not have a full diary, and said that it was ok. She confirmed that the interview was arranged for two days time.

Cornell found the address, which was an office that could be hired by the hour. The receptionist told him which office to go to. He knocked on the door. A female voice called for him to enter. Inside, he faced a very attractive woman in her thirties or forties. She told him to take a seat. He was asked a lot of questions, ranging from where and when he was born, up until the current period. He handed over his military records. She checked them against some papers that she had. She knew he was curious. She told him that they were the same as his. He did not ask how the company had acquired his military records. Once the questions were completed, she passed him four typed pages. Then she went through each page, confirming that he understood the details. It explained rates of pay, how and what expenses could be claimed. There were terms and conditions which he should read; and he needed to sign the last page. That page should be taken with him when he started his training course. He queried the need for training. The woman smiled and told him that the company had a policy and corporate procedures, so no matter the experience of the employee, everybody attended the three-day course. He was in and that was what mattered. Of course, what he did not know was that the organisation knew every last detail about him before the interview.

Thanks to the past efforts of Master Sergeant Stamp, he was a model employee, and devoted himself to the training course and the tasks to which he was assigned. Most of the work was escorting VIPs; or going into countries which the US could not openly enter in order to undertake an assignment. Months passed into a year; and it was at the end of his second year that he was summoned to an assessment meeting. He was given an address which turned out to be an isolated farm house. From the formal corporate image that he had grown used to, this was a step back.

Having driven along a long track, he parked the car in front of the house which had seen better days. His hand checked the gun, held in a shoulder holster hanging on the left side of his chest. He got out of the car, and slowly walked over to the porch and up the steps to the front door. He knocked on the door. It opened, and he faced a man who he thought was in his sixties. He was wearing a check shirt and denim bibbed trousers. His hair was grey and he was unshaven. The man asked him what he wanted. Cornell told him that he had been told to come to the address for a meeting. He showed the man the letter he had in his hand. The man looked at the letter and indicated that Cornell should sit down on one of the seats on the porch. He did as indicated.

The man didn't give a name, but looked him up and down. Cornell thought he was a bit simple. He did not speak, but waited for a reaction from the man. It was a strange situation, and reminded him of his first meeting with Master Sergeant Stamp, all those years ago. The man got a pipe out of a pocket, then some matches, and lit it. He puffed away to get it going. He looked at Cornell: 'So what yah doin ere?'

'As the letter says, I have come for a meeting – and this is the address they gave me. If it is the wrong place, I won't take any more of your time.'

Then the man changed character, 'Welcome, Mr Cornell, you have indeed found the right place. I am Lt Col Lee Chambers Jnr.' He chuckled, and put the pipe down. 'I like to have a little game. Many candidates just go and get in their cars, and go back to their company office.' He waited a moment, then asked, 'What made you stay, Mr Cornell?'

'I don't run away, sir.'

Chambers nodded. They chatted generally about his past life, and the work he had done whilst employed by the company. Chambers asked how he saw his future. Cornell knew that he could not say that he favoured going round assassinating people that the company identified as targets. So he kept it general: that he was open to any progression in his career. Then Chambers asked if he had ever heard of the Black Eagles. Cornell, like many others, had heard rumours; but nobody ever identified whether they really existed, or if it was just a name put about to scare people. Chambers gave nothing away, but stood and told Cornell to follow him. The pair entered the house through the front door. It looked as if it needed a good deal of work doing to it. Chambers clearly did not have a wife or a housekeeper. He went over to a door and opened it. They walked into another world. This was a modern room, where a younger man sat at a desk working with a computer. He did not look up when they entered, but continued with whatever task he was doing. Chambers said something to the younger man, and he stood up and left the room without saying a word. The man went to a wall that had a large map of the world on it. He pushed one half to one side, then the other to the other side. It exposed a two-way mirror.

On the other side was another room, which was stark and which was painted in one colour, a sort of off-white. A twin-tubed fluorescent light lit the room, and there was no window. Cornell saw that there was one person in the room. A male, who was sitting on a wooden chair, and leaning on a wooden table. There was nothing else in the room. Cornell studied the male, noting that he was unshaven, skinny, wearing jeans and a dirty faded 'T' shirt. He was looking around the room, and at what was a mirror on his side. He probably suspected that it was a two-way mirror. His eyes were puffy and red. Without looking at Chambers, Cornell spoke: 'Who is he?' Chambers answered, 'He, Mr Cornell, is a drug dealer and user. He ran a large number of other dealers; and his main customers were children. Some of the children died of overdoses, and others between 12 to 15 years of age had become hooked on the drugs, and became prostitutes to pay for fixes.' He turned and looked at Cornell. 'That is one serious down-side of this country. The system, if it caught them, could not or would not deal with them effectively. There are too many do-gooders wanting to save their souls. They would be locked up for a while; then, once outside, carry on where they left off.'

Cornell was shown some photos of the victims, as well as some of the press coverage that had followed the individual. Chambers then asked Cornell how he would deal with them. Chambers explained that it was easy. 'You snap their necks and they deal no more.' Chambers, devoid of any emotion, nodded. He indicated a door that led to the room. 'Well, Mr

Cornell, would you please demonstrate your option for dealing with the problem.' Without any hesitation, he walked over to the door, opened it and entered. He closed it behind him. The man, still sitting, looked up. He stood up and said, 'How long are you bastards going to keep me here? I've been kidnapped and kept prisoner, and there's gonna be shit to pay if you don't let me go.' He then confirmed the statement: 'If you don't let me go right now, somebody is going to pay.' Cornell told him it would not be long, and walked round behind the man. It took seconds to grab him, put an arm round his neck, grab the side of his head and jerk it round to hear his neck snap. The man became a dead weight, and Cornell let him fall to the floor. The door opened, and Chambers entered the room. Still devoid of any emotion, he said, 'Well, Mr Cornell, you have just become a member of the Black Eagles, the assassination department of Worldwide Executive Management. Cornell grinned: he had made the big time.

4

John Finch decided at an early age that he wanted to be involved in science, but it was many years before he moved towards the more focused and secret world of chemical and biological warfare. His interest was heightened at University, where he met a fellow student who had survived a chemical weapons attack and managed to escape. There were still the scars and lasting medical problems – but the individual had decided to devote his life to the eradication of such weapons. The young Finch was captured by the random devastation of the weapons, and the types of people who were prepared to use them. He was aware of the gassing of soldiers in the First World War, and had read up on the use of gas produced and the effects on its victims. That was horrific enough; but now despotic leaders were developing and acquiring chemical and biological weapons to use on civilian populations, as well as on enemy military forces. At an early age, John was classed as a "boffin", today; he would probably be called a geek. He was a swot who was quite at home experimenting, gathering data and pondering issues. He dressed the part: he remained conventional, and the relentless changes in fashion did not enter his head. He wore what he considered was comfortable and appropriate for him.

He began to accumulate information about the germs and chemicals that were available, and how they were or could be delivered to a target. He realised that it did not require volumes of a product to produce a disaster. A very small quantity could kill thousands. Whilst he had a passion for that aspect of science, his early employment was in laboratories, where he worked on various less exciting research projects. Much of the work was for overseas countries, and as a result he developed contacts with numerous like-minded individuals in many parts of the world. His thoughts always returned to the warfare aspect, and he discovered that the major powers of the world had such weapons in their war stocks. They used them as a counter-threat, or even as a threat of blackmail against an enemy considering employing them, or putting down a country's own population. The reason that most countries gave for the development of such products was that they could thereby develop and produce antidotes. They would be available should such an attack occur; or for selling on at big profit to countries who needed antidotes because they were facing threats. The supplies of chemicals and bugs were to a degree controlled, but with a lot of unscrupulous people in positions of authority, germs and chemicals became available to the wider world; and so into the hands of the wrong people. The one thing Finch realised from the beginning was that no one person could stop the proliferation of the deadly materials. Power and greed were the driving force, and that spread to all nations. None were immune.

With a doctorate in microbiology, his collection of data and global contacts, he was an ideal candidate to be recruited by the Ministry of Defence (MoD). A major threat of bio-chemical weapons came at the time from the Soviet Union, and he took up a post as a technical expert in the interpretation of data emanating from the Soviet Union. It followed that in due course he was appointed to a post in biological defence at Porton Down, the British centre for bio-chemical weapons and warfare. He was now immersed in a world of the deepest secrecy, where the object was to determine exactly what potential threats there were, and from where. Scientists could then work on antidotes and suitable clothing for working in contaminated areas. He progressed to become a senior adviser to the UN inspection agency, Unscom; and when the organisation began to undertake inspections in Maspamia, he led the first biological weapons inspection mission. He knew that President Akrawi had used such weapons in previous wars, and had also used the weapons to attack his own people. The weapons were dangerous, and so was the man responsible; and the west would be heading towards a conflict with him.

That was the future, and he would become deeply embroiled; but now, Dr Finch checked his notes for a final time. He was waiting his turn to take centre stage in a conference about bio-chemical weapons. He had been selected to represent the UK. In fact, he had no need to check his notes, as he knew the subject inside out; but then so did others who were attending. His task was not to challenge or discuss specific aspects of the subject, but to educate those attendees who did not know about Chemical-Biological Warfare (CBW). The chair of the conference waited as the applause for the previous speaker died down to give time for Finch to take his place on the dais.

'Ladies and gentlemen, our first speaker gave us food for thought about the changing world we live in, and the politics that are emanating from those changes. Now we have the great pleasure of hearing from Dr John Finch, from the British Ministry of Defence, who will provide an overview of what Chemical-Biological Warfare is all about. Dr Finch has made it his personal mission to examine such weapons, and to assess their impact on potential targets. He has gathered data from around the world, and has made valuable contacts in many countries. He is among the most knowledgeable scientist on the subject, and holds academic achievements in microbiology. Ladies and gentlemen, please welcome Dr John Finch.'

Finch nodded to the chairman and looked into the audience. His eyes scanned the sea of faces, as he waited for their polite applause to die away. He was aware that such a topic could be boring to some, and he had to hold their attention. He would watch those faces because they would be the indicator. The yawns, the looking down, the eyes looking around the room instead of towards him. He would, however, focus on those who were listening and taking onboard what he was saying.

'Good morning, ladies and gentlemen.' He paused, 'I would like to thank the organisation for inviting me to speak on a subject of special interest to me.' He paused again, 'Chemical-Biological Warfare, or, to use its acronym, CBW, involves the use of chemical and biological agents as weapons. Generally, the chemical agents used in warfare are substances such as gases, liquids and solids. They are used because of their poisonous effects on people, animals, and plants. The other group are the biological agents, which are harmful microorganisms, more commonly called germs; and it is the toxins, or poisons, that they produce that causes the harm.'

His eyes scanned the audience: no yawns, no snoring, even some interested note-takers.

'Once you have CBW's in your weapon store, they can be directed against an army, civilian population, plant and/or animal life. In this way, large areas can be affected. Take, for example, water supplies that we all take for granted. Our water supply reservoirs can be easily contaminated. It takes just one person to deposit an agent which would affect every person who has access to that water. The quantity of agent needed can easily be carried by one person; and, once released, spreads rapidly.

To a degree, chemical or biological agents can be used to

contaminate a limited area through the use of localised dispensers, such as aerosol sprays, hand grenades or mines. For example, a suicide bomber could have a device which when it explodes, spreads a toxin in the area that would affect the rescuers and the people who are close by. This could occur in a crowded place, so that those who survive the explosion die from the toxin.'

He paused to allow the information to be absorbed.

'For an attack over a large area, the use of artillery shells, bombs, aerial sprays, or missiles are the usual delivery systems. However, there are risks to those delivering such weapons, as it is almost impossible to devise adequate protection: gases and biological agents, once employed, are difficult to control – and their effects are unpredictable. For example, in the First World War, when gas was used, it was reliant on the wind direction. A sudden change of direction, and the gas you had delivered on the enemy would come back to you. Such weapons are indiscriminate, and kill unless there is rapid use of an antidote, or the use of protective clothing. Evidence shows that those who have used such weapons have little regard for those victims who were not the intended targets. Where civilian targets have been attacked, and the military who went in to secure the area were not adequately protected they themselves also died. It was probably cheaper to get more soldiers than to provide protective equipment. Such weapons can be very small, but can have devastating consequences. A person could carry a very, very small container into this room and release a toxin that could kill all of us in a few minutes. It would not destroy the building or the room. That could be cleaned. Those seeking a terror war with access to such material would, and, I think, will create havoc.'

He allowed just enough time for the words to sink in.

'The question is, what agents are out there and available?'

Again a pause. 'Well, for a biological agent to be used as a weapon against humans, it needs to have high infectivity, high virulence, little to no access – or even availability – of vaccines; and there needs to be an effective and efficient means of delivery. The production of the biological agent is not an obstacle, as many such agents used in weapons can often be manufactured relatively quickly, cheaply and easily. The problems come when it needs to remain effective after a prolonged period of storage. In addition, there has to be a delivery vehicle to a vulnerable target; and that poses significant problems for, say a country wanting to deliver the weapon onto another country. For example, if one country decides that it wants to attack another that is located several thousands of miles away. It has to have a weapon that is accurate, reliable, and which can reach the target. That is most important if the delivery system has to over-fly a country which is not involved in the conflict. There is nothing worse than dropping such a devastating weapon on unsuspecting recipients. Those using such weapons will require a supply of an agent or toxin that is "in date" to be effective.'

Finch turned a page of his papers.

'One of the most effective agents, and one known to be held by a number of countries is Anthrax, or to use its scientific name, *Bacillus Anthracis,* which can easily be controlled, and can even be created in a garden shed. It is considered an effective agent for several reasons. It forms hardy spores that are perfect for dispersal using aerosols. The organism is not considered transmissible from person to person, and so rarely if ever causes secondary infections. A pulmonary anthrax infection starts with ordinary influenza-like symptoms, and progresses to a lethal hemorrhagic mediastinitis within 3 to 7 days, with a fatality rate that is 90% or higher in untreated patients. The one advantage is that personnel can be protected with suitable antibiotics. However, there are technological difficulties in the production of this agent that relate to its storage.'

He looked again at the sea of faces.

'There is a long list of agents and toxins that are available in varying degrees. For those who are interested, I have produced a list that can be found at the end of my paper. I will not read out the list, or focus on any particular one. You may recognise some names in the list; if not, you can research any that you are interested in.'

He took a sip of water.

'The development, production, and use of chemical and biological agents has been a controversial subject for a long time. There are those who argue that such weapons provide a military weapon at a relatively low cost. They add that such weapons provide a combat alternative to the use of conventional armaments and nuclear warheads. They will also say that most CBW agents are intended to incapacitate, rather than kill – which, of course, most conventional weapons do. Those who oppose such weapons argue that CBW agents are dangerously unreliable. Their use could result in countless human casualties. I will quote one example: one ounce or 28 grammes of botulism toxin could kill 60,000,000 people. Imagine that in hands of terrorists in a city or town.'

Finch continued and took the subject into the more complex arena of anti-crop/anti-vegetation/anti-fisheries and anti-livestock. He showed a series of photographs of the effects of CBW weapons. His summing-up was equally focused:

'We have to monitor and control those countries who have, or can develop, agents and toxins and who, most importantly, we consider has or will use them. I focus on Maspamia. I do that because they are known to have such weapons, and to have used them on their own people. Using our teams of weapons inspectors, we search for such weapons; but we have to have access to a country, and they have to allow us to inspect any facility. Those we find, we can destroy; but it is a most difficult task.

He paused for effect.

'So, the work done by Chemical and Biological Warfare Inspectors is vital. It is dangerous, with high risks for the inspectors, as well as for those who are being inspected. When something is found and has to be inspected, the question is always: what will we find? The Inspectors do not get treated as important guests and looked after. It is quite the reverse. They are not wanted. Added to the problem is the fact that in say, a country, where we anticipate there being such weapons, its authorities can, whilst being inspected, move any material to other parts of the country, or even to a neighbouring country. That country may well get rewarded with a supply of such material for its own purposes. The task is never-ending, and the threats from such weapons must never be underestimated.'

He looked at the audience, then at the chair, 'Thank you.'

He was greeted with a warm and extended round of applause. The chair thanked him for his contribution.

At lunch time he spoke with colleagues, some of whom he had met face to face, others through telephone calls or e-mails. One person he had had no previous contact with introduced herself to Dr Finch as Rosie Portray. She said that she was a translator, and that she had been assigned to escort him on his inspections in Maspamia. Born in the Middle East, she was fluent in a number of languages including Arabic and English; and she was now an American citizen. It was not lost on him that Rosie was a very beautiful woman. However, she was an interpreter who had been assigned to the UN's weapons inspection team, and that was where it ended. He was unaware at the time that she was with American military intelligence, and probably trained to cultivate anyone who might be able to help her in her intelligence work.

5

President Dexter S. Franklin sat behind a large desk in his official office. He was studying a report from the defence department. As he flipped through the pages, it was clear that the build-up of troops and weapons close to Maspamia was well underway. He had a deep-felt anger towards President Akrawi of Maspamia, and wanted him gone. They had had one war in an effort to unseat him, but because of the UN limitations, they had stopped short of a real victory. Akrawi took advantage of the situation and rattled the sabre, threatening all sorts of retribution – including chemical and biological weapons – if anybody should attack him again. Franklin vowed that this time, there would be no stopping. A man of medium build, round-faced, dark-haired and with a slight southern drawl to his speech, he was noted for not being a good public speaker, but instead just shrugging off any comments. He had been elected because there had been no alternative worth speaking of, particularly in the opposition. Most importantly, he would do what the hawks wanted; and the hawks ran the country. The US had seen some poor decisions made by the doves, and had decided an eagle was what was required. They got a President who could be steered by eagles, and now many of the people regretted it.

There was a knock on the door and, before he could respond, the door to his office opened, and he looked up to see

Sam Crompton, the Vice President, enter. They exchanged brief greetings and engaged in general conversation whilst they waited for their trusted and selected aids to join them. Crompton was, and remained, a successful businessman; and he headed some very large, powerful corporations. Rumours abounded about what were alleged to be unsavoury business methods, but he just shrugged off any questions posed by the media. They, for their part, never found evidence to prove anything. One of the most controversial topics was his close links to the private security firm Worldwide Executive Management. It was alleged that the organisation operated with unorthodox methods in the way it conducted its business. Speculation abounded in the media about its possible operation of death squads against its political opponents. It was further alleged that they were killing the wrong people in the wrong countries – and that those countries were finding out about it, or at least that there was a suspicion that the countries might find out about it. Those who tried to find out more were stalled or, so it was said, assaulted, or at worst, eliminated. It remained, however, just speculation until somebody had the evidence to show otherwise.

Franklin swivelled round in his chair to face Crompton, who had sat on the other side of the desk. Franklin placed his hands together, fingers pointing up and touching, and said, 'I've heard from the joint chiefs of staff that the build-up is going according-to-plan.'

Crompton nodded, and added, 'We will just need to decide on a date to get in and kick arse.'

Franklin picked up the report of military deployments, and said, 'With what we've got, they're gonna wish they'd never heard of us.'

Crompton grinned. 'I've started to have draft contracts drawn up for a rebuilding programme, for after the event. We flatten the country, then rebuild it. We will also be the sole recipient of the oil revenue, once we have got it back on line. I say that, because the bastard will set fire to the oil fields. It's the oil money that will pay for the rebuild programme. We're talking billions of dollars.'

'What about those oil fires?' enquired Franklin.

'It's not a big problem. I have one company in mind that specialises in putting out oil fires, and another that gets the oil back on line. They are planning for the operation as we speak. Teams will be moved out there once the action starts, and some of the operatives have worked on those oil fields. They will follow the military in, and sort out the mess,' replied Crompton.

'That's good, so we have most bases covered.'

'Not all: there is one left,' added Crompton.

'What's that?'

'We are sitting holding this lot, with no real direct support from other countries, although some are making the right noises. We need help to get the UN onside. At this time, it's us against the world,' declared Crompton.

'We will have the UK onboard, it's just a matter of time. Proffitt needs to sort his people out. Some are talking about it being an illegal war, and forgetting that it's a war on terror.'

'He needs to sack them or buy them off, but we do need some action soon.'

Franklin raised another matter: 'We need evidence of chemical and biological weapons, and we don't have it. We have got people looking, and we've got people looking at those doing the looking; but nothing has been found. Proffitt's got his head scientist out there, but no progress has been made.'

Crompton was not happy. 'Why can't these people make it happen? If I had run my businesses like that, we would have made no progress.' He looked around the room. 'Who is this scientist? Do we have a name?'

Franklin moved some papers on his desk, and found what he was looking for. 'Dr John Finch, he's a specialist in bio weapons.'

'Not much of a specialist, if he can't find chemical and biological weapons in Maspamia!' countered Crompton.

There was a knock at the door and, after a short pause, an aide opened it. Franklin looked up, and told those waiting to come in. The three aides who entered were trusted with the highest of the countries secrets, and they knew that this was another unofficial meeting. There were no notes or minutes to be taken. Crompton, the hard, powerful businessman enjoyed the politics and the additional power it gave him. They knew that he had been pushing the President to set a date for the invasion of Maspamia. To him, it was simple: the country held the third largest reserves of oil in the world and the US had to have control over it. In fact, Crompton was adamant that the US have control over it. His argument was that the very existence and survival of the US relied on it. Franklin had listened to all the arguments, and endured the pressure from the powerful war lobby, the very same people who had made him President. Oil was not the only key part in the game; the arms manufacturers were also keen to go there to test their weapons, and of course to keep the production lines open. But Franklin hesitated. He argued that they needed the support of the UN, and from countries outside Maspamia. He knew that his best option was to get the UK Prime Minister's support for a war. Franklin had already spoken to Proffitt about the plan to topple President Akrawi and free the country. But he needed visible support.

The three men, Danny Davis, Cy Santana and Chris Champion, were told to take seats, which they did. Franklin brought them up-to-date with the state of the US military build-up at various locations around the world. At the right time, they would move forward, ready for the invasion. He explained how he needed credibility and support, and that this could come from the British. If Proffitt went with him on this, others would follow – or at least not intervene. However, Proffitt had hesitated: not that the electorate mattered, but he, like many government ministers, was planning his future – and that was based upon financial security. If he was hounded out of office for joining them, then he needed a safety-net that would provide the support and wealth that he sought. Franklin knew that Proffitt could see an opportunity, and that he would have to exploit it. Now that was Crompton's language: he knew how to deal with that.

Cy Santana, a tall slim, southerner, raised a question: 'Sir, there is a lot of talk suggesting that to invade would result in an illegal war. How do we stand on that?'

Franklin thought for a moment, then responded, 'Getting the UN to support an invasion would be the best option, but you all know how they pussy about. I'm told we could use the old mandate; but that falls short of actually getting Akrawi out of power. That has to be the main objective, otherwise we are wasting our time.'

'That's what I thought,' responded Santana, then added, 'so we have to give them a cause, and the best cause is chemical and biological weapons, and that Akrawi is prepared to use them.'

Franklin mulled over the point. 'That is the answer but, as I was saying to Sam before you came in, the inspectors who are out there looking for them have not found any. I agree that if we found some evidence that would show that they have such weapons, we would have a just cause in the eyes of the UN to go and make the place safe, ousting Akrawi at the same time.'

Compton grinned. 'What we need is evidence, and for that we will need scientists to find it – or we need to get them to say that they have. They can have some photos taken, and provide the UN with a report: we can do that. Hollywood could make it look real good.'

Franklin nodded, then told Santana to look into the situation, and see if he could get a report from scientists to the effect that Maspamia did have chemical and biological weapons, and that Akrawi was prepared to use them. The focus of the invasion would then be based on stopping their use, and not on toppling the leader.

Santana added, 'Mr President, I've already pre-empted that, and set the wheels in motion; in the strictest confidence, of course.'

Franklin sat back in his chair, and said, 'Well done.' He liked people taking bold pro-active initiatives. It gave him somebody to blame if it went wrong.

Crompton added that the opportunities for US companies were good for the US economy. Mega bucks would be earned. With that in mind, he also added to the conversation that he fully supported the military concept of a massive air and missile bombardment of the infrastructure. Once Akrawi was deposed, the country would need to be rebuilt. So, after victory, a friendly leader could be installed – and the oil could be sold to the US at a "special price". So America would gain all round.'

Franklin saw the picture unfolding, and pressing his finger tips together, spoke in a slow drawl to all in the room: 'Ok, so we are agreed that we need others to participate in this. Going it alone will place all the crap on us. We also need to find these dangerous weapons that threaten the region.'

'Well, as you have always said, we do have a special relationship with the Brits, and Proffitt would probably have no qualms about going to war,' added Santana.

'I agree; but I anticipate that Proffitt would want some inducement to join the war,' replied Franklin.

'That wouldn't be a problem; we could help him to get

established when he leaves office. He could take places on company boards with remunerations. He would want some contracts in Maspamia for UK companies, but the bottom line seems to be that it's what goes into his pocket that counts, not Brit businesses,' concluded Santana.

Crompton added to the debate: 'I'll talk to some people outside the US, and set up some deals. We are providing support to a few countries, and I'll call in some favours. I will also get him put on the board of one of our financial organisations as an advisor. He'd be on the board but have no input: he'd just be receiving big cheques.'

Franklin nodded agreement, then added: 'We all know that another thing that motivates Proffitt is being the centre of attention. He just loves himself and hearing himself talk. He is so far up his own arse...' He paused, then continued: 'I agree that he is motivated by an overpowering desire for money, and lots of it. So we give him those things, and he will bring the Brits into the war with us. In fact, he is so full of crap that he may even get support from other European countries who listen to him.'

Santana smiled, and said, 'Yes, that would work.'

Franklin turned to look at Davis, who was over six feet tall, of stocky build with good looks, and who sported blond hair. He was a charmer when he wanted to be:

'Danny, will you get in touch with Proffitt and tell him to get his arse over here. He needs to get here as soon as possible. We will meet at the ranch and keep it low key, that way we will be out of earshot of any snoopers. Also, tell him there are to be no wives. Mrs Franklin does not like Mrs Proffitt.'

Danny had been tasked with dealing with Proffitt on many occasions, and knew how to sort that out. He responded that he would get straight to it when he left the meeting. Chris Champion was often described as geeky, but that belied the fact that he was smart, very smart. He was about five feet six tall, slim going on thin in build, and he wore large glasses. He was not outgoing, but would sit quietly in a meeting, absorbing all that was being said then, at the appropriate time, would add a show-stopper idea or solution. Now was that moment. 'Sir' He always addressed Franklin formally. 'We could also offer Proffitt a Presidential award, for services against, say, terrorism and for peace. That could be at a gathering, where we could get together a group who would listen to his speech, and then make a lot of appreciative noise. We could hold the event after we have invaded, and when it suits us. I was thinking that if, following the invasion, there were still questions being asked of us, we could bring him in to carry some of the flak. As you say he's so full of bullshit, when he speaks some may actually believe him.'

Franklin thought that it was a great idea, and directed Champion to put a proposal together.

Crompton added, 'So the plan is: we need evidence that we can present to the UN showing that we have a rogue state which possesses chemical and biological weapons, and the need to get in and kick arse before they are used against us and our friends'.

'Gentlemen, that just about sums it up. Keep me advised on progress; but we do have a tight time frame.'

With the main business completed, the aides checked diaries, and dealt with other minor matters which needed clarity or confirmation. The meeting closed, and the three men departed, leaving the President and Vice President to continue discussions. Danny Davis had a vision of them working out the bonus profits they would each receive; and who else would get a share. He put the thought right out of his mind, as he knew that thoughts like that did not get you fired, they got you dead.

6

The telephone rang and Proffitt answered it. The operator who dealt with his telephone calls stated that it was President Franklin's office. He was put through to Danny Davis of the Presidents office. Davis apologised that the President had not made the call personally, but that he was conveying a request for an urgent meeting. Proffitt asked Davis if there was a proposed agenda, and about the level of urgency. Without going into detail, he told him that the meeting would be at the President's ranch, and that it was being held to discuss the growing threat in the Middle East. He added that the meeting would be very low key, and then, that no wives were to be included. Proffitt understood, and said that he would speak with his secretary, and sort out the earliest date he could travel, and that his people would get back to the President's office. The call had come in during the night, and now, at breakfast, he pondered the visit as he helped himself to another slice of toast. The family were getting ready for their day's activities, when his private advisor, Edward Reilly, joined them. He had free access to the home when it came to matters of state. Proffitt relied on Reilly, who was outside of the official political jungle, and who told it how it was. Proffitt could take or leave the advice; but when dealing with ministers or senior civil servants who opposed him, Reilly always had an answer on how to deal with the situation. It was an unusual situation: Reilly, as an unelected member of Proffitt's parliamentary inner sanctum, had attained a position of considerable power, and was not answerable to anybody other than Proffitt. That caused him to be distrusted, even hated, by the majority of those whom who he encountered. That did not bother either of the men.

'Ah, just the man!' exclaimed Proffitt, as he indicated a quiet part of the room. 'Had a call from Franklin's office. He wants a meet. Didn't give any details, but it is about ousting Akrawi.'

'Do you need me to come over with you?' enquired Reilly, taking the cup of coffee and plate of toast offered by Mrs Proffitt.

'No, it's a restricted low-key meeting. It's a case of fly over, then fly back. Probably spend more time in the air than on the ground,' replied Proffitt, then added: 'The one thing that concerns me, is that there is no UN mandate to invade. So, if we are to be involved, we need a bloody good story to sell it.' Proffitt looked at Reilly: 'What do you think?'

Reilly had been thinking of little else. 'What we need is a dossier, put together by a combination of the Foreign Office, the MoD and the Security Services and identifying a serious chemical and biological weapons threat. If the evidence is strong enough, then the UN will provide a mandate to remove the threat; and that way we will be saving the world. I also think we should refer to the threat as 'weapons of mass destruction', WMDs: it sounds better, gives it a bit of impact.'

'What about Dr Finch? He is leading a UN team in Maspamia, why has he not found anything?' enquired Proffitt, although it was more of a thought than a question.

'Bloody government scientists, put themselves above everybody else, and do not put the country first,' responded Reilly.

Proffitt considered for a moment, and then added: 'Well, we can't make him find things that are not there, but we can get the departments to use what data they have and put it together.'

Reilly then proposed a plan: 'I think that the information should come to the Cabinet Office, where I can control what goes in the dossier. If there are any gaps, then we can fill them in.'

'The dossier will be read by Finch, so what do we do if he makes claims that the evidence is not true?' asked Proffitt, who was looking for a credible document.

'Who is going to listen to him? He is not even a senior grade civil servant, just a scientist doing a job. If he claims that he has not found anything, then that's one thing; but we can claim that our spies in the Middle East have provided other information. Of course we will not be able to divulge the source, as that could put lives at risk, and we need our spies. The Cabinet Office will produce the document that will convince the UN.' Reilly was happy with his plan.

'OK: you get to work on it, and I will formally announce that Maspamia has WMDs, and, we are preparing a dossier showing the threat. When it is published, it will be presented to the UN and the USA. It will also stop the critics in the government.'

Proffitt phoned through to his private office and enquired about his diary: what could be changed, and when was the earliest he could travel? As soon as they had sorted that out, they could get in touch with the President's people and arrange the meeting.

Proffitt looked at Reilly and said, 'We are moving closer to war.'

'We just have to rebalance the scales,' added Reilly.

'Yes; but it means more body bags and more questions.'

Reilly shrugged and said, 'People join the military to go to war, and they have to carry the consequences.' He took a bite into a slice of toast. 'This is good!' he muttered.

7

Proffitt flew first class on a scheduled flight. He had argued for an aircraft to be at his disposal, to replicate the one available to the US President. The whole idea had been criticised, and it was one argument he had lost, for the time being. Landing in America, he did not have to go through the formal immigration process. Leaving the aircraft via the walkway, he was guided by security agents to a door and stairs that took him down to the stand where a car awaited him. It was not the normal entry he would expect; it seemed to him like a back-door entry. No press or flag-wavers were on hand to capture the moment. The car, escorted by secret service people in another car, sped to another part of the airport, to stop alongside an executive jet. The car door was opened; he got, out walked a short distance and climbed the steps into the aircraft. He was greeted and welcomed by Danny Davis from the President's office. As soon as he and his luggage were onboard, the aircraft engines started up and it took off ,to head south. Davis had been briefed by Franklin, so that he, in turn, could brief Proffitt about the overall situation, and the object of the meeting. Of course, Proffitt realised that it was for the President and, Prime Minister to get down to the business of commitment for the pending war. When they landed, Proffitt stepped off the aircraft. Once again, there was no reception party, reporters or dignitaries, just a quiet airport in the south of the country. He, Davis and some security people walked across the tarmac to a helicopter, which they boarded. Proffitt reflected on the fact that he, as the UK Prime Minister, had travelled a long way; and there was no official greeting, no crowds and no media. The helicopter lifted off the ground, tipping its nose down to allow the rotor blades to grip the air and power it away from the airport. Proffitt had nothing to do but sit and admire the view.

Then, seemingly in the middle of nowhere, the President's ranch came into view. It was a large, two-story building that sat in an expanse of cattle pasture. The helicopter banked and headed for the heli pad, a clearly visible red H. It was set a short distance from the house, and allowed easy and private access. Proffitt noticed a large number of cars parked to one side of the house. The aircraft lifted its nose, and came to a stop; it hovered, then lowered down onto the ground. Once set down, the pilot closed down the engines, allowing the rotor blades to stop, whilst an aide ran across and opened the door, to allow the passengers out. Proffitt exited the helicopter and saw Franklin walking towards the aircraft. They both had large grins. The two men walked to greet each other with a hug and then shake hands. It was then that Proffitt realised that there were a number of reporters and camera crews present. His grin now became a permanent feature. The exaggerated shaking of hands for the benefit of the cameras, and the small talk completed, they both walked back towards the house. On the steps, Franklin turned, and with Proffitt beside him, faced the press who moved closer.

He waited for them to settle, then spoke: 'You are witnessing an historical event today, as I welcome Prime Minister Proffitt, of our British allies in troubled times, to our country and my home. We are, together, facing an enormous challenge posed by terrorism and, in particular, a certain Middle Eastern country. As you know, our combined military forces, as well as those of some other nations, are assisting with the fight against terrorism and those who conduct it. Intelligence from the British confirms our intelligence that Maspamia has chemical and biological weapons. They are in the form of missiles, and can strike our friends in the Middle East, as well as our troops in the region. It is on this basis that there are UN weapons inspectors in Maspamia, who are still looking for the weapons and production facilities. We know that those weapons can be moved about and hidden from the inspectors. That complicates the situation. To counter the threat, we are gathering a joint military force in the region, should we need to seek a mandate to defend the free world against a very real aggressor. This is a fight for our very survival.' He paused for effect. Proffitt nodded agreement. One reporter noted the pause.

'Mr President, is it inevitable we will go to war?'

'That is a very good question. We have continued in our endeavours to get President Akrawi to surrender his chemical and biological weapons, but he has failed to do so. He claims that he no longer possesses such weapons. We know otherwise, and we will be left with little choice but to disarm those weapons, before they do any damage.'

'Mr Proffitt,' called another reporter, 'is Britain in full agreement with this? And are you willing to go to war?'

'The British government, with myself as the leader, are fully in support of the President on this. We have weapons inspectors in Maspamia as we speak. We also have other intelligence suggesting that there are chemical and biological weapons to be found in that country. In fact, we think that they should be called 'weapons of mass destruction', WMDs, because that is what they are. This is a very serious situation, as we know President Akrawi is prepared to use them. I have come over to meet with President Franklin to review the situation, and to discuss the way forward on this very subject. Yes, we are onboard with you in this.'

Franklin then called a halt to the informal press conference, and the two men turned and entered the house. The media quietly departed to their transport and were then on their way to their various offices. These media people were selected as the 'good guys', who would follow the presidential line, and present the cause in a good light.

Once inside, Franklin looked at Proffitt, 'I like the "weapons of mass destruction" and WMDs tag.'

'Thought you might, it gives it a bit more emphasis,' responded Proffitt.

Proffitt was shown to his room, where his luggage had already been placed. He took a shower and changed his clothes. He then went to find Franklin, who was in his study. He was sitting with Sam Crompton. Greetings were exchanged; then the men found comfortable chairs in which to sit. 'That went OK,' said Franklin, opening the conversation.

Crompton, who had kept out of sight during the press brief, agreed, 'I thought it best to keep out of the way for that one, but we do manage a lot of the media, so I didn't expect any problems.'

Proffitt added, 'I wish I did, I get some real aggravation.'

Crompton looked at him and said, 'Well, sometimes you need to kick arse. That's what we do: kick arse, or move people out of their jobs if they don't follow the line.'

Proffitt did not respond to the statement, but moved the conversation on: 'When I left the UK, Edward Reilly, my advisor, was in the process of gathering what intelligence we have, and is producing a dossier to support the case for war.'

'Have you got the scientists onboard with WMDs or are they still searching for them? Don't they realise that the regime will just keep moving any stocks of materials around the country? It is not going to admit to having such weapons,' added Crompton.

Franklin picked up on some tension between the two men,

and brought them back to the focus of the meeting. 'OK, once we have the dossier from you, we will present it, along with our own evidence, to the UN. They are full of crap about these issues, but our legal people say we will have to do it. Once we have their approval, we will unleash the military. I note from the Chiefs-of-Staff that we are progressing well with the build-up.'

'Probably another week, two at the most,' added Crompton.

'What's the plan if the UN don't buy the dossier?' enquired Proffitt.

'We go with the previous UN resolution we used,' replied Franklin.

'My advisors say that those were different circumstances, and so we can't use it.'

'Sack your advisors, and get some that see the bigger picture and toe the line!' It was Crompton who spoke, and he was quite serious.

There was a knock at the door. Franklin called out, 'Come in'. His aide Danny Davis entered the room. 'Excuse me, sir, but there is a call for Prime Minister Proffitt.'

Proffitt excused himself, and left the room to go and take the call. He made a short walk to a small office, and Proffitt listened as Reilly spoke: 'We have been working on preparing the dossier, and adding in more intelligence to give it some clout. Should be ready for when you get back.'

'Good,' replied Proffitt, 'any major issues?'

'Just Finch! It appears that he is unhappy with the inclusion of WMDs because there is no evidence that there are any.'

Proffitt considered for a moment then said, 'OK, get his department to keep him in line. This is very important. I am supporting President Franklin with this, and we need a positive approach. When I get back, we need to agree the dossier and get it over here to the President, so it can go to the UN. Anything else?'

'Some of the committees are getting a bit jumpy over the information that is going into the dossier; they want to take Finch's line, as he is the expert,' replied Reilly.

Proffitt responded, 'Right, I need you to chair those meetings, and to keep them under control. Also, any member of the cabinet who becomes awkward, take them out of the information loop. If they complain, refer them to me. We have to keep everything on course: I am committed to the President in terms of military action.'

'Leave it with me,' confirmed Reilly. He relished the authority to weald power over ministers and senior civil servants.

With the call finished, Proffitt rejoined Franklin and Crompton. He told them that the dossier was almost ready for publication, and that it would be copied to them as soon as it was. They both nodded. Crompton asked if there were any dissenters. Proffitt explained about Dr Finch and his concerns about WMDs because, as the senior inspector, he had not found any. Crompton said that people like that had to be dealt with. He added that, if he continued to have problems, to let him know because he knew people who could deal with them. Proffitt did not respond to that statement; he had enough issues to deal with and didn't want to be bothered by veiled threats. The three men had spent two hours in discussion, when Franklin insisted that they go outside for a stroll. Some fresh air in a beautiful location would be a welcome break. As they left the building, one of the security detail joined close by.

Crompton spoke to the man, then turned to Proffitt. 'Neil, please meet one of our top security people, Mr Cornell. He works for a private security company, and deals with awkward assignments.'

Proffitt turned, and faced a man who, by appearance alone, showed that he could look after such matters. 'Hi, pleased to meet you.'

'Mr Prime Minister, I'm Chuck Cornell, I provide close protection and security. Good to meet you.' Cornell immediately moved back half a dozen paces.

'You get problems? Hire Cornell, and you have no more problems. You need help, just let me know, and I will speak to the main man in Worldwide Executive Management; he is a personal friend,' said Crompton.

Proffitt knew by instinct that Cornell was one person you would not cross, or get on the wrong side of; and he pushed the thought of Cornell out of his mind, at least for the time being. The meeting continued into the morning of the following day, when Franklin called a halt to the gathering. They had heard from a range of people, and had the latest updates. Then, as quickly as he had arrived, Proffitt was airborne on the journey home. He made notes to up his campaign to have a private jet dedicated to the Prime Minister, and to those who tagged along.

8

Whilst Proffitt was out of the country, Reilly had remained in London, keeping a close eye on the activities of ministers and civil servants. He was described by many as an 'outspoken renegade', who owned up to a plan when it went well, but dumped it on some other poor sod when it did not. This was an occasion when he owned a plan that had to go well. But, cautious as ever, he already had the fall guy, engrained in his mind. He had ordered the Cabinet Office to gather information and prepare a dossier. He needed it done by the time the Prime Minister returned from America. The initial task of gathering data had already begun, and involved the work of a special adviser to the Foreign and Commonwealth Office (FCO). He had put together a document that was initially called 'the Middle East Weapon Status', and was comprised of information that was publicly available. The document, when completed, was presented to a Parliamentary group for consideration. In essence, the document described a number of countries whose leaders posed a threat. It singled out President Akrawi of Maspamia as being one of those who was considered a 'demonstrable threat to the stability of the region', and argued the case for the UN weapons inspectors to continue the search of the country. It also hinted that a military option might have to be adopted, if the threat remained.

Whilst the document set the scene, it needed to be more specific, with facts and intelligence data added in. This meant that, once the document had been reviewed by interested parties and commented on, Proffitt could commission a dossier to be produced. It would focus on weapons of mass destruction (WMDs) in four countries. One of those countries was Maspamia, and it would highlight the fact that President Akrawi was actually threatening to use the weapons and destabilize the region. At the same time, the Cabinet Office had produced a document on the history of the United Nations Special Commission (UNSCOM) weapons inspections. The document was shown to the appropriate people at the Foreign and Commonwealth Office, including Dr John Finch. The problem was, that if there was a conflict between the written sources and Dr Finch's expertise, the latter having been actively involved on the ground, the committees and departments would tend to go with what Dr Finch said: after all, as they pointed out, he was the expert. That was exactly what Reilly did not want. He wanted a case for war.

The first draft of the dossier was produced, and it comprised a number of separate sections. There was a section on Maspamia's WMDs; a section on the history of UN inspections, drafted by the FCO with the help of Dr Finch; and a section on President Akrawi's human rights record. The first dossier was published and circulated to the FCO, the MOD and Downing Street. It was classed as a document for comment.

A reporter seeking more information about the Prime Minister's dossier met Dr Finch at a London hotel. It was not unusual for reporters to cultivate a relationship with civil servants, particularly ones with specialist knowledge of issues such as WMDs; and, most importantly, those who really knew what they were talking about. Difficult questions were asked, but the answers sought were not forthcoming. Secrets were secret; and the boundary could not be crossed without a good deal of problems for the person making the breach. The reporter wanted to know about any weaknesses in the dossier, especially ones that may discredit the Prime Minister and his ministers. It was simple: Finch could not and, even if he could, would not tell him, because he did not know all the details. He explained that many hands were involved in the drafting process, and that he had to concentrate on the small part he knew about and had specialist knowledge of.

The Prime Minister read the dossier, and concluded that it lacked real evidence of the serious threat of the use of WMDs; with which the UN could be approached for their immediate approval of an invasion. Reilly thought it was weak and rather pathetic. He immediately issued a directive for its modification to the departments involved in its creation. It needed more focus on the threat and the weapons available, to a degree that would paint for the world a very real and probably an exaggerated picture of pending disaster. The whole document needed to be both more upbeat, and to promote the idea of the threat. The heads of the departments involved in its production were very wary of Reilly. It did not help that the bottom line was, that the dossier was the basis for a war where President Akrawi would be toppled. It was not a course of action that the UN would consider accepting, no matter how it viewed the man, unless the threat was real and the prospect of discussions ruled out. Of more concern was the idea that they were being told by a person with no legal or elected authority to prepare a dossier that would allow a conflict with global implications. Those who had looked at, or commented on, the legality of such a venture were sidelined. The real problem was the fact that none of those who were reviewing the dossier had seen one shred of evidence that would support the assumption of the existence of WMDs ready for use. They knew that the Prime Minister was playing a very dangerous game, and that Reilly was in the driving seat: a man who, like his leader, was expert at deflecting the blame if things went wrong.

* * * *

Sandy Crossman, the Head of MI6, was concerned about the way events were heading, and telephoned Lord Clive Smithson, the Attorney General, to seek an urgent meeting. Lord Smithson was expecting some mad plot to evolve, and this appeared to be the beginning of it. The two men made space in their diaries as a matter of urgency, and met at a private members' club. Ensconced in a quiet corner, Crossman revealed the instructions he had received, and from whom. Lord Smithson waited until he had finished. His immediate reaction was, that he understood that it would be illegal to go to war without a UN mandate giving approval, and that that needed solid evidence of the existence of WMDs. In addition, there needed to be evidence that such weapons would be used, or that there was a very serious threat that they could be used. He made it very clear that just deposing a despotic dictator would be a blatant breach of international law. Crossman agreed, but added that Reilly, apparently acting on behalf of Proffitt, was running around various departments, ordering the fabrication of a dossier. Those who challenged what was happening were taken out of the loop and ignored. Lord Smithson asked if there was any evidence in the dossier that supported the WMDs option. Crossman had focused on what was happening in the preparation of the dossier: neither he, nor his department had received any information to support such statements; in fact, the opposite seemed to apply. The weapons inspectors were drawing a blank and, on the ground, spies could not provide any positive information. Smithson asked who was in the "team" for putting together a dossier.

Crossman was able to provide some names; but the one who was only reviewing the dossier who, and, in his opinion was the one that really mattered, was the bio warfare scientist, Dr John Finch. Smithson thought that his opinion would be the most appropriate, but noted that he did not support some of the details being proposed for the dossier. Crossman said that he had spoken to Finch, and that he had advised that the inspectors had found no evidence to support the case for WMDs claims.

Smithson raised the point that 'everybody knew' that, in the past, Akrawi had used chemical weapons against his own people. However, following the earlier conflict, the weapons inspectors had found – and destroyed – what could have been WMDs, but had not found any other evidence since. Lord Smithson enquired as to whether there would be any input from other inspectors, as they could come under interference from Reilly. Crossman had considered that point, but it appeared that they all concurred with Finch. He added that he himself had to agree with Dr Finch, as the UK's leading expert on chemical and biological weapons: he had spent months in Maspamia looking for just such weapons, and his reports had concluded that there were none. The plan was that Dr Finch was to continue the search, along with other specialist inspectors, but that at this time there was no hard evidence. Smithson concluded that, until there was hard evidence, Proffitt should not rattle sabers, as any military action would be illegal. He would write an official note to Proffitt telling him this. The two men parted company, knowing that when Reilly found out that they had met, and were to all intents and purposes debunking the plan, all hell would break loose.

9

Reilly entered the meeting-room, located in one of the grand buildings in Whitehall, and used by the civil service and committees to conduct its business. A long table with matching chairs from a past era added to the grandeur. It had been set up for a Joint Intelligence Committee meeting. Members of the committee were present and awaiting the call to start the meeting. Some were standing and in discussion with others; some had taken their seats and were exchanging words with those sitting alongside. Reilly ignored everybody, as he walked up to the seat next to the chair of the committee and sat down. He placed his papers in front of him, and told the chair that he was himself chairing the meeting. Before the chair could say anything, Reilly leaned over, and said that if he did not like the arrangement, then he could go and take it up with the Prime Minister. Reilly called the meeting to order. The attendees looked first at Reilly, and then at the leader of the committee. He asked the members to do as requested, and to take their seats. The meeting was scheduled to review the content of the updated dossier, and then to give the committee's approval for its adoption.

Reilly addressed the meeting: 'The Prime Minister has instructed me to chair this very important meeting.' He paused to allow the statement to sink in, then continued: 'Has everybody received a copy of the dossier and read it?' He looked around the room for any dissenting voices. There were none. He continued, 'The Prime Minister is not happy with the contents of the first draft of the dossier, because he considers that it does not have enough impact, and that there is a lack of evidence about weapon's of mass destruction. These are chemical or biological weapons or as we now call them, WMDs; and this is a serious matter. What this means is that those responsible for its drafting have not been forceful enough in their use of language.' He again looked at the faces of those around the table. 'I have to remind you all that this document is the foundation for a war on a country that has the potential to create serious collateral damage and loss of life.' He emphasised the key words. He then added, 'The Prime Minister is focused on supporting the US in its war on terror, and we now have a country with a rogue leader, President Akrawi, who has created a threat that has to be dealt with.' He then explained, 'To pacify the UN, and the rest of the world, there needs to be justification – and we are tasked with producing the evidence.' Reilly then ensured that each of those attending the meeting had been provided with a list of the changes that he had suggested to be made to the original dossier.

'Chair,' summoned one committee member.

'Yes,' replied Reilly.

'You talk about WMDs but Dr Finch refers to them using their original acronym CBWs, or, to give them their full title, chemical and biological weapons. Why has their title changed?'

'We have decided to give the threat more meaning.'

'What, to sort of "make it look more cool"?' responded the committee member.

Reilly did not reply.

'Chair,' summoned another committee member.

'Yes,' replied Reilly, annoyed that somebody had not got the message, and had wanted to question him or the changes sought.

The member addressed his question by looking at the real committee chair, and not at Reilly: 'The information you want to add talks about Maspamia having weapons of mass destruction, and quotes this a number of times; it is included in the forward provided by the Prime Minister. It also states that there is a 45 minute time element for launching these weapons. I have not seen one piece of evidence that supports this. The question I would ask is: where exactly does this information come from?'

'Intelligence,' snarled Reilly. 'We have gone to a number of sources, including intelligence sources in Maspamia, and those reliable sources have provided us with that information.'

The committee member continued, much to the annoyance of Reilly. 'When this document was prepared, Dr Finch, the UK's chief weapons inspector, addressed this committee; he stated that no such weapons were found, let alone a time frame for the delivery of such weapons. In fact he showed us evidence of what the UN inspectors have been doing, and that the country itself was in a bad way, following its previous war. In summary, Dr Finch has found no evidence whatsoever of WMDs, and he doubted that there was a capacity to manufacture such weapons. Are you saying that there is evidence that contradicts his report?'

Reilly was annoyed. 'There is more than one source of intelligence, and so Dr Finch must be wrong.'

Another member signaled to Reilly and joined the debate. 'Mr Chair, I have to support my fellow member's questions, because you are asking us to agree to this country' committing itself to a war, when there is no substantive evidence available, none that we have seen anyway.' He paused just for a moment, then continued, 'You say Dr Finch must be wrong, but he has been in Maspamia specifically to look for WMDs – and he is the UK's leading expert.'

'There is evidence,' replied Reilly, who was getting quite

angry. He waved a document in the air, 'there is evidence.'

Another member joined in. 'Mr Chair, you are waving a document about and saying that these are evidence that chemical and biological warfare weapons can be launched in 45 minutes. But what credibility does it have? The weapons inspectors have not found anything; the secret service has not provided us with information. Surely this committee has a right to know where the information comes from?'

Reilly was angry. He did not like to be challenged, especially in meetings. The committee members knew that, and also that those who questioned Reilly would have to watch their backs. One member leaned over and whispered to another that the devil was brimming with fire and brimstone.

Reilly whilst angry, was still in control. 'I am telling you that this information is correct, and that we need to act now to deal with a regime that will use them.' He almost hissed the words out. 'Further more, the information is accepted by the Prime Minister, and so your acceptance should automatically follow.'

Another member joined the debate: 'Mr Chair, the matter of whether the Prime Minister accepts a report is not a matter for a committee that represents all parties. We examine, the evidence both verbal and documentary, and produce our own report based on the findings. We have done that in this case, and found no evidence to support the claims now being made. I would suggest that, as a committee, we would not change our view.'

Reilly hated these committees. 'The evidence you seek is in the documents you have been provided with; and they spell out the situation very clearly.'

The next question came from the other end of the table: 'Mr Chair, the members are clearly concerned about what is to be added into the dossier. I would like to raise an issue. In the current dossier, we already have information on page 12 which is an evaluation of chemical and biological weapons in general, and a reference to Maspamia in particular.'

'Yes,' responded Reilly, who really wanted the meeting over.

The member's words were slow and deliberate, 'My own research has shown me that this particular section offers us such a gloomy picture because the information has actually been plagiarized from an American university student's thesis. In fact, what makes it worse is that it has been quoted almost word for word, with only a few words added in order to make it more forceful. I have a copy of the thesis, the student's name and university. In his own words, he confirms that the information is not factual, but a synopsis of what could possibly happen in the future.' He paused for effect then concluded, 'What you are in effect proposing, is adding more fiction to an already flawed document.'

The room went silent. Many members felt a great deal of satisfaction, but of course did not show it. Nobody spoke; and all eyes were on Reilly. There was a long pause before Reilly responded. 'The dossier you have in front of you was produced by Downing Street. Everything in it is factual with regard to the topic we are discussing. I propose that the additional information about the 45 minutes to launch WMDs should be added to give it strength, and so provide a basis upon which the Prime Minister can go to the UN and seek a mandate to go to war. I know nothing about a university thesis, or an American student; and nor do the people who have drafted this document.'

Reilly waited, but nobody spoke. There were no more questions. He then said, 'I take it that your silence approves the amendments and the production of the final dossier for distribution.'

The committee's elected chair added the closing words: 'It is fair to say that this committee has reviewed all available evidence, and has concluded that there are no bio-chem weapons to be found in Maspamia at this time. We had not heard from our colleague about the university thesis. That is a matter that clearly needs to be reviewed. On that basis, I would propose that, unless there is a proposal otherwise, the committee does not accept the current dossier or the additional material.

Silence befell the room. Nobody accepted the dossier.

Reilly looked around the table and announced: 'The meeting is closed.' He stood and walked over to the minute-taker. 'Are those the notes of the meeting? he asked. The man nodded. 'OK, I will take them and get them drafted and distributed.' He left the room.

Back in Downing Street, Reilly tore up the minutes and vented his anger about the Joint Intelligence Committee on Proffitt, who had already heard about the meeting via telephone calls expressing concern. Once Reilly had calmed down, he identified the dissenters in the meeting; but Proffitt was aware that he was treading a very thin line and, unlike Reilly, did not want to rock the boat. Reilly departed to delegate the task of amending the document to civil servants, and not to the intelligence services whom he now considered untrustworthy. Reilly wanted the dossier to be really damning – and he was out to get Dr Finch.

10

The Joint Intelligence Committee report was ignored, and the final draft circulated to various departments. It included details of the weapons of mass destruction. There was a claim that Maspamia had probably dispersed its special weapons, including its chemical and biological weapons, and that that was why the inspectors had not found them. It now included a section where Intelligence sources indicated that chemical and biological weapons could be ready for firing within 45 minutes. The plagiarized American university student's thesis also remained in the amended dossier. The dossier was circulated, and carried a note to the effect that it was going to be printed and distributed, and that the need for any urgent amendments should be communicated as soon as possible.

Dr Finch's line manager at the Defence Intelligence Staff (DIS) arrived at the office, and found Dr Finch engrossed in a copy of the revised dossier. He was aware that the contents of it were in dispute; its inaccuracies were the talk of the department. He soon discovered that most staff who had knowledge of the situation were unhappy with some of the information in the dossier. He knew that they were right but, if the political master decreed a course of action, as a civil servant he and his staff had to follow. He also recognised that there was a real need to manage the staff with regard to the media, and not just at the junior levels but amongst those holding more senior positions. Dr Finch was particularly concerned about some of the dossier's contents. As the country's leading chemical weapons expert, he knew that there were statements in the dossier that did not accurately represent the assessment of the intelligence available.

The following morning, a meeting was convened as a matter of urgency. Dr Finch was among the participants. Their objective was to review the dossier, and to identify the incorrect statements. After a number of hours, the outcome resulted in a number of pages with detailed comments entitled: "Chemical and Biological Weapons Dossier – Department's Comments on the Revised Draft."

A copy of the comments was sent to, and received by, the Cabinet Office. Reilly took the time to read them, then flung them on a desk in anger, leaving an administrator to pick them up. He contacted the Prime Minister to advise him of the situation. They discussed the options, and Proffitt made his decision: the comments were to be ignored, and the dossier was to be sent to the printers'. The title of the dossier had now changed to: "Maspamia. The Chemical and Biological Weapons Threat"; and as such it was published.

Dr Finch was one of a few who had actual practical knowledge and experience of WMDs. He and some of his colleagues read the parts of the dossier where the information was unreliable. It was evident that large portions of the dossier had been cut and pasted from articles available on the internet. He had already heard about the inclusion of a PhD thesis, where the student had gathered material that was in the public domain. He was alarmed to discover that some of the information was 12 years old. When it was checked, it was found that the wording of some of the plagiarised material had been altered. What this meant was that Downing Street had "plagiarised and manipulated" academic material by inflating figures and exaggerating Maspamia's weapons capability. The dossier now included a statement that weapons of mass destruction were available and ready for use within 45 minutes.

Dr Finch despaired, because there was not one shred of evidence to support this statement; it was completely incorrect. The 45-minute claim was not just an added detail, but was the very foundation of the evidence that President Akrawi posed an imminent threat to the world. Finch was incensed because the claim was repeated a number of times in the dossier, including by the Prime Minister himself in the foreword. Reilly had insisted that the claim should be included, and did so against the express wishes of the intelligence services and the government experts in WMDs. The Prime Minister and his advisor had produced a document that would show the world that a war was the only option.

John Finch watched the television as the Prime Minister announced the publication of the awaited dossier at a press conference. He had met with the President of the United States of America, and it seemed that they, too, also had intelligence that had been gathered to show that there were WMDs in Maspamia that could be launched in minutes. The country and its despotic leader were shown to be a real threat to world peace. The Prime Minister said that Britain would support its ally the USA in the invasion of that country in order to rid the world of these dangerous weapons. He focused on the fact that the despotic leader had used such weapons on his own people, and on those of a neighboring country. He closed by saying that the British military were preparing for battle. Finch turned the television off, and immediately received a phone-call which was to be the first of many. Some calls were from colleagues who were angry that the authors had failed to take account of credible intelligence. Like him, they were aware that nothing could be done. Dr Finch knew that this was no "intelligence failure". There was no intelligence with which to fail. The dossier was a complete fabrication.

* * * *

Following the publishing of the dossier, there was a second meeting between a journalist and Dr Finch at a London Hotel. Knowing that he had upset a number of people in key positions, and probably the Prime Minister himself, he was very guarded as to what he said. He also knew that he was not alone in his communication with the media. There were a number of people in positions of authority who would relish the opportunity to drop the government in the mud; and they had far more media contacts than he did. There was also the fact that, in such delicate proceedings as these there was always somebody further down the chain to carry the can when it all went wrong.

It did not take long for the media to report that 'a source involved in the drawing-up of the dossier' had made the comment that 'the government probably knew that the 45 minute figure was wrong, even before it decided to put it in'. The source had also said that Downing Street had ordered the dossier to be 'made more exciting'; and had then ordered more facts to be discovered. The source further claimed that, in the run-up to publishing the dossier, the Government had been obsessed with finding intelligence on immediate threats, and had been desperate for information which could be released. The figure of 45 minutes was seized on. It was that which became the focus of the media's attention. Finch gave out no such information or details. It was considered to be an accumulation, of information gathered by a number of sources and combined with a journalist's flair for filling in the gaps of a story. Finch reflected on the old adage: 'never let the truth get in the way of a good story'.

In his role as Attorney General, Lord Smithson wrote a letter to Proffitt, telling him that the deposing of Akrawi – even though he was a despotic leader – through the invasion of Maspamia, without just cause, would be a blatant breach of international law. It was intended to make Proffitt call off his plans to join the US in its invasion. As he signed the letter, he knew that he would be ignored, and even targeted as a trouble-maker. His view was that he had done his duty, and that now the responsibility lay with the Prime Minister. He knew that Proffitt could talk his way out of any situation that developed, and that Reilly, unelected, would just dump any fall-out on civil servants. Lord Smithson's letter, addressed to the Prime Minister, was not read by Proffitt until after a Cabinet meeting. That was when Ministers were secretly told that the US and UK were set on 'regime change' in Maspamia.

That decision went against all sound advice. The war could not be justified purely on the grounds of 'regime change'. The United Nations rules permitted military intervention on the basis of self-defence; that did not apply in this case, because Britain was not under threat from Maspamia. The UN could allow "humanitarian intervention" in certain instances, but that was not relevant in this case. The letter, when read, caused utter pandemonium in Downing Street. Proffitt was furious. Reilly was even more furious, declaring all sorts of retribution. By writing the letter, Lord Smithson had placed on record information that both Proffitt and Reilly wanted to remain private and outside of the public domain. Reilly was tasked with telling Lord Smithson that he should never have put his views on paper, and that he was not to do so again unless told expressly by the Prime Minister himself. Lord Smithson questioned the response. He argued that it was his job to advise the Prime Minister on legal matters, particularly if it was in the national interest. He was told that the reason was simple: if the letter became public, it could make it impossible for Proffitt to fulfill his secret pledge to back President Franklin in a war to oust President Akrawi. More importantly, it could never be removed from official records, as copies were stored in the archives as well as in the Attorney General's office.

Then the full force of the Prime Minister's fury was revealed when Lord Smithson, who had Cabinet status, was told verbally that he could only attend meetings in the future when specifically invited. Proffitt, under guidance from Reilly, liked to do things with no note-takers, and in unofficial conditions. That way, there was no record and everything could be denied. Following the issue over the letter, Lord Smithson barely attended another meeting until the eve of the war. Proffitt also wanted him kept out of meetings in order to reduce the chance of spreading dissent to other Ministers. Proffitt even went as far as concealing information from his own Cabinet, fearing it would spark an anti-war revolt. The only people Proffitt told were a handful of his close cronies, who were sworn to secrecy, and who were at his beck and call. Even they were monitored, and reported on by Reilly.

11

President Franklin and Vice President Crompton had become preoccupied, and even obsessed, with President Akrawi and Maspamia; they had clearly decided that they were going to bring about a regime change. The question of a threat from Maspamian weapons of mass destruction was the foundation of their policy in the lead-up to the invasion; but they, as indeed did Prime Minister Proffitt, really needed more solid evidence to support the case for war. The decision had already been made, but to keep public-opinion on side, they needed to show the people that the case was real, and that American lives were at risk. Neither Franklin nor Crompton actually believed that the country was still producing and stockpiling WMDs; what they really believed was that any attempt to prove false their assertions that Akrawi did have such weapons was most unwelcome, and had to be dealt with.

The dossier produced by the British proved to be of value in the case put to the UN. All of the flaws in its content had been kept secret. However, it was very evident that Dr Finch, the leading British chemical and biological weapons scientist and weapons inspector had, behind the scenes, rocked the boat. During the preparation of the dossier, he had challenged details within it. His main point was the fact that the weapons inspectors had not found any evidence of weapons. Finch had been flagged up as a concern to the US Administration and the

Pentagon because he was a prominent expert, but was not on board with the scheme. Franklin, and in particular Crompton, had never really had faith in any of the United Nations' weapons inspectors, even their own. They considered that they were much too professional – much too neutral – for their liking. That was the reason for the insertion of secret service operatives into the weapons inspection teams associated with the operations in Maspamia. They travelled in and out with the inspectors, but it was never explained why they were there and what they were doing. As far as the weapons inspectors were concerned, they just seemed to hang about and watch what was going on.

* * * *

The lack of any evidence that Maspamia had weapons of mass destruction did not stop the coalition action; and the war machine, once under way, was almost impossible to stop. The world watched a massive aerial bombardment, as aircraft and cruise missiles destroyed key targets over a number of days. The emphasis was on the capital and the seat of government, as well as military targets. One outcome of the 'dodgy dossier' was that troops waiting to move into the country on the land warfare side spent a lot of time dressed in chemical warfare suits, awaiting the threat of WMDs to become a reality. With the main impact of the air war completed, the ground battle groups moved in, with the country's capital in their sights. The main cities were virtually destroyed by the air attacks; thousands were dead; the oilfields were set alight; and the elite Maspamian Guards were decimated. Everything was going according to plan, and President Akrawi was on the run. The anti-war lobbies were in full cry, and Franklin and Proffitt were desperate for somebody to find some WMDs. With boots on the ground, allied soldiers searched for the weapons of mass destruction, and as soon as it was safe to do so, weapons inspectors were deployed.

President Franklin was asleep when the telephone rang. His orders were specific, in that he was to be kept informed of any developments, and so, as he reached for the telephone, he had no idea what sort of message he would receive. The main strike was over, cities and towns were captured. The population had been freed of Akrawi and his henchmen, but now allied troops remained in position and they would become targets for terrorists and remnants of those loyal to Akrawi. He knew that the death toll of the military would continue to rise, and that the anti-war lobby would become more vocal. The voice at the other end announced that they were from the Defense Intelligence Agency (DIA), and that they were calling about Maspamia. The message he was given was straightforward. Ground troops had captured two mobile biological warfare laboratories mounted on trailers. Franklin's first thought was that that explained why the weapons inspectors had not found them: the Maspamians had kept moving them. Full details and photographs were being transmitted as they spoke. Franklin was more than pleased, he now felt vindicated against the claims that it was an illegal war.

With the message delivered, Franklin called Crompton and gave him the news. Crompton sounded surprised as he asked, 'They actually did have WMDs, then?'

'Well, they had the means to make them, and that's good evidence,' replied Franklin, who was smiling.

They agreed to meet at the White House early the following morning, so that they could get the media bandwagon underway. Franklin then called Proffitt.

Because of the time difference, there was a short delay whilst Proffitt was found and brought to a telephone. With the good news delivered, the pair indulged in self-gratification. It was agreed that Franklin would announce the news to the world;

after that, Proffitt could follow up the story in the UK. In the meantime, it would remain a secret until they were ready to go public.

A press conference had been called, and a flurry of reporters, photographers, and TV channels had people in place. Franklin walked up to the dais and stood with a hand either side holding on. A smile beamed from his face. 'My fellow citizens, today I can tell you that we have found weapons of mass destruction in Maspamia. They are, in fact, mobile biological weapons laboratories. Allied ground troops in ongoing operations discovered and captured two trailers. As you know, the existence of WMDs has been central to the case for war – and now we have the hard evidence that proves we were justified.' He paused among the clicking of cameras. 'Their existence had long been predicted by the Administration, and so, with the leader defeated, the evidence that we and our allies had been looking for is now a reality.' Franklin answered a number of questions, but avoided detail. He was leaving that for others.

In the UK, Proffitt called a press conference, and made the information public. The US forces on the ground had done what the weapons inspectors themselves had failed to do: they had found WMDs. Dr Finch had not heard the news, and it was a telephone call that alerted him to the situation. He was dismayed that those in authority were proclaiming a dramatic find. He knew what the troops had found, and they were not related to WMDs in any way. He also knew that, as the media delved into the story, they would soon come up with the same conclusion. Why had such a stupid statement been made public?

* * * *

Franklin was at his desk in the White House when Crompton joined him. 'Dexter, I've got real bad news, we are deep in the crap', declared Crompton.

'Can't be that bad,' grinned Franklin, still on a high following the WMDs news.

Crompton slumped down in a chair, 'Worse,' he said.

Franklin was all attention.

Crompton leaned forward, his hands clasped together tightly enough to make them change colour to a bright red, with white gleaming at the joints of the fingers. He looked at Franklin. 'The message you were given about the WMDs was crap. Pure crap. What we were not told was that the Defense Intelligence Agency had already produced a three-page summary of a secret authoritative report. That report had been commissioned by the administration two days before you gave the press statement about the trailers. The conclusion of that report was, that the trailers that had been found were not mobile biological warfare laboratories. We had not been given that information because it was deemed unimportant intelligence.'

Franklin sat motionless whilst Crompton laid out the details of the political disaster.

Crompton concluded, 'The DIA could not identify who actually made the telephone call to you. But it came from the DIA building and so they are reviewing security to track down the individual.'

When he had finished, the two men sat in silence. Franklin broke the spell by picking up the telephone: 'Get Danny Davis, Cy Santana and Chris Champion as quick as possible. When they arrive, send them in straight away.' He pondered for a moment, then added, 'Put me through to Prime Minister Proffitt as a matter of urgency.' Champion was the first to arrive, and Franklin briefed him on the news.

'Who called you with the information?' enquired Champion.

'Somebody from the Defense Intelligence Agency.'

Santana joined them.

'Do we know where Davis is?' asked Franklin.

'He is at the Defense Intelligence Agency building,' replied Santana.

'What is he doing there?' quizzed Crompton.

'Getting some action on the telephone call, as far as I know,' responded Santana.

Crompton did not say anything, but wondered how Davis knew about the report and the telephone call, when he had just mentioned it to the aides. That was a matter to look into later.

Addressing the two aides, Franklin wanted it chapter and verse, who had done what, when and why. He had gone on national television and declared that WMDs had been found. Somebody was going to have to go and tell America that there were no weapons or facilities to make them. They would have to bury the report.

Franklin asked Crompton about the report itself.

'We have a copy on its way, but others may have seen it already.'

'The press?' enquired Franklin.

'Seems not,' added Crompton, 'or they would have been crawling all over the place. No; I think we can keep the lid on that. At least until we get our shit together.'

The telephone rang and Franklin answered it. He listened, then replaced the phone. 'That was the press office. They have had enquiries about the trailers' not being intended for making WMDs. They are denying everything until told otherwise.'

The four men sat in silence, which was broken when the telephone rang again. Franklin spoke to Proffitt and told him the bad news. When Proffitt grasped what had been said, he sat down. He had managed to appease some of the cabinet and had been given ammunition with which to fight the opposition and the mass of other dissenters. If the report were to be made public, then he would have to retract the statement and defend the argument that he had tried to deceive the public with a made-up story. When the call was over, Proffitt telephoned first Reilly, and then other key players who were close to events, in order to break the news to them.

The background to the issue evolved. As soon as it was safe to do so, the Maspamian Survey Group, formed by the secret service and made up of US and UK weapons inspectors, flew to Maspamia's capital. They were tasked to check out anything the ground forces found. Dr Finch should have been one of the team, but he was not allowed into the country. He had to do the round trip and return to the UK. It was during this period that the allied forces found two trailers. The troops thought that they could be mobile chemical warfare equipment. The experts inspected them. They were not impressed, and found that there was no chance of the trailer equipment being able to make biological weapons. In their report, they were able to conclude definitively that the trailers were not mobile laboratories, but were intended for the manufacture of hydrogen for weather balloons. They produced a report to that effect.

Dr Finch returned to Maspamia and was allowed in. He met Rosie, and was taken to inspect and photograph the trailers on behalf of the British government and the UN. At the site he spoke with operatives of the equipment and carried out a full examination. He was also adamant that they were not mobile germ warfare laboratories, and confirmed that they could not be used for making biological weapons. He added that they did not even look like mobile laboratories. They were, in reality, facilities for the production of hydrogen gas to fill military balloons. Finch investigated further, and found that they were hydrogen generators used by artillery units. He added to the misery when he reported that the systems, now confirmed as artillery meteorological equipment, had actually been sold to Maspamia by the British back in 1987.

Even with all of this evidence to the contrary, the US Administration defended its position by saying that their information was provided by an unidentified chemical engineer who managed one of the mobile plants. The political situation was such that the US Administration considered that this source was clearly of a higher calibre than the experts, who had unanimously concluded that the function of the trailers was to produce hydrogen. The question that prevailed amongst the media and weapons inspectors was: what was the point in sending experts to look for WMDs and assess objects like the trailers, if their unanimous voice was to be ignored? It seemed that if the experts had returned with evidence to support Franklin's and Crompton's own determinations, then they would not have been ignored. It was evident that intelligence was only useful and desirable, if it reinforced the preconceived policy situation. Prime Minister Proffitt told Parliament that, in respect to the trailers, investigations into their role were continuing. The Defence Secretary told the House of Commons that the mobile laboratories were 'within the technical description of mobile WMD laboratories.' In the US, Crompton had the full 122-page report stamped 'secret' and promptly filed away as quickly as possible, never to see the light of day again.

Franklin and Crompton insisted that the trailers were part of the WMDs system. They directed the CIA and the DIA to proclaim that they were confident that the trailers were used for mobile biological weapons production. They released the story that the hydrogen production explanation was a cover story, issued as part of Maspamia's continuing policy of denial and deception.

Dr Finch was unhappy with the spin cascading from the White House and Downing Street. He maintained his doubts about the 45-minute claim in particular, and totally disbelieved the official line in respect of the trailers found in Maspamia.

Dr Finch was deeply aware of the dishonest manipulation of intelligence for political purposes. It was far from the truth and, because he maintained the truth, he felt he was being led into an abyss.

12

Dr John Finch did not like being in London, particularly when he had been summoned to a meeting by Julien Clayton, the Director of Personnel. The two men despised one another. Dr Finch saw a pompous bullying senior civil servant who, at about 1.7m in height, was what might be called overweight. He always had the look of somebody who had smelled something nasty and turned their nose up at it. It gave him the appearance of looking down his nose at those he spoke to, which was also the reality. He had no personnel management experience when he was appointed to the job, a situation in the senior civil service that was not unusual. In fact, he had no personality or skills apart from jumping to a ministers call and doing what was requested. Clayton, on the other hand, hated the fact that Dr Finch had such a high professional status both in the UK and around the world. That status allowed him to work from home, where he had government computers and secret communications equipment as well as secret files. He had a direct line to MI6 and other government departments. He was a trusted holder of state secrets, and was seen as being extremely professional in his work. Clayton resented the fact that he could not fully control and manipulate the respected Dr Finch as he did others. Without such controls, he had deliberately gone out of his way to ensure that Finch was kept at the lowest grade possible, and had ensured that his salary had not been increased to complement his added responsibilities.

Clayton now revelled in the knowledge that he had something against Finch; he was going to enjoy the coming foray. With the approval of the Prime Minister himself, he had devised and put into action a plan to get Finch out of the Civil Service, using his name as the source, of the leak to the media about the failings in the dossier. The basis would be that Dr Finch had become embroiled in a dispute between the British government and the media over the contents of the dossier for war. A reporter claimed that he had been given information, to the effect that the government had exaggerated the Maspamian danger of weapons of mass destruction in its dossier. That had then justified an invasion of Maspamia. This was, in his opinion, at the minimum a breach of the civil service code, and possibly a breach of the Official Secrets Act, even though legal advice argued otherwise. The situation that Finch faced was deemed by Clayton to be so serious that he had directed that he be subjected to action under the Personnel Departments conduct code. That meant withholding any pay increase for a three-year period. This was most harmful to Finch now that he was approaching retirement: it would seriously impact on his pension. In fact, Clayton would like to see Finch forfeit his pension.

Another issue between them was that Finch had been told, prior to the Maspamia events, that there was to be a reorganisation within the department which would mean that Finch would get a sizeable increase in salary. That did not happen. Finch wrote several letters to Clayton asking why the changes had not been made; but he received no explanation. Finch now knew that it was because he would not go along with the deception spelled out in the dossier.

Dr Finch had voluntarily disclosed to the department his contacts with the media, as was the normal procedure. When the accusations were made against him, he maintained that he had not provided the information that was now being attributed to him. The problem was that Proffitt was furious because the focus was on him for the wrong reason. He had taken the country into a war alongside the Americans, and Finch was saying that he did not agree with key parts of the dossier. That would mean that the war was illegal. Clayton had interviewed him and reported to Proffitt, stating that he could make a case against Finch as being the source of the leak. Proffitt was out to save his own skin and was looking for a way out at any cost; Reilly pulled strings wherever he could, to get people onboard and behind the Prime Minister. Manipulation was easy within the civil service. Reilly identified those seeking to save their own jobs or those who would in the terms of the expression 'sell their own grandmother' to get some recognition and eventually some form of reward. That was the easy part; the difficult aspect was when Proffitt and Reilly conspired to get Finch before the Joint Intelligence Committee to get them to publicly degrade Finch.

The twist was that Proffitt and Reilly became further outraged when Dr Finch, having been hauled before the Joint Intelligence Committee for an inquisition, was not lambasted as planned. He answered all of the questions thrown at him, which were numerous. His answers were structured and honest. At the end of a gruelling session he had convinced committee members that he had not provided the information to the media. Then the committee delivered another blow when it reported that, in their united opinion, the Government had treated Dr Finch very poorly. Those comments really did not go down well with Proffitt, Reilly or Clayton. Reilly spoke to Clayton, 'Do whatever it takes to get him discredited and out of that job. That includes the loss of pension.'

Dr Finch, having endured a thorough interrogation by the Joint Intelligence Committee, was pleased with the outcome.

He had received messages of support, both from within the department and also from his many contacts outside. He now faced another interrogation, by a bully who was probably focused on a knighthood for services to a dodgy government. He took the lift up to the top floor of the building. Leaving the lift, he made his way along the corridor to Clayton's office. He already knew the reason for his presence at the meeting, and even knew the outcome. The department and the Government were pointing the finger at him, because he had found serious flaws in the reports on weapons of mass destruction. They now wanted to discredit him by saying that it was him who passed on his views to the media. He also knew that whilst the review by the Joint Intelligence Committee had gone his way, that fact would also be held against him in this meeting. He knocked on the elaborate heavy wooden door and entered the secretaries office without waiting for a response. She looked up and gave the expression that a bad smell had just entered the room. He reflected that that was possibly a common trait within a government personnel department.

'Dr Finch to see Mr Clayton,' he announced.

She checked the diary, then told him to take a seat. She telephoned a message about Dr Finch's arrival through to Clayton. There was a wait of about ten minutes before the office phone rang. She answered and, replacing the receiver, told Finch that he could go in. Finch stood and walked to the door, turned the handle and entered. Clayton sat behind a large and rather ornate desk. There was little to clutter the desk: just a photograph frame, a telephone, and a green table lamp. In front of Clayton was an open file, with a pen lying alongside it. Finch thought to himself that was just what you would expect from somebody who did nothing useful.

'Good morning, Dr Finch, sit down,' said Clayton, not looking up.

'Good morning,' replied Finch, who sat down in a leather chair. He had been in the office before, and noted again that it was well, decorated and – furnished. He reflected that the troops fighting in Maspamia had poor equipment, but that here there was some real opulence. He reflected that that just about summed up the situation but; that he was just a lowly civil servant: what did he know about such matters?

Finch watched as a pompous Clayton leaned back in his large leather chair; it was much larger than the one that he was sitting on. 'Dr Finch, I thought we had better have a chat about what is a very serious matter.' He paused then said, 'As you know, information has been leaked to the press alleging false claims being placed in the dossier on bio-chemical weapons. The Prime Minister is most disturbed about the situation, as indeed are we in the department. The problem is that we have found no other source for the information other than from youself.' He waited a moment for any response; but none came. 'You have denied that it came from you, but the media are pointing the finger.'

Dr Finch kept very calm and reiterated, 'I did not speak to the press in the manner that I am accused of. I gave evidence to the parliamentary committee about that very issue. I was quizzed about it for a whole day, and they concluded that the information had not come from me.'

'Oh, yes: that's another matter that I would like to address. The committee allege that you have been poorly treated by the Government and by this department in particular. Well, that is simply not true.' Clayton paused then said, 'You have been afforded every courtesy, and been treated in line with the Civil Service Code.'

'The answer to that question depends on which side of the desk you are sitting on. So, my reply is: does the Code provide for being found guilty where there is no evidence to support that claim, and having to prove one's innocence?' Finch paused for a fraction, then added, 'I had always thought that one was innocent until proven guilty.'

'Certainly not! There is evidence in the media saying that you had a meeting with one journalist in particular.' exclaimed Clayton.

'A lot of people have spoken with the media, and they had access to the same information as me. In fact a lot of those people had a lot more input than me. Are they being investigated? From where I am sitting, you are telling me I am guilty even though there is no evidence. Evidently none was given to the committee who investigated my case.'

Clayton became unnerved as he glared at Finch.

'You disputed the claim that chemical and biological weapons were available and could have been used at short notice, and that is the claim the media are making.' He gave a really snooty look and asked, 'If it's not you, then you can help us, me, to identify the source perhaps?'

Finch maintained his posture, 'I have no idea who it is, but I can assure you that the information produced in the press did not come from me.'

Clayton retaliated. 'You do realise that if you are named as the source of that information, then there will be no choice but for me to take formal action which, of course, could have serious implications for you.'

At this time what Clayton knew, but did not tell Finch, was that the department intended to confirm Finch's name as the source to the press if any reporter mentioned his name: a charade devised to lead to Finch's name. The Prime Minister approved the move, and Reilly managed those involved. Finch was set up as the fall guy to take the pressure off Proffitt.

The meeting continued with Clayton accusing Finch of wrongdoing, whilst Finch quietly stood his ground and denied complicity. At a lull in the proceedings, Finch asked, 'Am I going to be allowed to go back to Maspamia to continue with my work?'

Clayton moved the papers on the desk in front of him saying, 'It will be dependant on any reports that appear in the media. If you are named as the source, you will not be going back, but will face disciplinary procedures.'

Finch still did not have a definitive answer. 'Do I continue with my current schedule of work?' he asked.

'Yes, you can continue at present but; if the situation changes, then the matter would be reviewed and we would notify you. As required in the civil service code, you will receive a letter following this meeting.'

The meeting ended abruptly and Finch departed the office. He made his way down to speak to colleagues in his department. They all knew the system and so did not dwell on the outcome of the meeting. Clayton smiled to himself as Finch left the office. He reflected that the scientists always seemed to want to get above their station. He picked up the telephone and pressed the buttons. 'Good morning', he chirped when the phone was answered at the other end. 'Clayton here', he paused for the name to register, 'could you please pass on to the PM that I have had the meeting with Finch. He will not conform with our requirements. He is under no illusion that we have done our best for him. I have explained that he has been the leak of official information, and that when he is named by the media, then he will face disciplinary action.' He waited while the message was read back to him. 'That's correct,' he cooed and ended with a crisp 'goodbye.'

No sooner had he put the telephone down than Reilly contacted the head of the department and ordered a press conference. It was there that through a series of disclosures to the press, they would allow the media to give the names of possible sources. When the name of Finch, who was the main scientist in the search for CWBs was announced, they could confirm him as the leak. Then Clayton could begin the process to suspending him from his post. Reilly informed Proffitt that the wheels were set in motion for the disclosure of Dr Finch as the source of the leak undermining the Government by challenging that there were no WMDs which would have made the invasion illegal.

Reilly was prepared for the fact that once, Finch's name was out, it would make him a resentful employee; so he made a call to Sandy Crossman, head of MI6, to update him on the course of action. Crossman wanted to ease back, as the parliamentary enquiry had pointed out that they did not believe Finch to be the source and that they believed that he was being treated badly by his employers. Reilly did not like to be challenged. He stated that the Prime Minister himself had ordered Finch to be exposed, and that the head of MI6 would view Finch as a security risk. In turn, Crossman did not like to be used by an unelected rabble-rouser, possibly exposing his good name, should the whole mess backfire. Crossman also pointed out that Finch had for years maintained his silence in terms of his extensive knowledge of the bio-warfare weapons; and that he himself did not view him as a resentful employee who could be considered unstable and a security risk. Reilly was an arrogant bully and did not like his instructions being questioned. He confirmed the course of action, emphasizing that there was no mediation or other option in this instance. Of course Crossman could always resign if he did not like it.

Proffitt telephoned Franklin to reveal the course of action that was being played out. People were going to be protected at the cost of one scientist. It was a small price to pay in the scheme of things. Franklin called Crompton and updated him. Crompton had been considering the situation. 'Dexter,' he said in the slow speech that he used when he was thinking. 'This

Finch might get thrown out of his job but, having read his resume, he's no third-rate striker, he's at the top of his game and knows a lot of stuff. Now, he's gonna be pissed off when he gets his arse kicked and, if he should write his memoirs, then a whole lot more crap will drop on us.'

Franklin considered for a moment, then replied, 'Well, we will be out of it by then, and who bothers about history? Maspamia will be old news and there will be a new war to worry about. Anyway, what do you have in mind?'

'I was thinking of speaking to my buddy at Worldwide and seeing what he thinks. Perhaps he could send somebody over to check out the good scientist, and make sure he doesn't involve us in his recollections of germs and bugs.'

Franklin's response was not well thought-out. 'Well, if you think it's necessary, there can't be any harm in checking it out. Make sure that Proffitt and that side kick of his are kept informed.'

Crompton was one step ahead, 'Oh, they are in it already: they get the rewards, then they take the crap.' He then made a couple of telephone calls. There was serious work to be done.

13

The battle for Maspamia was over. It was a matter of containment by the troops on the ground. The oil fields had been brought under control, and were online pumping oil. Parts of the capital were being subjected to the work of bulldozers as part of the rebuilding programme. It was during this period that Cornell received a telephone call. He was directed to go to the isolated farm house that he had visited when he became a member of the Black Eagles assassination team. He made the journey, and arrived to find Chambers, the grey-haired, unshaven former Lt Col still puffing on a pipe whilst sitting on a chair on the porch.

'Howdy, son,' he offered by way of a greeting.

Cornell grinned, 'howdy to you, sir.'

'Hear you been doin' good things.'

'I do my best, sir,' said Cornell, pleased that the organisation was satisfied with his work.

'Well, sit yourself down. Wanna beer?'

Taking a seat alongside the man, Cornell replied, 'That would be good.'

'Two beers!' the man shouted.

Nothing more was said until after the younger man came out of the house with the two beers. When he had gone back inside, Chambers spoke: 'We've got a special job for you.' He picked up a file that was lying on a small table next to the seat.

Opening it, he took out a photograph, and handed it to Cornell. 'That is a Dr John Finch. He is a Brit weapons of mass destruction expert. He lives in the UK. He is also a UN weapons inspector. He was in Maspamia looking for WMDs; but it seems that he did not find any. Now we all know that Maspamia had them and could use them at short notice, but this guy would and will not go along with this. He said that information in a dossier produced in the UK contained dodgy information. Now, we all went to war based on the contents of that dossier. The army or the marines found some trailers, and somehow the President was told that they were mobile WMDs equipment. Well, he then went on television and told the good people of our country that they had found the evidence that then took them to war. It turned out that the information was bullshit, and so our President Franklin was not at all happy. In fact, he was right pissed off.'

'Was this Finch involved in that?'

'Not to begin with, because we managed to keep him out; but, because he is the Brit's number one man, we eventually had to let him in. But he just confirmed what we already knew.'

'Who threw the curved ball?'

'We don't know, but we are searching the bastard out.'

'What's the plan with this Finch?'

'The Brit's are putting him under a lot of pressure, so we need you to help. We propose that, under all this pressure, he may decide to commit suicide, you know, takes off to the woods and tops himself. Probably takes some pills and then cuts a wrist.' He pursed his lips in contemplation, then added, 'If that happens, we then have one less problem. It appears that the man may need some assistance, and that is where your experise comes in.'

Cornell nodded.

'The outline we have been given at the moment is that you

fly to London Heathrow airport. You will be met by one of our people, although he is a Brit. He will guide you through and get you to the location, but you are in charge. His name is Spider.'

'Spider?' questioned Cornell.

'That is the name he goes by,' replied Chambers. He pulled a map from the envelope and continued, 'This Finch works from home, and takes a walk most afternoons. He can be grabbed on one of these walks. There is a river close by,' he pointed to the map, 'and the plan is to use a boat which will be your base. It's not far from the wood, where the body can be dumped.'

Cornell studied the map. 'Where does Finch live?'

Chambers leaned forward, studied the map, then made a circle with a pencil, 'Here.'

'Not a lot of ground to cover,' added Cornell

Chambers continued, 'In addition to Spider, there will be another operative. Not sure who that will be yet. We have other help in the UK, which is led by somebody high up in their Government. I don't know who that is and I don't want to, nor do you. The plan is that you will be given a mobile phone with a couple of numbers already installed, and they will give you instructions and provide any support you need.' Chambers looked at Cornell, eye to eye: 'Do what they say and don't go off and do your own thing. This is political, both sides of the pond.'

He paused for effect, then finished, 'Once you have fulfilled the contract, you will be got out. They have not said how yet, but they will not want an assassin running loose all over their country.'

Cornell understood, but had a question. 'Why don't they just do it themselves?'

'Simple,' replied the man. 'If anything goes wrong, the Brits will stand back and deny any knowledge. If you get caught, you will be the fall guy, a mad assassin. They will haul your arse into court and send you to prison. Should that happen, we will get you extradited back home as quickly as possible and back into work.' Chambers grinned, 'Don't worry; they don't have capital punishment and the prisons over there are soft; and you will be well-rewarded.'

Chambers called for two more beers. They sat without speaking until they were delivered.

When the young man had gone, the man returned to the map. He opened it up, laid it on the table in front of them and went over the plan again. 'So, this is the area you will be working in. Finch lives here,' he said pointing, to a pencil mark. 'He walks in this area. This is the river and that is the wood. You will need to do a covert reconnaissance of the area, so that when you get intel that he is on his walk, you have decided on the location where you'll grab him. Take him to the boat and keep him alive. You will get instructions about what to do and when, but you will take Finch to the woods in this area,' he pointed on the map, 'then follow the instructions for disposal. You will then be got out.'

'Looks OK,' replied Cornell.

'One more point: let Spider do any talking. He's English, and your accent would stand out.'

Chambers looked at Cornell, who was studying the map.

'If anything goes wrong, and you are not being hunted, then make your way to this place.' He pointed to a church a few miles from the area. 'Phone either of your numbers and stay put out of sight. They will come and get you. The church is only used on Sunday's so there should not be anybody about.'

Cornell shrugged, 'What can go wrong?'

Chambers, always patient, speculated: 'There are people in the country who are involved. We do not know who they are, that's their business. Those who will be involved in the front line search, such as police and medical people, will not be in on what is happening. You will only meet some of the dodgy dealers; you won't learn their names, but you will have to rely on the services they undertake.' Chambers took a swig of his beer. 'With so many people involved, a number of things can go wrong.'

Cornell began to respond, 'In that case, we just fight…'

'No,' interrupted Chambers. 'We have the President and the Brit Prime Minister in the frame, and so it needs to be clean and quiet, no high action. You clear on that?'

Cornell heard the sternness in Chambers voice. 'Real clear,' he replied.

'OK, once you have completed the assignment you may get details of another operation. They've got a problem with somebody. His son was killed the first time round. For some unknown reason our fly-boys hit Brit armour. The son was one of those killed. Ever since, he has run a campaign against the Prime Minister for not getting the pilots over for questioning. We've been asked to deal with the problem. So, it's an aggressive mugging and job done. Spider will also be with you on that job. They will then get you out of the country..'

Cornell nodded, then shrugged, 'That's fine, sir.'

'Good,' responded Chambers. 'You need go and pack a bag, you're on the move as of now.'

Cornell finished his beer. The two men stood and shook hands. Chambers watched as Cornell drove his car down the track towards the road. He then went into the house to report to his superiors.

14

Spider met Cornell at Heathrow airport. He was holding a piece of card with his name on it as the big American walked through the arrivals door. It took time to get to the short stay car park, and the men said little. Once on the road, they headed away from London. On leaving the motorway, they were soon driving down narrow lanes. Spider eventually guided the car through the gates of Apple Tree Boatyard. He parked by some offices that had seen better days. A man who had been sitting on a dilapidated bench stood and walked over to the car. He introduced himself as Leo Crogan, the third member of the team. 'The boat is round the corner on the jetty. It's called *Windward*. I've had a look at her and she's fine for what we need. I have some food in the boot of my car, not a lot as I was not told how long we were likely to be, also a bag for each of us with clothes for the operation.'

'The operation will be as quick as possible,' responded Cornell, who was unsure of Crogan's accent, but did not ask.

Crogan nodded, 'First we need to check in with the boatyard, to sort out the paperwork.'

Cornell looked at Spider. 'Can you do that?' Without waiting for a reply, he walked away to find and have a look at the cruiser.

Spider and Crogan went into the office and signed the documents. The money transaction was by a credit card that had been supplied for the job. The owner's wife took them to the cruiser, where Cornell was standing looking at the river. Onboard she took Crogan through the operating procedures and the do's and dont's whilst onboard. When the formalities were done the woman went back to the office, leaving Spider and Crogan to collect the food and the bags. As soon as everything was onboard, they cast off and moved up-river to find a mooring close to the wood. For those on holiday, it would have been a pleasant journey, passing through the green English countryside. For the three men it was a mode of transport and it was work. They were pleased to find the location was devoid of any other craft. Food was next on the agenda.

As evening approached, Cornell and Spider carried out a reconnaissance of the wood, leaving Crogan onboard to look after the cruiser. They found a spot that was secluded but accessible from the cruiser at its mooring close to the path. They noted that the path was not well used, and that was a bonus as it reduced the chances of them meeting anybody. They moved about the wood and were able to view through binoculars the village and the track leading up to the wood. There was nobody about; it was just a warm summer's evening. Having got the lie of the land, they returned to the cruiser. They checked their kit. Each had been provided with black police combat-style trousers, polo shirts and black boots. The plan was that if they were seen, they would, from a distance, look like police officers and not raise immediate suspicions. Cornell made a phone call to one of the numbers on the phone. He confirmed that they were on location and had the appropriate equipment with them. When he finished he just told the others that they were to wait for a call that he hoped would send them into action the following day.

* * * *

John Finch spent hours in his book-lined study, where he immersed himself in the secret murky world of chemical and biological weapons. Through his computers he was linked to Britain's intelligence services MI5, MI6, GCHQ, the Ministry of Defence (MoD), the Foreign Office and numerous foreign spy agencies. One computer was used for his contacts outside of the official ones. His lap top was where he kept his personal records and data. He had an office in London at the Proliferation and Arms Control Secretariat, and another at Porton Down, the British government's chemical, biological and nuclear weapons establishment. To him they were the realms of officialdom and interference by senior civil servants who had no idea of what he and the rest of the department did. For that reason he preferred to work at home. It was also why he kept his secret data at home, including tens of thousands of documents and photographs. He was not a spy, but was the closest you could get without actually being one. He was highly trusted and respected. He knew that if he were not then he would not have the freedom that he had been granted. Whilst he had no real faith or trust in the majority of senior people or the ministers they served, he was trusted and he would never break that trust. He would give information as requested, and it was up to those who received it, to use it wisely. The fact that anybody could consider that he would breach that trust was hurtful but, as he and his colleagues knew, it was those who had a lot to lose or sought a high profile who could not be trusted. Callers from all round the globe consulted him about biological weaponry because he was a world-renowned microbiologist expert in the field of biological and germ materials that could be used for warfare or terrorism. He was an honorable man.

It was a warm day as Finch sat in his office looking out of the window. He noticed that the garden looked good, and that the weather was a mixture of hot sun shielded by the occasional cloud. The weather forecast had advised that there might be showers, but so far it had been fine. He found that at home he could get on with his work without the interference that surrounded him at either office, but particularly the London office. His work routine was not 9 till 5, Monday to Friday. He received calls all hours of the day and night as well as at weekends, unlike those in the office who pontificated and worked the regulation hours. The morning found him absorbed in answering calls, sending e-mails and reviewing documents. He was preparing to return to Maspamia to continue the search for weapons of mass destruction. It was the part of the job he loved, out on the front line, checking and quizzing those who may hold the key to any lethal weapons. He received a regular call from Rosie, who would again be accompanying him in Maspamia, to get an update on a departure date. He would fly from the UK; she would fly from the USA. They would meet in Maspamia.

His wife left him to his work, and only interrupted at meal times, when he took time out so that they ate together, always making best use of the garden if the weather was good. Their talk was not of work, but of his pending retirement and of what they planned to do. He had in mind moving to America, where he could get consultancy work or a research post in a University utilising his knowledge and experience. Some of the ground-work had been done when he visited the US to attend meetings or give lectures. Rosie had also been active in promoting possible options. Until he could retire he had to live a double life, with his secret world and that of a family man. Whilst he loved the job, politics ruled and he disliked that, in particular he resented being pressurised to lie, not by his superiors but the the minions who pandered to ministers. His view was that if Maspamia had biological weapons and was a threat to other countries, then his job, along with other inspectors, was to find them. He objected to being told that they had such weapons and could and would use them. It was that which had come to a head in resent weeks. He had a meeting with a journalist who, as the saying goes, would never let the truth get in the way of a good story. He had not divulged anything but, because the inaccurate information in the dossier had entered the public domain, those in power had decided that somebody was going to be in the frame. He had already formed the view that that somebody was going to be him.

He reflected on the fact that Clayton, as the head of personnel, had called him to a meeting and had been most objectionable. Of course, there were no witnesses, nor any notes of the meeting taken by Clayton or himself. He knew that he could have had somebody with him, but it would have served little purpose. The Civil Service would manipulate the situation in their favour. Clayton had made his mind up that he was dangerous to the organisation and had to go. It was just a matter of when. He pondered the possible loss of pension. He had been told by others who were in the know, that only traitors met that fate, as the Government was always worried about opening a can of worms. He smiled as he reflected that he was witness to one big can of worms, but was mindful of the Official Secrets Act and the ramifications of any breaches.

He had propped up a letter from the Ministry of Defence that had landed on the doormat that very morning. He had not bothered to open it as he knew what the contents would be. It would at the very least be very threatening. Well, it was designed to silence him, because people in government and the Ministry of Defence had "discovered" that not only was he talking to journalists, as he had done many times in the past; they had also heard that he might be planning to write a book about his work with chemical and biological weapons, once he had retired.

His mind came back to the matter in hand, and he finished an e-mail listing all of the media people he had met over the years, where he had met them and in what context. It was agreed that the list would be sent to the Joint Intelligence Committee after he was exonerated of any wrongdoing. When it was completed, he e-mailed it to his line manager in London. A short while later, a colleague from the London office rang and, after some pleasantries, checked some points in the list. It was then confirmed that his flights to Maspamia were booked and he was given the dates. The tickets were being sent by e-mail. When they had finished talking, Finch checked the clock, which showed it to be almost 3 pm. He got up from his chair to look out of the window, where he saw that it was still cloudy with glimpses of sun. It was time for his ritual walk. He found that when he worked at home, he became so engrossed that a walk of about half an hour at the end of the working day was a necessary way of unwinding.

He walked out of his office and went through to the kitchen to find his wife. She was busy preparing a meal for friends who were visiting later. When he walked into the room she smiled, told him not to be long, and reminded him that they had friends coming over. He said he would be about half an hour. He went along the hallway to the front door. Looking at his green-waxed jacket hanging on the coat stand, it crossed his mind as to whether he would need a coat. He opened the front door and stepped out. It was warm even when clouds hid the sun. He scanned the sky and decided that he would be alright without a coat, but his stout walking shoes were a must. He closed the front door and, walking to the front gate, surveyed the front garden. Passing through, he closed the gate, then turned right and walked along the street.

He never noticed the car parked on the pub forecourt with its lone occupant. Tasked with observing the house, the woman had become bored there being no activity. She had thought that somebody from the pub would have come over to enquire what she was doing, but nobody did. Had they done so, she would have told them that she was a customs and excise officer, and to check with the local police station for verification. She was not with that organization, and local police did not know who she was. It was a ploy: the very mention of customs and excise caused people to get into the spirit of some big crime bust, and so they would leave her to it. When Finch left the house, she used her mobile phone to call and give that information, and the direction in which he was walking. That done, she started the car and drove away, going in the opposite direction to that of Finch. Aboard the cruiser, Cornell took a call. When he finished, he looked at Spider. 'OK, we're on. Crogan: you look after things here, and if there's any problem let us know.' Crogan nodded. Cornell and Spider wasted no time. They dressed in their dark uniforms and were soon moving up the hill towards the wood.

Finch walked along the footpath of Springfield Road, which had once been a busy main road. A by-pass had changed that, and the village had become a quiet backwater, much to the delight of the inhabitants. There was not very much traffic at any time of the day, and as he made his way along a short distance, there was none. He crossed the road and turned up into Orchard Lane. As he walked along the lane he passed a number of houses but did not see anybody. He followed the road under the bypass and continued along the lane. When the lane met Grove Road he saw Mrs Braithwait, and stopped to pass the time of day. They did not really know each other but, if she was in her garden when he took his walk, he would stop and speak to her. Their short conversation was about the weather and the pending joint villages fete which she was organising. Then they parted, she continued with her gardening and he with his walk. Crossing Grove Road, it was a case of following the lane up to the village of Hillgrove. He then turned off onto Blossomhill Lane which led to a point where it stopped being a lane and became a track. At a number of places he could have taken a circular route that would have returned him home. Because the weather was holding good, and the news had come that his trip to Maspamia had been sanctioned, things were looking better; so he decided to follow the track.

The track, well used by those walking their dogs, was deserted and he strode purposefully up the slight gradient. He noted that one field had a good crop of cereals whilst the other had been harvested and now looked bare. The sun, when it came out from behind the clouds, was quite hot. He maintained a reasonable pace to get his body moving. The track, if followed, went past Bluebell Wood and down to the river. He usually walked about half the length of the wood, and turned left to follow a wider track through it .At the end of the track it joined a smaller track, where to the left, it led back down to the village and was clear of undergrowth. The track to the right was almost overgrown. He was at the point where the field met the wood when he stopped to look back. He contemplated the surroundings and felt a million miles away from the dirty tricks manipulators in London. Walking on, he came to the larger track and tuned into the wood. Like many who walked the track, he did not know all the species of trees or species of wildlife that could be seen and which varied on every walk. The trees provided some shield from the sun and it felt cooler, but he kept up a good pace and that kept him warm.

When he was almost at the end of the track, he spotted a person emerging from the undergrowth. He could see that it was a male, white, about 1.8 metres tall; but the curious thing was that he was dressed all in a dark military-style uniform. As he approached the man, he could see that he was wearing black boots, dark combat-style trousers and a dark polo shirt. His immediate thought was that he was a police officer. As he came up to the man, who appeared to be alone, he greeted him with a 'good afternoon'. The man did not respond, but just stood and stared at him. In those brief seconds he became uneasy, and he reflected on something he had heard: that in intelligence circles, if there was a "target" then they might be found "dead in the woods". He dismissed the thought because this was England on a sunny summer day. That sort of thing did not happen in real life, not in England!

Dr Finch never heard the person approach his back, and was totally unaware until a very powerful arm wrapped around his neck and a cloth was placed over his face. The cloth contained a modern anaesthetic agent that caused unconsciousness in less than a minute. He struggled but the grip held firm. He felt himself starting to be overcome by the substance on the cloth. As he struggled, he breathed deeper and became more engulfed. He was losing consciousness and could do nothing to stop it. He could not shout because the assailant's hand was holding the cloth across his nose and mouth. His body became limp, and then there was blackness in both mind and vision. Spider played no part in the action, leaving it to the large American, Cornell. Dr Finch was allowed to drop to the floor, unconscious. Cornell told Spider to check for any other walkers. He did so without question, and it was a quick task to check the track which, when followed, took them to the river. Spider returned and gave the all-clear. Cornell bent down and hauled Finch up and then onto his shoulder. They joined the track and, with Spider keeping a good look-out, Cornell, with Finch draped like a rag doll over his right shoulder, moved quickly towards the river.

As they reached the end of the wood, Spider was scanning the ground between them and the river. He turned and said it was all clear, so they moved at a fast pace down the gentle slope to the river. The track joined the river pathway. They turned and almost ran a short distance along the path to the cruiser moored at the riverbank. Spider leapt aboard the boat and, with Crogan, helped Cornell manhandle Finch aboard. Once they were aboard, Crogan used the binoculars to scan the wood, track and path for signs of anybody who could have seen the strange activities. Nobody was observed which was, just as well as the orders were simple. If the men in black were seen, then they had orders to eliminate any witnesses.

Aboard the cruiser, Finch was taken below. His hands were secured together using soft cloth to avoid marking the skin. His feet were tied together in the same way. He was laid on a bench seat, and it was a case of wait for him to come round. Cornell went up into the wheelhouse, and made a call on the mobile phone to a number he had been given. The number, being pre-programmed, meant that he just needed to push a button to connect. It rang a few times before a male voice answered. Cornell identified himself through a code name he had also been given. He then added that the package had been collected in good condition. He said that he would examine it later and call back. With Finch still unconscious, Spider was sorting out some food and coffee. It was going to be a long night.

It was about an hour before Finch regained consciousness, and his head was foggy. It took time for him to realise where he was. He determined that he was on a boat, and so had not travelled far following his forced abduction. His hands were tied and so were his legs. He was lying on a bench seat and it was damned uncomfortable. He was aware of somebody close to him and, although his speech was not clear, he questioned what was happening and why.

Cornell went over and pressed his face close to Finch. 'So, you're awake. Now, if you behave I'll sit you up, yeh?' questioned Cornell.

Finch breathed out, in a wheezy voice, the word, 'yeeeees.'

Cornell hauled Finch into the upright position and propped him up with some cushions. Looking at Finch, he thought he looked awful.

'You wanna drink?' grunted Cornell.

Finch tried to nod and say yes at the same time.

Cornell looked at Spider, 'Give him a drink.'

Spider was pissed off with the Yank giving orders, but said nothing. He got a water bottle and held it to Finch's mouth, allowing some to be drunk and some to run down his chin and onto his lap. Finch was still getting over the ordeal whilst trying to understand what was happening to him. Cornell got up close again and stared into his eyes. 'I've got some questions for you. Can you hear me OK?'

Finch grunted and attempted a nod of the head, aware of the American's face and bad breathe overwhelming his face.

'My boss says that you're a bad bastard. He says you're gonna write a book about chemical and biological warfare shit, and he wants to know if that's true.' Finch did not respond. Cornell continued to stare at him. 'Well, are you gonna write a book? It's a simple question.' Again Finch did not answer. Cornell knew he could get the information, but he was under strict orders not to harm Finch unless he was told to.

'Well, old man, you're gonna tell me what I want to know. You can do it the easy way or the hard way. If it's the hard way, it's gonna be painful for you.'

Finch knew that the focus was, whether he was or was not going to write a book, so why go through pain? 'Yes, I am going to write a book'. His eyes were looking anywhere other than at Cornell.

'See, that's great, you can do it.' He moved his face up close. 'OK, who is the publisher?' he enquired.

Finch knew that they would have that information as well. 'World Books Press, based in London.'

Cornell added, 'Good, any other publishers?'

'I am speaking to a couple of publishers in the US, but nothing is agreed yet.'

'Where is the manuscript?' demanded Cornell.

'I have not written anything yet,' replied Finch.

'Well Doctor Finch, I don't believe you. If you are speaking to publishing people, then you will have something written. Is it on a lap top at home?'

'No, there is no manuscript,' he muttered.

Cornell moved his face back. 'My people think you will write about there being no WMDs in Maspamia, and that that was made up so as to justify going to war.'

'If I write about that, it will be the truth.' He paused, 'Can I have a drink please?'

'Now that is just what my boss does not want to hear. That's the problem. You see, they did have WMDs and so the war was justified. You and some of your scientific colleagues going around saying otherwise is embarrassing.'

Finch feared for his safety more than at any time in his life. 'Scientists work on factual evidence, and we did not find any such weapons.'

Cornell grinned, 'You see, Doc, your problem is that you just have no imagination.'

He stood and, passing Spider, told him to give Finch some more water and then continued up into the wheelhouse.

'Seen anything?' he asked Crogan.

'Some people further along the path, but nobody close by.'

Cornell surveyed the area. Spider climbed up to join them, handing out some food.

He did not give any to Finch. 'What happens now?' asked Crogan.

Cornell looked at him. 'We wait until somebody calls and tells us what to do. You OK with that?'

Crogan shuffled and felt uncomfortable. 'Fine by me,' he replied.

When they had finished eating, Cornell went below. Finch still sat propped up on the bench seat.

'You OK?' enquired Cornell.

Finch nodded.

'So, Doc, you're gonna write a book and tell about WMDs?' asked Cornell.

Finch, able to concentrate better now, looked at the American. 'When I retire, I am going to publish a book about weapons of mass destruction, so, as I have already said, the answer is yes.'

Cornell nodded, 'Well, my boss is not happy about that prospect, and that posses a dilemma.' He paused. 'You see, we invaded Maspamia because of the threat from these weapons which you say did not exist.' He paused again. 'Well, you saying that has pissed everybody off.'

'I spoke as I saw it. We never found any weapons or materials before the war or after.'

Cornell added, 'Well, our troops found two chemical trailers which you guys missed.'

'They were nothing to do with chemicals. They were for weather balloons.' Finch was very serious. 'Do the Americans have a problem with me?'

Cornell looked at him, 'It's both: my people are pissed off and your Prime Minister is pissed off cause you're making it look as if they went to war for no good reason.' He paused, then added, 'People listen to you and what you're saying, and that is not good.'

'You want me to tell lies?' questioned Finch.

'Now you got the message,' said Cornell, 'but it's a bit late, in fact it's too late.'

'So what happens now?'

Cornell became matter-of-fact in his reply, 'I will do what I have to when I get orders, and that is what I am waiting for.'

It was at that point that Finch realised that he was not going to survive. They wanted him dead and this thug was going to do the job.

15

When, after about four hours had passed and Finch had not arrived home, Mrs Finch began to worry. Their friends Doug and Beth Sayer had arrived as arranged. They went out in different directions to see if they could find him. Each time they returned to the house without a trace of him. He had seemingly just vanished. They checked the pub and walked to the small shop which was also close by. Nobody had seen him. They knew that he had his mobile phone and that he kept it on and charged up because people were always calling for work matters. He did not use it to phone home and say he was delayed or that he was in trouble. He had not gone out dressed for a long walk. Mrs Finch called his number several times, but the phone was switched off. She was reluctant to contact the police because of all the grief her husband had been subjected to in the past weeks. She concluded that he would not want to rock the boat, cause trouble and make matters worse. She was a witness over the years to the destructive power of the civil service.

The evening pressed on and eventually, after one last search, Doug managed to persuade Mrs Finch to call the police. She was so upset by this point that it was Doug who made the call. He rang Clifton Vale police station and reported Dr Finch missing. When the police sergeant realised who it was that was missing, he said that police officers would be at the house straight away. About ten minutes had passed when two police officers knocked on the front door. Doug opened it and let them in. It was now almost midnight. They went into the lounge and met Mrs Finch. Beth went to make some tea. The officers were told that Dr Finch had gone for a walk just after three o'clock, and that his walk normally took about thirty minutes. So he was about eight hours overdue. They sought information and made notes recording what he was wearing when he went out. They asked: did he have any other friends whom he might have gone to visit. Had he taken a car? Did he have a bicycle, and was it still at the house? This was general background information' and they explored all options. They then asked if they could look round the house and garden, explaining that this was normal procedure in such cases. Doug showed them round, leaving Mrs Finch with Beth sitting in the lounge. Whilst they were upstairs, two more police officers arrived at the house; while a female officer sat talking with Mrs Finch, her male colleague joined the others in their search of the house and grounds. They found nothing and returned to the lounge. One of the PCs radioed the police station and gave a brief report. The first two officers were told to return to the station and to leave the other pair at the house.

At Clifton Vale police station, Sergeant Doug Kennedy was in charge of the case. He had received the information about Dr Finch being missing, and about the search of his home and garden which had revealed no clue as to his whereabouts. For him, it was a normal missing persons report; but instinct told him that it might be wise, in this case, to go further up the command chain. He did, and was told to wait for further instructions. Those instructions were not long in coming. He was told to prepare a Major Incident Record Log. He was instructed to record the actual commencement as 2pm on 17th July, which was one hour before Finch had departed for his walk, and many hours prior to the missing person report being completed at 11.40 pm on that day. Having done that, his instructions were to carry out a search as defined in the force procedures. He consulted the Missing Persons Search Manual, which contained the procedures and contact details of those who he could call on. A quick check identified that a helicopter could be used. Whilst he himself could call one up, it had to be authorised by a higher ranking officer, as it was an expensive exercise in what was in fact the early stages of a missing person incident. Had it been a child or a female, the reaction would have been quicker. Also in the equation was the fact that Finch was a high profile defence scientist, and senior management was involved. It was 'political'. But he did have volunteer searchers, some with dogs. They were OK, and they did not cost the force anything apart from some expenses. He could call on police officers, some of whom were trained in search techniques; but he had to be careful about overtime. The same applied to the police diving team, should he want to search the river. He decided to leave that option until a search on land of the surrounding area had been made.

The two police officers who had arrived at Finch's home had returned to the police station and reported to Sgt Kennedy. They told him what they had seen and heard at the house. Having reported in, they left to resume the beat in their patrol car. Kennedy, a very experienced police officer, began to formulate a plan of getting officers on the ground and a helicopter in the air. Before actioning the plan he sought clearance from a Chief Superintendent. That was given and he proceeded to activate the search procedure. He had two officers at the house and now called for a helicopter to deploy over the area. He requested one that was equipped with a heat seeking locator, as it would show a body that was still warm. This would be helpful for covering the farmland and woods in the area. Expecting that the local police helicopter which

116

was ready and available would be deployed, he was surprised to learn that it was a helicopter from well outside the area that was to be sent to undertake the aerial search. Given no reason by senior officers for the selection of that particular helicopter, Kennedy was told that he would not have air support for three hours.

Sergeant Kennedy was contacted by a senior police officer who said that because of who the missing man was, it was 'political' and he had been directed to get a mobile communications vehicle sent to the house. In addition a tall mast needed to be set up. A communications vehicle was requested by Sgt Kennedy, and the officers who operated it were called in. They would contact Clifton Vale police station as soon as they arrived. The mobile comms vehicle parked outside the house and a medium height mast was erected. Then one of the police officers went to the house and spoke with Mrs Finch. He explained that in order to have better communication, they needed to put up a larger mast, and that they would need to do that in her back garden. She had little choice, as a group of officers were already at work erecting the larger mast. She was told that they had planned to use the usual mast, but that they had been instructed to use the tallest mast available. The police thought it very unusual. Doug asked why such a large mast had to be deployed for an operation in the local area. He was told that whilst the police radios did work in the area, they wanted to make sure that there were no glitches in maintaining communications.

It was 3am when Assistant Chief Constable Timothy Long was called by the Chief Constable and advised of events; he was told that he had been assigned the case, which was high profile. Long knew immediately that it was 'political' and that spelled trouble. Long contacted Sgt Kennedy to explain the situation and get an update. He told him to continue with the search plan and asked him to arrange for all the key players

117

in the search to be at Clifton Vale police station at 5am for a briefing. Sgt Kennedy was then informed that the helicopter had arrived early and begun its search of the area. It was fitted with and was using its heat seeking equipment to scan the ground below. After just over an hour the helicopter departed the area to refuel, which took about half an hour. It then returned to the search area. It had not identified any heat source that would have indicated a human being. It was decided by the Chief Constable that the helicopter could be stood down as it was no longer required as part of the search operation. Long arrived at Clifton Vale police station and took over responsibility from Sgt Kennedy. Following the first briefing at 7am police officers were notified of the search plan and were to be assembled at the house. PCs Mike Devlin and Roger Palmer were to be responsible for the actual search, being trained in search methods. In addition to the police officers, civilian volunteer searchers were being contacted. Particularly those with trained search dogs. They would be deployed as a matter of urgency.

* * * *

A police Inspector was now in charge of the investigation at the house, and was contacted by Long. It was done through the secure police communications link. He needed to speak in confidence and so the officer entered the van, sat down and put a headset on. The other officers stepped outside to take in some fresh air as it had been a busy night, with a lot of communications flooding the airwaves. Long introduced himself and identified that he was in charge of the search operation. Then his tone changed: 'I am sending a couple of officers over to your location, including a search dog and handler.'

'Right, sir,' replied the Inspector.

'Give them full access to the property and grounds. Whilst they are in the house, I want the occupants out. Put them in the back garden. Don't ask why, just do it. Tell them it will allow the dog to search without distraction.'

The Inspector was mystified by this particular order; but if that was what had to done, so be it. 'OK sir, no problem, any idea when the officers are due at our location?' he enquired.

'In about 5 minutes,' replied Long.

'OK, sir, I will sort things out. Is there anything else?'

'No, not at present.'

The Inspector stepped out of the van and walked back to the house. He now had to tell the family that there was to be a dog search of the house, and that they had to wait outside. The Inspector had just got to the front door when a van containing a search dog and its handler arrived. He walked back to the road to meet the dog handler and they exchanged greetings. They knew each other and had worked together on other operations.

'What's the score, sir?'

'We are getting our orders from up on high, and we need you to do a search of the house with the dog.'

'Am I looking for anything in particular?'

'No, but the occupants have to go outside into the garden while the dog searches.'

The handler shrugged his shoulders.

The Inspector told him he had to undertake the search with two other people who had just arrived. The Inspector and the dog handler stood by the front gate and were joined by two men. They introduced themselves as police officers, but they were not local. They said that they needed to inspect the house, and in particular Finch's office. Neither the Inspector nor the dog handler made any comment.

The Inspector said that he would ask the occupants to leave the house, and that then they could undertake their search.

Mrs Finch was quite shocked to be asked to go out into the garden in the early hours of the morning whilst a dog did a search of the house. Doug objected and asked why. They were told these were orders from senior officers. Although they grumbled, they did as the Inspector had requested. Once they were outside the house he went and told the others that the house was clear. Three men and a dog entered through the front door. The dog handler walked the dog into each room and allowed it to sniff about. He was mindful that he needed to keep control of the dog and so kept her on a lead. He had no idea what he might be looking for. So he opened any doors, including those on cupboards and wardrobes. The other two had put on surgical gloves and had their own agenda. One raced upstairs and had a quick look round each of the bedrooms. Then he went into the bathroom. Opening a cupboard, he saw a box containing blister packs of pain killer-tablets. He checked his list and found them on it. They were powerful pain-killers. He removed thirty tablets, and replaced the box where he had found it. With the blister packs in a pocket, he then raced downstairs to join the other man. He had been busy downstairs, and had placed a green-waxed jacket in a black holdall that he had carried with him. The jacket had hung to one side of the coat stand in the hallway, close to the front door. In one pocket he found a pruning knife. He had also found a cap. He was given the tablets. All of which went into the black bag. Opening the fridge, the other man took out a 500 ml bottle of water, and handed it to the other. He would need that to take all those tablets. A nod was the only reply, and the bottle went into the bag. The last item to go into the bag was Finch's private laptop computer. Both men departed out of the front door, speaking to nobody. They went to separate cars: one sped off towards London with the computer, the other made a quick call on his mobile, then turned the car round and headed to the top of Blossom Hill lane. The dog handler completed his search, realised that the two men had gone, and reported to the Inspector. He said that he had searched and found nothing of interest and that the others had gone. The Inspector went into the garden, apologised again for asking them to wait outside, and advised them that they could now return to the house. The Inspector and the dog handler made notes in their respective pocket notebooks.

16

Proffitt flew to Washington in grand style on a chartered aircraft. It was as if he were the conquering hero returning home: for many, the problem was that he really believed that to be the situation. He had, in the course of the build-up to the war, become subservient to the Administration, in particular to President Franklin and the driving force of Vice President Crompton. Now they were going to thank him officially. Mrs Proffitt was with him and was going to maximize the global exposure, particularly as her husband was talking about relinquishing power as Prime Minister. They could then really get on the world stage and market themselves. They had tasted the high life and now wanted a lot more of it. Also part of the entourage was Edward Reilly, the advisor who masterminded the controlling of ministers and the closure of difficult situations and questions. Now, having endured the onslaught of negative public opinion, Proffitt was going to get some of the rewards – albeit in the USA; and to hell with those at home who had rallied against him, and continued to do so.

In America he was greeted as he had become to expect, like a king; but he had not attained that title yet. Franklin used the British Prime Minister because he had a manipulative way with words, something he himself lacked. That was, in part, why the President and the Administration were hugely grateful for Proffitt's decision to join them in the invasion of

Maspamia. Of course most of those bestowing the plaudits were unaware of the considerable incentives that had been offered. The press was in attendance and all offered photo opportunities, but the cream of interviews was only available to selected media, those who supported the cause. The whole show was a charade. Proffitt was to be awarded the US Golden Medal of Honour.

When it was proposed that Proffitt should be awarded this particular medal it caused a storm of protests in Congress, and one congressman made a passionate plea against him being given the award:

'I stand before you today in strong opposition to this proposition of presenting Prime Minister Proffitt with a Golden Medal of Honour, for a number of reasons. First, I believe that in doing so is to place a burden on our people, who have to pay tens of thousands of tax dollars to give a golden medal to a foreign leader. It is both immoral and unconstitutional. Second, though these golden medals derive from American tax dollars, at least in the past we have awarded them to great humanitarians and leaders. These medals normally go to deserving individuals, to recognise a life of service and leadership, and not, as in this case, for political reasons. This means that the current proposal is different. I know that there is no claim that the British Prime Minister has given a lifetime of humanitarian service or demonstrated historical leadership; so why is the proposition being made? The British Prime Minister is being given this medal for one reason: he provided political support when international allies were sought for our attack on Maspamia. In my opinion, this overtly political justification degrades both the medal itself and the achievements of those who have been awarded it previously. I would like to draw your attention to a British television poll that found Prime Minister Proffitt to be the most unpopular man in Great Britain: and I urge a 'no' vote on this occasion.'

This was high-level politics, and it was an issue that the administration was not going to lose. The vote went against those who sought the 'no' option; and so the scene was set for Prime Minister Proffitt to be awarded the medal. It was to be a public display of thanks from the President. The remainder of Proffitt's visit would be low-key. For now, Neil Proffitt was to be the focus of the American nation. People might not have liked him at home, but the Americans seemed to adore him and that, for him, was a wow factor. However, as Franklin and Crompton had planned, the audience was selected and restricted to those who supported what was happening. That was an easy task, as those who opposed did not want to witness the event. At the ceremony, Franklin set the scene and then made the award. He stood to one side to allow Proffitt to give a speech. This was his real moment of glory. Television cameras beamed the ceremony and his speech on numerous TV channels, and he made the most of it. The worries of an illegal war were a world away. He was being rewarded as he would expect. The chosen audience was in a gracious mood and they gave him numerous standing ovations.

Whilst in America, Proffitt had private talks with Franklin who was still smarting from the UK's "dodgy dossier": the fact that it had not been endorsed by the UK's leading scientist had been picked up by the media. Crompton, who had been involved in supporting Franklin, remained in the background. That way, the snooping media would not easily put together the whole picture. There were already allegations that when Proffitt left the office of Prime Minister, he was to have a place on the board of a major financial institution as an advisor. He would not have a vote, but it would net him $2million in the first year, then a million each year after. He would also be asked to be an advisor to a global insurer. He was to be engaged as a consultant by some selected governments and have a place on the board of a foreign oil company reaping

$2.5million a year. Crompton had managed to achieve these discreet positions, avoiding at all costs any connection to any company he was directly involved with. He had long ago reached the decision that Proffitt was a waffler and not a businessman. He was always amazed how people flocked to listen to him speak, and would never understand why any country or organisation would seek his advice, as he had clearly screwed up his own country. But that did not matter because Proffitt was on a high, and he departed the US heading for the Far East. The ovations were still ringing in his ears and the gold was in his pocket. The world was his and, he thought, rightly so.

17

The car journey from Finch's house up through the country lanes to the top of Blossom Hill lane was undertaken without any problems. The driver stopped in an area where cars could turn round. The car faced uphill so the driver could see anybody approaching. The black holdall was on the seat next to him. He would rather have been taking the laptop to London than sitting in a shitty country lane in the early hours of the morning. Nothing moved and there was no sound. He moved to make himself more comfortable. His brief was to go to the end of the lane where somebody would collect the holdall. So where was that somebody? He would give them an ear pounding when they showed up. The driver's door sprang open and he fell towards it. His hands grabbed for the steering wheel to steady himself. Then he felt the cold of the gun barrel on the side of his head. Fear ran though his body and he did not move. A voice uttered the word, 'Holdall.' Without speaking, his hands moved slowly to the side and gripped the handles. He lifted it up and passed it between his body and the steering-wheel. He moved in slow motion. 'Move it,' commanded the voice. He passed the holdall from his left hand to his right and then out of the car. It was pulled from his grip. Then the holdall, the cold steel of the gun and the individual were gone. He waited a few moments, then looked around. There was nothing. He closed the door and started the engine, switched on the headlights. There was nobody. He put it in gear and swung the car round to head back down the lane. He was breathing heavily and sweating. All his training had told him to lock the doors and keep alert. He had been caught out. He asked himself why he hadn't been able to take the laptop; then he would have been OK.

Spider had enjoyed that little bit of excitement, and he made his way in the darkness along the track and down to the cruiser. Cornell checked the contents of the holdall. He put the pruning knife, tablets and bottle of water on the table. He replaced the jacket and hat back in the holdall. Spider watched the process. Cornell had received a call on the mobile. He checked his watch, and said, 'We will carry him up to the woods, then force feed him the tablets; then we cut a wrist. When they find him, it will look like suicide. We just have to wait for a call to do it. Once we go, Crogan will take the cruiser back to the boatyard.'

'How do we get out?' enquired Spider.

'We will get told that when we get our next orders.'

Spider made no further comment.

* * * *

Sarah Hardy's telephone rang. She awoke and looked at her bedside clock. It was just before 6am. She picked up the telephone to find that the caller was Sgt Kennedy at Clifton Vale police station. He explained that there was a missing person and asked whether she was able to assist with the search. Sarah was a volunteer member of the local search team along with her collie dog, Rusty, who had been trained in search techniques. She was self-employed and reasonably flexible with her time, and said she was available. She was asked to be at Clifton Vale police station with her dog for a 07.15 briefing. She got up and quickly prepared herself for the occasion. Suitable clothing, walking boots, two large flasks filled with coffee and snacks were her priority, and they went into her rucksack. Then she got Rusty's grab bag which contained dog food, water and two bowls, a couple of towels and some treats. From experience she knew that these searches could mean long, tiring days, so her motto was to plan for the worst. Lastly, she fitted Rusty with his search harness and departed the house. She found the volunteering to be good for her, and Rusty loved it, even though there were often some unpleasant times. The sky had some cloud and so the weather would be unpredictable.

The police station was busy for the time of day as she made for the briefing room, where she met Simon Roach, also a search volunteer. The briefing provided only limited information. A male, a government scientist in his late 50's, had left home the previous day at about 3pm in the afternoon. He had planned to take a walk of about half an hour or so but had not returned home. Sgt Kennedy asked Sarah and Simon to search the area up from Hillgrove village to Bluebell Wood and the wood itself. With Rusty in the back of her estate car, they began the journey which took about 15 minutes. When they arrived at Hillgrove, they drove up to the end of Blossom Hill lane and parked the car. Sarah noted the time as being 08.00. She opened the rear door, allowing Rusty to jump out. He ran about sniffing the ground and relieving himself, his tale wagging in excitement at the idea of another long walk. They set off up the track leading to the right-hand side of the wood. They did not rush, as Rusty needed to absorb the smells and delve into the undergrowth. Sarah would keep calling him back and then allowing him to rush off again, his nose working overtime. They reached and passed a couple of paths that ran through the wood, but they continued on to the end of the wood. The path continued down to the river. As Rusty had not picked up any unusual scent or object, they continued down to the river.

On the boat, Crogan had spotted the searchers on the river path and gave a warning to the others. Cornell had prepared for just such an event. Finch was in the cabin, lying on the bench seat in what seemed to be a semi-conscious state. Crogan, previously all in black, was now in jeans, trainers and a green sweatshirt. He stood by the cockpit door, which was open to the river-bank. Spider had come up from below and was similarly dressed. He went and stood close to Crogan. Below, Cornell kept out of sight, as he wanted to avoid talking to strangers with his American accent; he also wanted to make sure Finch kept quiet. He took the container and poured some of the anaesthetic agent onto a cloth. The fumes affected him slightly and he jammed the cloth over Finch's nose and mouth. It caused almost immediate unconsciousness. Cornell was aware that too much use of the chemical could cause serious harm or even death. That, of course, was not a problem, as it was destined that Finch was going to die. From his bag Cornell took a large volume syringe; he found a suitable place in the left wrist in which to take blood from Finch. Because his body had closed down, it was not an easy task; but he managed it. Having made a number of attempts, it had marked the skin; but that was the wrist that was to be cut, so it would be covered up. He followed the instructions for the safe storage of the blood until it was required. Cornell then heard Spider speak, and so became aware that there were people on the bank.

Sarah and Simon walked up alongside the cruiser. Simon called out, 'Good morning.'

Spider replied, 'Morning, you're about early, s'pose the dog needs a walk.'

Simon told them that they were part of a search team looking for a missing man. He explained that the man was in his late 50s, white shirt, jeans and brown walking shoes. He had gone for a walk about 3 to 3.30 the previous afternoon but had not returned home.

Spider responded, 'We've not seen anybody like that. There was a helicopter flying about in the early hours, otherwise nothing.'

Simon questioned him about the helicopter: 'Was it overhead, over the wood?'

'It flew about all over the place, but it was difficult to see. It didn't have a search-light or anything,' replied Spider.

Sarah did not like the other man, who had said nothing but just looked at them. She was aware that Rusty was giving signs of unease, and this was a dog that loved everybody.

'You guys on holiday?' asked Sarah.

Spider responded, 'Sort of, we are trying out the cruiser to see if we want to buy it.'

Sarah had begun to ask another question when Simon interrupted her, and said that they should be going. 'OK, bye,' said Sarah and the pair walked back along the path to the track that led up the hill. Once clear, Simon said, 'I didn't like that pair one bit, so we were best out of the way.'

'Do you think that they might be connected to the missing man?' asked Sarah.

'I don't know; but we are best out of it and we can let the police know when we speak to them.' Sarah still had an uneasy feeling about the men on the cruiser but they were tasked with searching for the missing man.

Onboard the cruiser, the two men watched the pair walk away and disappear from sight at a bend in the river. Crogan had been holding an automatic handgun fitted with a silencer. It was out of sight of the pair, but had the need arisen he would have shot both searchers in quick succession. They had in fact had a narrow escape. Once the pair had gone, Cornell came up and joined the two men. Crogan asked if he should deal with them. Cornell said that everything was going to plan so there was no need to complicate things.

Spider changed back into his dark combat-style outfit. Cornell, still in his dark outfit, answered the call to his mobile phone. It was a one-way conversation with Cornell listening. He ended the call with a 'Yes, sir.' Cornell told Spider to get Finch ready to move, and to untie his hands and feet. They manhandled Finch, who was still unconscious, up from the cabin into the cockpit area. Crogan then used the binoculars to look out for people. Spider went below and grabbed the holdall with Finch's personal items in it. Cornell knew time was short, as the searchers would head up to the wood: so they needed to be there first, and to dump the body ready for it to be found. The three men carefully lifted Finch from the cruiser to the river bank. Without ceremony, Crogan climbed back onto the cruiser and started the engine. Cornell and Spider let loose the moorings, and Crogan steered the cruiser out into the river and away from the scene. The pair, now looking – from a distance – like police officers, began their journey up towards the other side of the wood, keeping as much as possible to the undergrowth. Cornell, with Finch draped over his right shoulder, set a fast pace, with Spider carrying the holdall behind him.

Cornell moved through the undergrowth that had consumed part of the track. He entered a clearing and noted the oak tree on his left. He moved quickly over to it and, with help from Spider removed Finch from his shoulder. They lowered him down so that he lay flat on the ground. Cornell told Spider to get the tablets, water and pruning knife out of the holdall. Cornell popped some tablets out of the bubble packet and opened the water bottle. He then got hold of Finch's head and pulled his jaw open. Finch was regaining consciousness and was vaguely aware of what was happening. He tried to struggle but only succeeded in knocking his head on a tree stump, producing a couple of slight cuts. Cornell was a powerful man and he took control. He forced Finch's mouth open sufficiently to allow Spider to push in a couple of tablets. Water followed. The process was repeated. Cornell decided that Finch had probably swallowed enough tablets for the deception.

Working against time, Cornell moved to Finch's left side. He grabbed his left arm and removed the wristwatch from his left wrist. Spider had taken the pruning knife from the bag and handed it to Cornell. He made some rough cuts before he pushed the blade in on the side closest to the body where the ulnar artery is located. He then drew the blade from the inside of the wrist across away from the body. It created one deep wound that severed the ulnar artery but not the radial artery, which is located much closer to the surface of the skin. Blood did not pump out, as would be expected when cutting an artery; the wound just bled. Because Finch had tried to move his arm, it had moved into an awkward position. Cornell looked at his handywork. It was the first time he had been told to recreate a suicide in this way. Spider had watched the proceedings from the other side of the body. He was going to speak, but thought better of it. You did not challenge Cornell when he was at work. What Spider had realised was that Cornell had cut away from the body, whereas if Finch had cut his own wrist, the cut would have been towards the body: this would have severed the radial artery first, which would also have been more effective. Spider hoped that they would be long gone before the medical specialist got to the scene, as they would know immediately that the wound had not been self-inflicted.

Finch's body had almost shut down. His head rolled to one side and he vomited. It ran down the side of his face to his ear. Cornell realised that most of the tablets he had managed to force into Finch had probably now come out. He did not have time to worry about that. Those higher-up would have to cover up issues like that. Both men then lifted Finch so that he was slumped up against the tree. Cornell then took from the pocket on the side of his combat-style trousers a small syringe. Removing the cover from the needle, he pushed it into the cut wrist and pushed the plunger. A potent, untraceable poison was in the syringe and it delivered the fatal blow to Finch in seconds. When he had finished, both men stood and looked at the body. The scene looked as if Finch had sat down, taken some tablets and then cut his wrist. It was suicide.

Cornell, aware that the searchers could find the location at any time, told Spider to retrace their steps back along the track. He moved away, carrying the holdall with items still in it, including the remains of the bottle of water. Cornell did a final check of the site and then followed. They moved into thicker undergrowth until they found a suitable place to hide. Once out of sight, Cornell made a mobile phone call. The orders were to stay out of sight until somebody came to find them. Both men reflected that their lives revolved around high action for short periods, then long periods of hanging about doing nothing.

* * * *

Sarah and Simon retraced their route back along the river footpath and then turned onto the track that went up the hill. They continued along the edge of the wood, allowing Rusty time to rush about in the undergrowth. When they reached the wider track that went into the wood, they turned and followed it. At the end of that track, there was a narrow track to the left which led down and round the bottom of the wood to join the path that led down to Hillgrove. To the right, the track was much less used and went through some heavy undergrowth and down to the river.

Sarah was aware that Rusty was behaving a bit strangely: he was stopping, sniffing, looking back at her then moving a short distance and doing the same thing. Both Sarah and Simon had a good look round but found nothing. They headed in the direction of the river and passed an area that was well overgrown. Rusty had rushed ahead, seemingly less agitated, and was back to rushing about sniffing. He had disappeared into the undergrowth when they heard him barking and he suddenly appeared, running back to Sarah. This was most unusual behaviour because he was a trained search dog, and would wait at the 'find and bark' until Sarah arrived. He went to Sarah and sat on the ground looking up at her. She realised that he was alarmed by something and so she told him to stay. Sarah began to walk into the undergrowth where Rusty had come out.

Simon had been looking elsewhere but was now a short distance behind her. The undergrowth was rather thick but she suddenly entered a clearing. It was then that she saw the body, with the head and shoulders slumped against the base of a mature oak tree, almost in a sitting position. She called to Simon who came to join her. They both stood for a few moments, looking at the body. It was a male, and they presumed it was the person they were searching for. Sarah checked for a pulse but did not find one. She noted that he had vomited, and that the vomit stain ran to his ear. She got her notebook out and recorded the details and time. The man's legs were out in front of him. His right arm was lying by the side of him. His left arm had a lot of blood on it around the wrist and hand. It was bent back in a strange position. She recorded that there was not much blood around the body. He was dressed in jeans, had sturdy brown shoes and wore a white shirt. She did not notice any objects close to the body.

Sarah realised that Rusty had not followed them, which was really odd. Whilst she continued making notes, she asked Simon to call the police station. He got his mobile phone out and, using the telephone numbers they had been given, called the police station at Clifton Vale. He was unable to get through, called 999 and received an immediate response. He gave details, and asked the police to call him back. He gave the mobile number. About two minutes later, Sergeant Kennedy, the duty sergeant at Clifton Vale, called. Simon explained where they were and described the scene. He told them not to touch anything and to walk back down to their car. He was dispatching police officers who would meet them at the car. He asked that they show the officers when they arrived where the body was. They confirmed that they would leave the body and walk back down the track to the car. They left the site as they found it and, once out of the undergrowth and on the footpath, Sarah found Rusty sitting waiting for her. She made a fuss of him and they began the walk back to the car. Rather than walk back through the wood, they decided to follow the track that ran down outside the wood to join the path below.

They had just started to follow the track when they confronted two men and a woman coming up the track towards them. The three were dressed in civilian clothes. Upon meeting, one of them identified himself as DC Peter Munroe and said that they were police officers from Clifton Vale. He showed his identity card and did all of the talking. Neither Sarah nor Simon had seen any of the officers before. The other two never spoke. Sarah commented, 'That was quick.'

'What do you mean?' responded DC Munroe.

'We only just telephoned Clifton Vale to tell them about the body, and they said they would send officers over.'

'Who are you?' asked DC Munroe.

Sarah replied, 'I'm Sarah Hardy and this is Simon Roach, and my dog is called Rusty. We are from the Volunteer Search team, civvies who get called in to help look for missing people and stuff.' She paused, 'Were you not briefed.'

'No,' replied Munroe.

The two who did not speak glanced at each other, and Munroe looked up the track.

'So you found a body.'

'Yes, just up there,' said Sarah, pointing. She continued, 'It's a man, slumped up against a tree with cuts to one wrist.'

'OK,' said Munroe 'We will take it from here.'

Simon asked if they wanted to be shown where the body was. Munroe agreed that they did. Simon told Sarah to go back to the car; he would show them where the body was and then join her. Sarah, as a matter of course, checked the time and wrote in her notebook.

Simon led the short distance along the track to the area of heavy undergrowth. He stopped at the point where he and Sarah had pushed their way through.

He turned to Munroe, 'He's just through there: it opens into a clearing, and the body is slumped against a tree.'

'Did you touch or move the body?' enquired Munroe.

'No, it's just as we found it,' replied Simon.

Munroe looked at Simon, 'OK, you leave it with us and go back and join your colleague.'

Simon did not need to be told twice and departed the scene. When he reached the car, Sarah spoke, 'Everything OK?'

'Yes, no problems,' he replied.

'I see two of them have come back down,' she said, looking past him up the path.

He turned and saw the man and woman who had not spoken. As they reached Sarah and Simon they did not stop or acknowledge them, but continued walking down Blossom Hill Lane towards the village of Hillgrove. Sarah and Simon had poured drinks from the flask. 'That's odd,' said Sarah, 'Not like your usual copper who would have something to say. Wonder why they didn't stay with the other one?'

'Don't think they are local: and to be in the area before the search team is odd,' commented Simon.

* * * *

136

Munroe, having located the body, told his colleagues to go. It would mean less explaining to do once the police search teams arrived. When they had gone, he went along the track calling for Cornell. He did not go far when he confronted two men. 'You Cornell?' he asked the larger of the two.

Cornell nodded.

'OK, we've not got long,' added Munroe.

They all returned to the body.

Munroe took charge and told Cornell that they needed to put the jacket on the body. Cornell did not ask why, but did as he was told. The three of them lifted the body and, with Cornell and Spider holding it up, Munroe struggled to put the coat on. Once it was in place they lowered the body down. Now it was laying flat on the ground, the head close to a root of the tree. Cornell took off Finch's glasses and put them in the jacket pocket. He noted that there was a mobile phone in the pocket. There were three packets of tablets, some of which Cornell had managed to get Finch to swallow; the remainder he had stuffed into his own pockets. One had remained in the packet. He put the empty packets into Finch's jacket pocket. The wrist watch was put close to the body on the left side. The knife was put on the ground close to the wrist. The left arm was not now contorted and the right arm was laid up onto his chest. The quarter-full water bottle was placed upright by his head and the top by its side. His cap was placed on the ground, also on the left side. Cornell handed Munroe the syringe full of Finch's blood. He then began to apply the blood onto the wrist watch, knife and water bottle. Then more blood was put around the cut in the wrist, and some was smeared onto the jacket and shirt.

The three men surveyed the scene. Although it looked like suicide with all of the key elements in place, Spider thought that it looked too precise, with objects placed rather than dropped after use. And the cut to the wrist was done in the wrong direction. However, he was with two people who vied to be in charge, and were clearly not comfortable in each other's company. There was no way he was going to rock the boat, so he said nothing. The last task was to tidy the site; then Cornell and Spider were to leave and return to their hide, leaving Munroe to guard the body and await the police searchers.

Two uniformed police search officers, Mike Devlin and Roger Palmer, arrived followed by two para medics, Eddy Sale and Kate Hope who parked their ambulance close to Sarah's car. Mike Devlin had been delegated to lead the search on the ground. He asked Sarah and Simon what they had found. Sarah, with her notes, went straight to the point of describing the finding of the body, giving a good description of the man and the area. PC Palmer made notes as she spoke. Simon then added information about the three police officers in civvies, and how two of them had gone back to the village leaving one, identified as DC Munroe, with the body. Neither of the police search officers had heard of or had been briefed about a DC Munroe. The officers were not mentioned at the briefing. Nobody should have been with the body as it was a crime scene. Simon offered to show them where the body was located. He led the four up the path. Sarah stayed at the car.

As soon as they entered the clearing, PC Palmer took photographs of the body. The paramedics attended to Finch and checked for any signs of life. There were none. They opened his coat, then his shirt and fitted electrode pads to his chest. They attempted to revive him but were not successful. The paramedics lifted Dr Finch's eyelids, felt for a pulse and applied a heart monitor, but it was all to no avail.

PC Devlin approached DC Munroe and introduced himself, 'PC Devlin.'

'DC Munroe,' was the response.

'Have you touched or moved anything?' asked Devlin.

'No,' replied Munroe.

'How come you managed to get here so quick?' enquired Devlin.

'We were told to come and search in the area.'

'Not by our station,' added Devlin.

'No,' replied Munroe.

Getting little response from Munroe, Devlin went over to the body. Eddy Sale looked up as he spoke to Devlin, 'No hope, he's well gone.'

'OK,' replied Devlin, 'his description fits that of the missing man.'

'Roger, can you call the station and give them the details?'

Palmer nodded and moved away to make the call. Devlin turned to the paramedics, 'OK, what have we got?' he asked.

Kate Hope began, 'He's a male, guess he's late 50s early 60s. He is lying on the ground close to a tree. There are a series of attempted incised wounds, but one main cut.' She paused and moved slightly, 'The problem is the lack of blood around the body. When somebody cuts an artery, whether accidentally or intentionally, the blood pumps everywhere.' She looked around, 'As you can see, there's not a lot of blood. There is this small patch on his right knee, but no obvious arterial bleeding. There was no spraying of blood or huge blood loss, or any obvious loss on the clothing.'

PC Devlin nodded.

Hope continued, 'I think it is incredibly unlikely that he died from the wrist wounds.'

PC Palmer had finished his call and was making notes of what was being said.

Sale added, 'We are just paramedics but, having seen all types of trauma, I go along with what Kate has said: that this man did not die from a cut wrist, but then it's for a pathologist to determine.'

Kate added, 'He has vomited at some point.'

'Anything else?' asked Devlin.

Kate looked at the body, 'Well, what's strange is that there is the small bottle of water that has been opened, but it still has water in it, and it's propped up. If somebody cut their wrist I would not expect them to lean over onto the cut and stand a bottle up like that. There is a gardening knife, which is the worst possible knife to use if you are going to slit your wrists. You would use something sharper. There is the discarded and somewhat bloodied wrist watch, which I presume was removed to allow access to the wrist. I would question why it has blood on it if it was removed before the cutting of the wrist.' She looked up at the officers, 'But eh, what do I know? I'm only a medic!'

'OK,' said Devlin. He looked at Palmer, 'have you got all that.'

Palmer nodded and answered 'Yes.'

Devlin thanked the paramedics, who were recording their actions and findings for the official record. When they had completed the form, they collected all of their equipment and departed the scene.

PC Devlin had forgotten about DC Munroe but, looking round, he was nowhere to be seen. He asked Palmer if he had seen him go. He had not: one minute he was there, the next gone. 'Something is bloody strange there,' remarked Devlin. The police officers taped off the area as a crime scene and then moved to the part of the undergrowth where they had entered the clearing. They now had to wait for the police forensic team and the pathologist to arrive.

Bluebell Wood was quiet. The sun was shining and, apart from the fact that it was the site of a gruesome death, it would have been a pleasant place to spend some time. The two police officers had nothing else to do but wait. They did not know how long it would be, so PC Devlin decided that PC Palmer should go back down the track to guide the forensic team to

140

the spot when they arrived. Devlin had been alone for a few minutes when he heard the distinctive noise of a helicopter which seemed to be approaching the location. Nobody had communicated with him to advise of any helicopter activity. Were they bringing the forensic team in by air? Was it the media? Then he saw the helicopter: it was not one he recognized as being used by the police. It dropped down below his line of sight. Although he was guarding the crime scene, he decided to find out what was happening and who was on the aircraft. He pushed through the undergrowth along the track heading towards the river. He could hear it but not see it: then, through a break in the undergrowth and trees, he saw it.

It had landed in a field. Its rotor blades still spun as it sat on the ground. Then the side door opened, but nobody got out. He spotted three figures running across the field from the track further below him towards it. One was in civvies and two were in black police search uniforms. 'Shit!' he exclaimed to himself. Although he was not very close, he could see that the one in civvies was Munroe; but he had no idea who the other two were. The three climbed aboard the aircraft and then he heard the engines power up. It lifted off the ground and skywards before banking away from him, gaining height. Devlin made hasty notes of what he had seen then called the station on his mobile phone. He told Sergeant Kennedy, who was in charge of the search, about what had occurred. He was told that it was an operational matter, and not to say any more.

PC Devlin was quite relieved when the forensic team arrived, because it ended his involvement. After a formal hand-over, he and PC Palmer, who had led them to the spot, left the scene. Crime scene tents were erected and the forensic work began. They would have to wait for the pathologist to arrive to record the scene before the body could be removed for an autopsy. Walking down the track towards the patrol car they met with Sarah, still at her car at the top of Blossom Hill Lane. Simon had departed, as he had to go to work. As ever, Sarah was well prepared and offered both officers a cup of coffee. Drinking coffee and absorbing the sun's warmth, Devlin asked Sarah if she was OK; it was not every day that she would see a body with blood around it. She said she was fine.

'Could we take a statement from you now?' asked Palmer.

'Sure,' she replied, and got out her note book.

'OK, start from the beginning.'

'I got a call at home from Sergeant Kennedy to see if I could help on the search. I agreed and was at Clifton Vale police station at about 07.00 hrs for a briefing at 07.15. The briefing just told us that a man in his late 50s had gone out for a walk the previous day at about 3.pm and had not returned home. I was paired with Simon Roach, and we were told to search up and around Bluebell Wood. We made our way over and parked the car here. We went up the path past the wood on our left and continued down to the river. Rusty was off his lead and searching for any traces or scents. We were not given any clothing belonging to the missing man to aid Rusty's search. At the river we noticed a cruiser, and went along to see if anybody was about and whether they had seen anything. There were two males on the boat, who were pretty uncommunicative. We thought there was somebody else onboard but we did not see them.' Sarah paused, 'I should say, I did not see who it was.'

The officers smiled.

'Did they speak to you?' enquired Palmer.

'Yes,' she replied, 'to tell us that a helicopter had flown round during the night and that they had not seen anybody.'

'That's it?' enquired Palmer.

'Oh, I asked them if they were on holiday.'

'How did they react to that?' enquired Palmer.

'The one who did the talking said something about trying out the cruiser as they were thinking of buying it.'

'What were they wearing? asked Palmer.

Sarah pondered, then said, 'One was wearing jeans, trainers and a green sweatshirt. He stood by the cockpit door. The other man was similarly dressed but I noted that his top was a brown colour.'

What did they look like? pressed Palmer.

Sarah thought for a moment; she had not made a note, so she was trying to picture them: 'One was well-built, muscular, dark-haired, with a mean-looking face. The other not so well-built, but I would say he works out. He was dark-haired, with a more open face. You know, friendly. He did all the talking.' She paused, then added. 'Oh, they were both white men.'

Height? pressed Palmer.

'Both just under 1.8 metres, I would think. They were on the boat and it was difficult to tell.'

'OK', said Palmer. 'You went back up to the wood?'

'Yes,' answered Sarah, 'When we got to the wood, we took the first path off and walked through, looking in the undergrowth as we went. Rusty was rushing about in and out of the undergrowth.'

'OK,' said Palmer.

Sarah continued, 'At the end we decided to turn right onto the narrow track going towards the river. We had not gone far when Rusty, who had gone into a dense piece of undergrowth, suddenly started barking.'

'You followed?' asked Palmer.

'Well, it was strange because normally Rusty would sit and bark to guide me to the spot, or come back and guide me.' Sarah paused, 'He came back and went behind me and sat down. He's never done that before.'

'What did you do?' asked Palmer.

'I saw where he had come from and called to Simon. I

walked through the undergrowth until I entered the clearing and saw the body.'

Palmer was still noting what had been said. 'OK, you saw the body, can you describe it to me?'

Sarah consulted her notebook, but did not need to as the scene was as clear as day. 'He was lying propped up against the tree, his right arm was lying by the side of his body, the left one was twisted away at a strange angle. The left arm had a cut at the wrist. There was not much blood, in fact hardly any. He wore blue jeans, brown walking-type shoes and a white shirt.'

'OK, how close did you get?' asked Palmer.

'Oh, quite close, in fact I touched him to see if I could feel a pulse but there was nothing.'

'Did you touch anything else?' asked Palmer.

'No.'

'Was there anything else at the scene?'

Sarah considered the question, then added, 'No, I did find it odd because he appeared to have cut his wrists, but there was no knife.'

'Are you absolutely sure,? questioned Palmer.

'No, there was nothing else at all,' replied Sarah. She then showed Palmer her notebook which she had written in at the time. It was a clear and full description.

'OK Sarah, what happened next?'

'Simon called Clifton Vale police station and spoke to the coordinating officer and gave details of our find, just as I have to you now.' Sarah was aware of the two officers glancing at each other. 'What's wrong?' quizzed Sarah.

'Nothing,' said Palmer.

'Well, we were told to go back down to my car and wait for you guys who would take over the scene. That's what we did.' 'But,' she added, 'we had just left where the body was when we met a DC Munroe and two other officers. They did not give their names, in fact I cannot recall them speaking at all.' Having paused and looked at her notes, she continued, 'We asked who they were, as we had been told that officers were on their way, not, already at the site. It was strange, but he had ID and who were we to challenge anybody.'

'What happened then?' asked Palmer.

'DC Munroe asked where the body was, and Simon showed him. I continued down the path. We thought it was rather odd when the man and woman who were with Munroe came down the path after us and then went on down Blossom Hill Lane. They never spoke as they went past.'

'Where was DC Munroe?' asked Palmer.

'I presume he stayed up in the woods with the body; I never saw him again,' said Sarah.

'Any idea how long he was up there before we arrived?'

Sarah checked her notebook, 'About half an hour.' Palmer finished writing then asked if he could take Sarah's notebook into possession. Palmer asked her to sign and date it under the last entry. She did it and handed it over. When he had finished drafting the statement he gave it to her to read. When she had agreed with the contents she signed and dated it. Sarah had completed the statement and that was her version of events. Devlin's mobile rang and he took the call. When he finished he advised them that it appeared Simon Roach had given a statement, and that it supported what Sarah had said.

'Would you look at the photos I took when we arrived at the body?' asked Palmer.

He moved to sit partly inside her car to get shade from the sun on the camera's screen. She studied the images, moving the camera to deflect any light off the screen, then with a clear view she could see the body.

She was quiet for a moment, then spoke softly. 'When we found him, he was propped up against the tree, not laying flat on the ground. He was not wearing that coat. His right arm was not lying on his chest as in the photo, but lying alongside his body. These things what appear to be a water-bottle, knife, watch or hat were not there. I would have seen them if they had been.' She handed the camera back to Palmer. 'None of that was at the site when we found him. There was nothing else.' Her voice was calm but firm.

Nobody said anything for several minutes, each absorbing the implications of what they had seen and what had happened. Devlin broke the silence. 'Well, as I see it, the only person we know who was with the body alone for any length of time was Munroe.'

'He was one of those who departed in the helicopter,' added Palmer.

'Well, if he did move the body and add the other things, then it would be logical that the other two who left with him were part of it,' said Devlin.

Sarah, having grasped the seriousness of the situation added, 'Well I know what I saw, and I know Simon saw the same. If it's different to what you saw, then the body was tampered with.' She paused and added, 'What do we do or say?'

Devlin said, 'If you want my opinion, we stick with what we each saw, that way it's the truth and you can't be criticised.'

Palmer agreed.

Sarah added, 'Yep, I know what I saw and I am not changing that.'

Devlin cautioned them, 'It must be a 'dirty tricks operation'. You don't get a helicopter to come in to get three people out, who we don't know about, if there's not something funny going on. They could easily have walked down the track and used vehicles like the rest of us, so it's a case of keeping your heads down.'

The first job when Sarah got home was to look after Rusty.

He had done a good job but had been upset by something, so he deserved a bit of comforting. Once he had settled she ran a hot foamy bath. Then it was a choice, wine or beer. A cool beer won. Relaxing in the bath, Sarah sipped her beer. Some spilled and ran down her chin. Wiping her chin, she put the drink down and lay back further in the bath, eyes closed. Then, her eyes open again, she remembered that the vomit stain on Finch ran from his mouth down to his ear. For that to have happened, his body would have to have been lying down, not slumped up against the tree. If you are sitting up, liquid runs down. The more she thought about it, her only conclusion was that Finch's body must have been moved after he vomited. When she had finished with the bath and was dressed, she texted Simon and asked if he would call in to see her when he was in the area.

It was about 4pm when Simon called round. Sarah opened the door, saying, 'Hi, thanks for calling round, come in.'

'I can't stop, I've got a job on.'

'OK, when I was with Dr Finch's body today, I noted that he had vomited.'

'Yep, I saw that.'

'Well, the vomit ran from his mouth to his ear.'

'So?'

'Well, when we found him he was almost sitting up, and if he had vomited, then it would have run down over his chin. Not into his ear.'

'Shit,' exclaimed Simon, 'I never thought of that, but you'r right.' He thought for a moment, 'There must be a logical explanation.'

'Well, there's none that I can think of,' she countered.

Simon was silent.

'Do you think we should tell the police?' asked Sarah.

Simon considered that option. 'No, leave it and say nothing. There was those two blokes on the cruiser who I wouldn't trust, then the three who arrived at the scene minutes after we reported the find. Something's not right about all this. As Devlin said, keep your head down. No, forget it.'

Sarah pondered, 'OK, we found the body, it's up to the authorities to sort it out now.'

18

The men and women who arrived and entered the mobile communications unit parked outside the Finchs' home were not police officers. The officers who were manning the equipment were told to leave. Police sergeant Kennedy had given a full briefing to ACC Long who, in turn, reported it to a senior police officer in London. The people who had arrived at the site were there to confirm the details and deal with any loose ends. Communications were first made to an aircraft heading from the US to the UK. It was due to land shortly and they needed to brief Reilly, who was a passenger in First Class. The man on the ground provided as much detail as possible, but the link was not scrambled. He was aware that once on the ground, Reilly would advise on the way ahead, as the Prime Minister was also airborne several thousand miles away, en route to the Far East. The Deputy Prime Minister was, in theory, in charge of the country but Reilly wanted him kept out of the loop. He didn't need things complicated. The situation was such that it needed to be handled with care and diplomacy. Reilly knew that they were not qualities that he possessed, but once on the ground he could call the Prime Minister.

Reilly departed the aircraft first and was met by an official who led him down steps to the tarmac. A car was waiting and, once he was in it it sped to the VIP reception area where a high-speed police car was waiting. The formalities were soon dealt with, and then he was being taken to the area of the incident. It was very low-key, and no journalist realised where he was. A search within the airport drew a blank. By the time they knew anything he would be back in London, rattling a sabre to get a plan of action underway. As they approached the communications centre, there were a few people watching the activities, including members of the local press. Reilly, who would normally show his face, bent over to lay down on the back seat of the police car. It drove up to the door of the unit, which had been screened off from prying eyes. Reilly lost no time in getting out of the car and into the unit. The first to speak was the ACC. Without any delay he gave a briefing to Reilly. When that was done, he left. Reilly used a handset and waited to be connected to Proffitt.

Prime Minister Proffitt was enjoying the luxury of a first-class flight aboard a private chartered aircraft flying to the Far East. Two senior members of the Cabinet sat in the first class area, along with Mrs Proffitt. One of the cabinet members was included in some of the underlying activities surrounding the dossier. One problem was that he and Reilly did not get on. Proffitt was still on a high from the reception in the US, but there was nobody to share the excitement with. Those accompanying him had either been present or had heard about it several times. In business class were some of the media who fully supported the Prime Minister and the government, and who had supported the war. Those who were not so loyal were in economy. It was, up until that point, a pleasant flight.

Proffitt came on the phone and the two men exchanged the normal greetings. Proffitt enquired as to whether Reilly had had a good flight, and Reilly replied by asking if he was himself having a good flight. Pleasantries exchanged, Reilly gave Proffitt a short and to-the-point briefing. He could speak openly, as the communications were scrambled to avoid eavesdroppers. With the message delivered, Proffitt was concerned as to how it would affect him and the government in general. Reilly explained that the lid was being well and truly kept on the pot, but he still asked Proffitt how he wanted it handled. Proffitt decided that whilst it was not yet news in the UK, he would hold a press conference when they landed. They discussed the options and Reilly advised that they should set up an inquiry into Finch's death. Proffitt agreed and asked him to set the wheels in motion. Reilly proposed that there be a formal inquiry with a very narrow remit. He would obtain a list of suitable chairpersons who could be approached and who would be sympathetic towards the situation. With that agreed, the media bandwagon in the UK could be brought into action. Of course, the Prime Minister and the government would regret the course of action that Dr Finch had taken, and would support the family at this traumatic time. With the plan outlined, the two men would speak later.

Proffitt, who had moved away from his wife to take the call, went back and spoke to her. He told her about Finch. Her reaction was to the effect that not only had he been a nuisance over the dossier, but had now decided to take his life when her Neil was just enjoying celebrity status in the US and indeed around the world. Proffitt then went to his two cabinet members and gave them the news. One, who was always willing to provide support mainly because Proffitt was having to support him with regard to his misdemeanors, asked how he could assist. Proffitt explained that they were setting up an inquiry and, until they were back in the UK, Reilly would be looking after affairs. Proffitt, joined by his co-conspirator, went into business class and gave an impromptu press conference. These were the sympathetic media, and there were not a lot of questions because they were in the air and communications would be restricted. Proffitt really did not want to go and address the media in economy, but was persuaded to do so.

When he entered the cabin, it seemed vast compared with the other cabins, and a small sea of faces looked up at him. He addressed them as they sat silently noting the words down. When he had finished he said that when they landed he would get more information and hold a press conference so that they would be fully informed. He was about to leave when the words rang in his ears, 'Prime Minister, does this mean that you have the doctor's death on your hands?' The words seemed to overpower him, and his cabinet minister stepped in. 'The Prime Minister was in the USA and on this flight when this tragic death occurred. He had no part in it. He will give more information once he has been updated after we land.' Proffitt returned to the safety of the first-class cabin; he was not looking forward to the next press conference.

* * * *

It was after 2pm when the pathologist Dr Robert Cley arrived at the crime scene. The walk up the hill to the wood had left him slightly out of breath. When he arrived he saw two police crime scene tents. One was for personnel at the scene and the other covered the body. He had been briefed about the situation, and that was one reason for the delay. Communications with a certain aircraft heading towards the Far East and carrying the Prime Minister had also delayed him. He had then had to speak with Edward Reilly, the Prime Minister's advisor. This was clearly not a run-of-the-mill investigation and it was going to be under the spotlight of the media. For him, it was just another job that had serious political implications. He had yet to see the body, but the focus was clearly on the point that the eminent scientist had committed suicide.

He walked over to and entered the police tent. Three or four people were inside. All were in white forensic coveralls.

He spoke with the senior police officer at the site, to ascertain an overall picture. It seemed straightforward. A body, cut wrist and blood were what they had seen. Possibly pills of some description had been taken. The details were down to the pathologist to determine. The entire site and body had been photographed. He found it was a bit unnerving when the police officer referred to the subject as a straightforward suicide. He thought there was nothing straightforward about discussing the situation with the Prime Minister who was on board an aircraft in flight, on the other side of the world.

He then donned a white forensic coverall and put on surgical gloves. It was a short walk to the other tent that had been erected over Dr Finch's body. Entering, he had his first sight of Dr Finch. The body was laying flat on its back, close to the base of a tree. He was wearing a green-waxed jacket, a white shirt and jeans. His left arm was flexed at the elbow and had a cut with blood at the wrist. His right hand, with the fist clenched, was resting on his chest. He knelt down and checked the pockets of the jacket. He found a mobile phone, glasses and three packs of ten painkiller tablets with only one tablet remaining in the blister packs. He placed each of the items in separate evidence bags. Neatly propped up on the left side, close to his head, was an opened bottle of water. It was about a quarter full and was smeared with blood. Next to the bottle was a bottle top. Also to his left side was a cap, which he noted had some blood on it. A wristwatch was also on the left side close to his wrist, lying face down on the ground. It also had blood marks on it. He noted that the watch appeared to have been removed whilst blood was already flowing, suggesting that it had been removed deliberately in order to facilitate better access to the wrist. He concluded that the removal of the watch in this way, and indeed the removal of the spectacles were consistent with actions that pointed towards it being an act of self-harm. Next to the watch was a gardener's pruning knife, its blade extended. It had blood marks on the handle and the blade. There was a pool of blood underneath it.

He checked and noted that there were no obvious signs of damage to clothing that might have occurred if there had been a life-threatening struggle. So there was no evidence to suggest Dr Finch had been restrained or subjected to a violent assault prior to his death. At this point, no consideration was given to the possibility that he had been drugged, as tests would need to be carried out at the morgue. There was no visible evidence of strangulation in any form, or the use of an arm hold. There was no evidence that he had been dragged or otherwise transported to the location at which his body was found. The doctor had considered the fact that the site around the body had been disturbed, firstly by the initial search team, then by the paramedics and then by the photographer.

Dr Finch's body was removed from the site and transferred to a hospital for a full post-mortem examination. After the preliminary observations were completed and noted, Dr Finch's body was undressed and minutely examined for blood marks, cuts or bruises or any other contamination. Dr Cley noted blood marks on some of the clothing. On the body he found heavy blood marks over the left arm; it was lighter over the back of the fingers and palm of the right hand. He did not identify the volume and spread of blood that would have come from a spurting wound to the wrist. He had no explanation as to how blood had got inside the jacket. There was evidence that Dr Finch had vomited, and it had run down the side of the face from the mouth to the ear. This indicated that it had occurred whilst he was lying down. He did not appear to consider that by vomiting, a quantity of any tablets that had been swallowed would have been ejected. At that moment in time, his first opinion was that Dr Finch had taken his own life by cutting his wrist. The pain was reduced by taking the powerful pain-killers.

Dr Cley recorded a series of incised wounds across the front of the left wrist. The largest wound was 6cm long and between 1cm and 1.5cm deep. It had completely severed the ulnar artery and partially severed the ulnar nerve. There were two deep wounds around 2cm long on the wrist. There were also a number of superficial cuts. He determined that the incised wounds over the left wrist were entirely consistent with having been inflicted by a bladed weapon. He concluded that the knife found at the scene would have caused such wounds. What was not considered in his report was how Dr Finch had made the deepest incision into the right side of the wrist and then drawn the blade across to the left. It is almost impossible to make such a cut. The logical cut would be from the left drawing across to the right. Dr Cley then went on to determine that many of the injuries may well have been inflicted over minutes rather than seconds or hours before death. He therefore considered that the nature of the wounds at the left wrist were typical of self-inflicted injury; but he did not elaborate as to how they would have been achieved. There was no evidence of any 'defence' wounds against either a sharp or blunt weapon attack.

Only a small amount of the pain-killing drug was found in Dr Finch's body. In fact the autopsy revealed that only a fifth of a tablet was found in Dr Finch's stomach. Moreover, the blood reading of each of the drug's two components was less than a third of what would normally be found in a fatal over-dose victim. This means that the volume of pain-killer found did not correspond with the volume of opened packs of tablets found with his body. In his report, Dr Cley determined that the toxicology findings showed that Dr Finch had consumed a significant quantity of these tablets either on the way to or at the scene itself. While the blood/drug levels were not considered particularly high and may not have caused death, it was said that the pain-killers may have affected the heart if there was low blood pressure as a result of bleeding.

Dr Cley's conclusions were that Dr Finch had killed himself at the place in which he was found. He determined that the main factor involved in bringing about the death of Dr Finch was the bleeding from the incised wounds to his left wrist. On the balance of probabilities, it was likely that the taking of an excessive number of pain killer tablets, if coupled with a coronary artery disease, would have played a part in his death. The fact that Dr Finch, in line with government policy, had had regular medicals and health screening because of the nature of his work; and that no coronary heart disease ever had been diagnosed was not mentioned. The die was cast: no foul play, just a case of straightforward suicide. The government had its ruling. The next step was to ensure that all the details were kept secret from the public for a very long time.

19

DC Munroe, Cornell and Spider sat without speaking as the helicopter sped over the English countryside. It was not a long flight and they were soon back on the ground. As they walked away from the aircraft towards waiting cars, the helicopter's engines were powered up, and they felt the down force from the rotors as it lifted up and away. Munroe thanked the two men for their part in what was seen as a successful operation, and indicated to a car. It was their transport for the next assignment. He walked over to another car, got in and it sped away. Cornell and Spider walked over to the car. On the driver's seat lay a brown envelope. Spider opened the door and picked it up. Cornell surveyed the small airfield. There was nobody to be seen. Spider emptied some papers onto the seat. He picked up a separate envelope with Cornell's name on it and passed it to him.

Spider had instructions to drive the car to a town in the north of England. Cornell had his separate instructions, containing the new assignment. He was in charge and would be supported by Spider. The yank was giving him orders again – and that pissed Spider off. He never showed any emotion that would upset the yank as it would certainly have resulted in a serious outcome. There was a sat nav device which had the details of the route and location already entered in it. There was a bundle of bank notes for expenses. He noted the demand that receipts were required. He contemplated that it must have been a government person who put the package together. In any event,he did not see that going partying with Cornell was on the cards. He checked the car and set up the navigation system.

Spider opened the boot and found two bags. He opened one and found civilian clothes. He checked the shoes, and from the size knew that the contents of the bag were for Cornell. He called to him and pointed to the bag. He opened the other one and removed the contents. On the deserted airfield he stripped off the dark outfit and put on the civvies. Somebody knew what they were doing as they were a perfect fit. He jammed the clothes he had removed into the bag, zipped it up and threw it into the boot of the car.

Cornell had taken a photograph from his envelope, and he looked at it long and hard. Then he read the accompanying note. It gave a name and address. It said that the target was a high grade risk against the security of both the USA and Britain. The target should be threatened so as to silence him from continuing his undermining activities. If he considered that the target would not cooperate, he was to be silenced. He was to be eliminated in a way that looked like a mugging gone wrong. Cornell hoped that the threats would not work, as he enjoyed a good beating to death. In fact he already knew that the target would not cooperate. He changed into his new clothes, the old ones going into the bag and into the boot. He was just about to get into the car when the mobile rang. He answered. The voice at the other end was monotone. 'Is that Cornell?'

'Yes.'

'Zulu 4 here.'

Cornell knew who it was. He had provided his own back-up, just in case, and had made use of their services. 'Met the target as arranged and followed. When in safe location delivered the message. The target has retired.'

'Got that,' replied Cornell. He ended the call.

Cornell was closing the trail behind him. When Crogan reached the boatyard and handed back the keys of the cruiser, he did not see the car from which Zulu 4 was watching. Crogan got in his car and drove towards London. He was followed. When he stopped to relieve himself, he saw a car stop and a male get out looking at a map. The male walked in his direction holding the map. Crogan thought he was lost and, being in a good mood, offered to help. Hidden under the map, the silenced hand-gun was unseen. Zulu 4 fired three rounds, leaving Crogan lying on the ground, hidden from the road by his car. It would be six hours before his body was found by a police patrol car.

The car sped north, with Spider unaware of the events surrounding Crogan, he was beginning to feel some of the effects of a lack of sleep over the past few days. The traffic was building up and the roads were going to be busy. Cornell looked at the countryside but absorbed none of it. It was just another country, but at least he could communicate with the locals. Although it was summer, the weather did what it always did in the UK and offered them a shower. It washed the car if nothing else. The first words that Cornell offered were that they should find some place to eat. The only option for them was a motorway café. Nobody would have given the two men a second glance as they parked the car, ate plastic motorway food, topped up the car with fuel and took to the road again. The traffic was still heavy, and Spider hoped that they did not run into one of the infamous traffic jams which could see vehicles stuck for hours with no escape.

Spider need not have worried as they approached the turn-off to the town where they were headed. Cornell now became more aware and took notice of the surroundings. It was an area of England with an industrial past, but the industry had gone, leaving rows of small houses that had once been home to the vast labour force. Now he noticed the mixture of nationalities, and that it was like parts of the US, tired and run-down. The sat nav guided them along the streets, and Spider kept to the rules of the road. He knew they would have a 'get out of jail free card' but; were never sure if it would work, and so he hoped never to have to use it. They also had two bags of incriminating evidence in the boot that they had yet to get rid of. The bosses did not like having to get involved and get their hands dirty. They restricted their input to power and money. The higher-level government officials also never wanted to get involved; they were waiting for their pension, a gong and a lucrative job in a private company for services rendered.

They had moved away from the rows of houses and had entered an area with neat semi-detached and detached houses with neat little gardens. They turned into one such road, and the sat nav announced that they had reached their destination. Spider drove along the road slowly whilst Cornell got to grips with the house numbering system. Spider spotted the house and continued past. At the end of the road it was a case of turning left or right. Cornell noted a sports field and a small car park just a short distance down the road to their left. He directed Spider to it. He swung the car to the left and, reaching the parking, area drove in. He turned the car round so that the car faced the exit. Cornell told him to stay with the car and got out. It was good to stretch his legs as he walked along the road to the junction. He noted that there were a few people about, some walking, others in their gardens. There was the occasional cyclist, and cars frequently used the road. He reflected how small everything seemed compared with the US.

He walked down the road, crossing it to be on the same side as the target house. He found the number, noted that it was a semi-detached house. There did not seem to be anybody about in the house next door. In fact it was all very quiet. He opened the gate and walked up the path to the front door.

Pushing the door-bell button he heard it chime. He stood waiting. He was beginning to think that nobody was at home when the door opened. A woman stood in the doorway. Cornell appologised for disturbing her and asked if it was the home of Mr David Pierce. She said that it was, that he was her husband. He asked if he could speak to him. She was going to ask what it was about, but decided not to. The man was polite, but there was something about him that she did not like but could not put her finger on. She said, 'He's in the back garden, I'll go and fetch him.' She left the door ajar. As she disappeared around the back of the house he gently pushed the door open further, enough to allow him to step inside the hallway.

David Pierce came through the house to the front door, to be confronted by a large, powerfully-built man. 'Can I help you?' enquired David.

'Good morning,' he grunted, 'are you Mr David Pierce?'

'I am, and who are you and what do you want?' It had not gone unnoticed by David that he was speaking to an American, and one with a military air about him. It crossed his mind that, after years of battling the Americans in his quest for information about the death of his son, somebody had listened, and that here was a messenger in person. Or it could be a religious person trying to convert him.

Cornell kept a quiet, calm voice as he spoke, 'I have to deliver a message to you: there are important people in this country and in America who are concerned about your continuing dialogue about the death of your son. The message is that you have to stop your campaign and forget how your son died.'

Instant rage flowed though David: 'How dare you come to my home and speak to me in this way! Americans killed my son, and I want to know why your people killed him and I want them to face an inquiry.'

Cornell spoke a bit more sternly, 'Mr Pierce, people in very high places are fed up with your activities, and they must stop, do you understand? You're not gonna get any Americans over here. It's in the past, forgotten.'

David looked at Cornell, 'Do not threaten me. My son died for this country, killed by your countrymen, and I want justice. Do you understand that?'

Cornell remained passive, 'I am the messenger and the message is simple. Stop the campaign you are running, tend your garden. It's in your best interest.'

David hissed through clenched teeth, 'What are you going to do to stop me? I will stop when I get the answers, and you can go and tell that to the bloody President and Prime Minister.'

Mrs Pierce, who had been listening from the kitchen, came out to join them. She looked at Cornell. 'We have had a bad time; David and I only want to know the truth.'

Cornell answered. 'The truth is that you must drop the campaign. Powerful people do not like it, and it has to stop.'

The Pierces had heard on the news that the body of Dr Finch, a government scientist who had been involved with the war in Maspamia, had been found dead in some woods. Mrs Pierce looked at Cornell and there was fear in her eyes. She knew that the messenger that stood before them was dangerous, very dangerous.

David spoke, 'When I get justice I will keep quiet; until then, my fight continues. Now leave my house.'

At this point, Cornell would normally have stepped forward and dealt with the problem his way. In this case he was under orders, and he now had to report back to a higher authority to get further instructions. He stepped back from the confrontation and walked down the path to the road and back to the car. Having closed the front door, David was muttering about being threatened and his wife was very concerned about the event that had just occurred. 'Should we call the police?' she asked.

'What's the use? They're in it as well.'

'Not all of them,' added his wife.

David looked at his wife. 'They are controlled and if the senior people want something covered up, then that's what happens. So there's no point.' He walked back through the house and into the garden.

Cornell made a call on his mobile phone as he made his way back to the car. He found Spider asleep. Cornell's orders were to wait; somebody would get back to him. He sat in the car, not liking to have to wait. He told Spider to drive round and park the car so they could observe the house. This was risky: anybody seeing them waiting in a car for a long period could get suspicious and call the police. It was a risk that Cornell was willing to take. Spider drove to join the road, then turned at the junction to find a spot that did not obstruct the road and enabled Cornell to see the house.

They sat for two hours, and throughout that time Spider was very uneasy; he was pleased when the call came, even though Cornell did not say what had been said.

'OK, let's go. Drive to the bottom of the road, and we will check right to see if there is a pub.'

Doing as instructed, Spider drove until they found a pub. It was within walking distance from the target's house. 'What do you think?' enquired Cornell.

'About what?' asked Spider.

'The pub! Is it worth going in to get a drink and something to eat?'

'Looks OK,' replied Spider.

He drove into the car park and parked.

Spider went in the pub and did the ordering whilst Cornell sat outside. There was not a lot said between them as they ate and drank. When they had finished they went and sat in the car. Cornell then decided that they should go back to the road and park the car so that he could observe the house. They did not park in the same place and nothing had changed. It was early evening when they spotted David Pierce leaving the house. He did not take his car but walked down the road. In fact he was going to meet up with some old work-mates at a pub close by. David liked this particular pub because he could walk to it. It was a very pleasant evening, and he had got over his earlier confrontation. He did look around more than he usually did, but saw nothing to cause him concern. In fifteen minutes he was at the pub. It was not like the old pubs with character, but had become a modern place, all plastic and gaudy with a horrible noise going on – what they called music. It served a reasonable pint and there was room outside to sit away from the confines of the noise inside.

Spider had driven the car, stopping and starting in order to follow David. They were on course for the pub where they had eaten earlier. When David entered the pub, Spider drove into the car park and parked. He was tasked with going into the pub and keeping an eye on the target. Cornell needed to keep out of sight, so he ambled along the route that David had just walked to get to the pub. Spider had to make two pints last two hours, not easy when in a pub on your own and bored out of your skull. Nobody spoke to him, there were no fruit machines, just small groups of people chatting amongst themselves. He sat and reflected that this was what he was paid very well to do.

After about two hours David, who had told his mates about the visit earlier, said he should get back to his wife, who was really concerned. They all said that they would walk back to his house with him, safety in numbers being the best option. David declined the offer. He had to live the rest of the time without such help, so he would manage. Spider had already made the call to Cornell that the target was on the move. David and his mates parted company, having arranged their next meeting. He walked along the path, following the route back home. It was still light; nobody was going to do anything in the residential streets of a northern town in the middle of the summer. At one point, David stopped and turned round. There was nothing or nobody to be concerned about. He turned back and continued on his way. He reached a driveway to a number of garages for houses that were not large enough to have them adjoining. Out of instinct he looked back along the road, to check that nothing was coming that might turn in.

He never saw the arm that swung round and grabbed him across the throat and shoulder. The arm belonged to somebody who was very strong. He was hauled into a hedge. Clear of the hedge and along the driveway he was hidden from the road. His body was swung round and the powerful blow to the stomach felled him to his knees. He struggled to breathe and he felt he might pass out. The next blow was to his face and it shattered his nose causing blood to flow. The pain was overpowering and blackness was descending. Powerful arms hauled him up. Another powerful blow was delivered to the kidneys. Then as he sunk again to his knees a fist smashed into the side of his face. He began to shake, there were pains in his chest; then there was nothing, only blackness. He fell to the ground. Cornell checked for a pulse. There was none to be found. He then removed David's watch, took money and credit cards from his wallet. Checking that nobody was about, he left the body and walked to the road. A call on the mobile summoned Spider who was with the car in the pub car park. They left as quietly as they had arrived. Cornell made a call and reported that the contract was completed. He was given an address where they were to meet and change cars. Cornell passed the information to Spider: their next stop was at a disused derelict warehouse, where they were to meet two men with a change-over car. To Cornell, it was just the right place for a double-cross and he trusted nobody. He told Spider to drive past and park up. Cornell checked his watch. They were early.

He told Spider to stay with the car and keep his eyes open whilst he went to have a look around the place. It appeared to be deserted but he was taking no chances. He normally worked, alone but for this operation he had been reliant on others and he was not overly comfortable with that. Making his way back to the car, he had already constructed a plan. 'OK, there is an open area at the front of the building. The lock is bust on the gates, so they can get access. I want you to meet them and get the keys for the new car. I don't know these people; so I will cover you; and if there are any problems, we take them out.'

Both men checked their weapons and Spider drove the car to the gate. Cornell got out of the car and opened it, allowing Spider to drive in. Cornell pushed the gates closed and ran across to the building. Whilst Spider parked the car, Cornell went into the building and found a good spot where he could see what was happening and be able to respond. They had not been waiting long when a black BMW arrived, followed by a second car. The driver of the second car got out and opened the gate. The BMW drove in and parked facing their car. The second car entered and parked alongside the BMW. The driver got out and walked across to Spider; he was carrying a red can. He looked about for Cornell but could not see him. He handed the keys of the car to Spider, who passed his keys over. The driver got in their car and drove it further along in front of the building. Having got out, he poured the petrol from the container over the inside of the car and lit a rolled paper, which he threw into an open window. The car was rapidly engulfed in flames. The driver then ran across to the BMW to get into the passenger seat. The BMW departed at great speed. Spider ran to the car they had been left and, by the time he had got it started, Cornell had joined him. Spider powered the car away from the building where their other car was well ablaze. They were on their way to Manchester airport.

David Pierce was found later, when an occupier of one of

the garages returned to park his car. The police and an ambulance arrived to deal with the situation. Although the medics could find no sign of life, they took him to hospital where he was certified dead by a doctor. He was identified from his driving licence, and the police made a call to the house. Mrs Pierce answered the door, and at the sight of the police officers knew it was not good news. One of the officers moved quickly to catch her before she fell to the floor. They carried her to the lounge and sat her on the armchair. An ambulance was summoned and a paramedic checked her. They discussed whether a doctor should be called or if she should go to hospital, but she declined. A neighbour came round to see if she could help, having seen the police car and the ambulance. Mrs Pierce had regained some composure: but she was really not surprised, following the earlier visit. She was angry, very angry. The police took a statement from her which included the details of the earlier visit and the threats. A police officer waited with her until her sister could make the journey over to stay. Mrs Pierce had lost a son and now a husband, and she knew that the government was to blame for both. Now the police knew that she had put it in her statement.

The following day two, detectives arrived at the house and questioned her about what she had put in her statement. They were of the opinion that her husband had been the victim of a violent mugging, because his cash, credit cards and watch had gone. They avoided the question of why the perpetrator had left Mr Pierce's wallet with his driving licence still in it, and had even put the wallet back into his inside jacket pocket after taking the other items. Mrs Pierce was still more angry that they did not believe her, or if they did, that they were not going to do anything about it. She looked for an address for Dan and wrote a letter. She did not have a phone number for the Foreign Legion.

* * * *

Spider had followed the signs to Manchester airport. It was an easy option to locate the drop-off point and he was lucky enough to find a space where he could stop. Cornell had barely spoken during the journey, and he would be pleased to see the back of the yank. Cornell got out and went to the boot which he opened; he retrieved his small bag containing the most basic of personal items. He closed the boot and walked down the side of the car to stand by the driver's door. Spider pressed the button and lowered the window just enough for the two of them to communicate. Cornell grinned. 'Still don't trust me? Can understand that. Thanks for your part in the operation, doubt we will ever meet again.' Spider sat waiting for some movement but it never came. Cornell walked round the front of the car and headed to the terminal building. Spider breathed out and relaxed. He closed the window, put the car into gear and drove away. He did have a smile on his face.

Inside the terminal building, Cornell checked his ticket against the departure board. He was early. He purchased a magazine, appropriately about guns, then a coffee. It was a case of waiting and he was very used to that. Checking-in was a straightforward process and his bag was light enough to carry onto the aircraft. It was noted that he only had the small bag and no check-in luggage. He walked through to the departure security and joined a queue of people passing through the process. He did not give a thought to the police officer with his spaniel dog. It was just another part of modern travel and the search for drugs which was relentless. The dog walked along the line of people, sniffing at each person, tail wagging; after all it was, for her, a game. Cornell's bag got an extra sniff before walking on. Once past the dog stopped, turned and her nose pointed at his bag. The police officer continued the walk along the line and, once clear, used his radio to alert other officers. Cornell reached the security check and watched as his bag went through x-ray. He passed through the detector arch. Nothing, after all he had nothing. Two armed police officers moved in and stood either side of him. A man dressed in a suit joined them and picked up Cornell's bag. Cornell was invited to go with them. This was not the first time airport people were curious about him. He was quietly and efficiently led away. He complied, he had nothing and his holiday in the UK had been uneventful.

In a room his bag was placed on a bench. The man in the suit spoke.

'Is this your bag?'

'Yes, sir,' replied Cornell.

'Do you have anything in it that should not be there?'

'No, sir, I have not put anything in the bag. Only clothes and some wash gear.'

'Do you have any checked-in luggage?' enquired the suited man.

'No, sir, just this bag.'

'OK, this officer is going to check your bag.'

'Fine,' responded Cornell.

A police officer wearing a white forensic suit and gloves opened the bag and began to remove the contents. Cornell watched, giving nothing away with facial expressions or body language. When the items were laid out along the bench the dog was brought in. With paws up on the bench its nose sniffed the air. It stopped at a rolled pair of jeans. The search officer carefully unrolled the jeans. Feeling in one of the pockets he retrieved a small oblong package. 'What is this?' enquired the officer.

'No idea, it's not mine,' replied Cornell, aware that the armed police officers now had their weapons pointing at him and ready to use.

'Well, sir, when you checked in you declared that you had packed the bag and nobody else had access to it.'

Cornell shrugged, 'It's not mine, I don't know how it got there, I don't do drugs.'

'The dog who identified your bag as being suspect is not trained to locate drugs, only explosives.' He looked hard at Cornell for some reaction. There was none.

A woman joined them and carefully picked up the block. The contents were wrapped in cling-film. She removed the film and took the slab to a table in the corner of the room. Using some equipment already there she conducted tests on it. They all waited. As an expert in explosives, she soon declared that the slab was a well-known readily available plastic explosive.

The police officer, who was a detective constable and dressed in a smart suit, began the formal procedure of arresting Cornell for being in possession of explosives. It was Cornell who halted the process. He looked at the detective. 'There is a letter in my coat pocket: read it.' The detective continued with the caution. Cornell shouted. 'Read the letter.' The detective stopped. Cornell repeated in a lowered voice, 'Read the letter.' The detective could also play games. He located the letter, opened it and read the contents. His sense of job satisfaction and bravado at apprehending a potential terrorist had evaporated. He looked at Cornell, and then told the armed officers to keep guard whilst he made a phone call.

In the police office, the duty officer handed him an alert for a well-built American with a military bearing who was being sought for a possible connection to a murder. He read the details. It was a police officer's delight, a murderer carrying explosives at an airport, his airport. Then reality took hold. The letter! He re-read it and phoned his boss. Full details of the letter's contents and the situation at the airport were given. He was told to do nothing until he received further orders. It started a chain reaction up through the command structure until the telephone call to Whitehall was made.

The detective could only wait. He returned to the search room and updated everybody that they were waiting for orders. He did not have to wait for long before he was called to the police office. There was a telephone call for him. Picking up the handset, he gave his name and rank. The voice at the other end identified himself. The detective recognised the voice as that of a superintendent based at their main police station. Listening to the voice, he thought it a bit strange. It was monotone but very precise. He was told that the order came from the very highest level of government. Cornell was to be allowed to go and board his flight to America. The explosive was to be removed from the site and disposed of.

He could not believe that he, a senior detective-constable, having passed his sergeant's exam and awaiting promotion, had to let go a person who was carrying explosives and could possibly be wanted for questioning for a murder. 'Sir, with all due respect, are we talking about the same person?'

The superintendent remained very calm. 'I understand your concern, but the orders have been given and we must carry them out.' Almost as an afterthought he added, 'None of the action that has been taken in this incident is to be logged. Do you understand?'

As a lowly detective-constable, orders were orders; but this was different. He was being asked to breach every rule in the book.

'Sir, with all due respect, I have a problem with what you are ordering me to do. Others are involved in the incident, and I can't tell them what to do. How can it not be recorded?'

The superintendent anticipated this response. 'A security officer and a police inspector will join you at the airport, if they have not already arrived. They have the authority to take delivery of the individual and place him on the aircraft. They will also organise the removal of the explosives. Neither you, or the others involved in the incident need to log any details, other than that it was just a routine search. No details of what was found are to be recorded. Have I made myself clear and do you understand? These orders are from the very top level of government.'

The lowly detective-constable could only answer, 'Yes, sir.'

'Good, now can you give me the names of all those involved? The inspector will talk to each of them so that they understand the situation.' The list comprised five people in total. In the search room the detective faced Cornell. 'It seems that you have friends in high places. I am instructed that you are to be released and that you will be allowed to board your aircraft, minus the explosives. We have to wait for other officers who will take over.' Cornell put his clothes back into the bag and waited. Two men arrived, one identifying himself as a police inspector, the other did not identify who he was. It was the second person who took the explosive. Then both men escorted Cornell to the departure lounge. The inspector returned to the search room to debrief those involved in the incident. The Official Secrets Act would bury the matter.

20

About an hour from their destination, Proffitt had been preparing a speech for the press. He gave the draft to his favoured cabinet minister who read it and made some comments. They discussed the issues that he wanted to avoid. Rather than blow the trumpet as usual, today he would be more measured. He must only show emotional sorrow at the loss of an important scientist. Then came the call from Reilly who was now, as some said, in London "ruling the roost" from the cabinet office. He gave an update on events at the scene and on the initial media reaction. It was not good news: the government was being blamed for Finch's death. The coroner had been briefed that it was a high-level security matter, as had the pathologist. In fact, the pathologist's report had already been classified as "most secret". Wheels were in motion to ensure that there would be no coroner's court hearing. To appease growing hostility, a suitable judge had been approached to instigate an inquiry and he had accepted the role. The narrow brief had been agreed and it would be followed. The inquiry would begin as soon as arrangements could be made. The outcome before the inquiry began was focused on the fact that Dr Finch had committed suicide; it was hoped that that would close the matter.

In the meantime Reilly warned that there were elements of the press who were baying for blood. The word quickly forming on the street was that people did not believe it was suicide. It was this last issue that concerned Proffitt, and they discussed ways of presenting a good case for themselves. People had seen on television how Finch had been hauled over the coals about the leak concerning the absence of WMDs. They had heard a Parliamentary Committee exonerate him from being the source of the leak. They had heard that he had been treated badly by the civil service, his employers. They knew that Finch had done a good job as an eminent scientist, and that he was due to go back to Maspamia to continue the work of searching for weapons, weapons that people did not believe existed. Whilst Reilly considered the options and developed a plan, Proffitt needed to say as little as possible; what he did say needed to be positive as far as the government was concerned.

As soon as the aircraft landed and parked at the terminal, Proffitt and his personal party were taken directly to the VIP lounge, an area of some privacy. The press corps exited the aircraft and were immediately on mobile phones to their respective offices in the UK, to get and give the latest information. When they had passed through immigration and collected their luggage, they made their way to the press area where they anticipated that Proffitt, updated by his people, would make a statement. When he did face the press, he had adopted his best "lost puppy-dog look" that begged sympathy from the press who crowded before him. The room, which was a-buzz with conversations, went quiet. 'As you know, during my flight from America I learned of the tragic death of Dr John Finch. I do not have the full details yet, but I am told he went from his house on a walk to some woods and there took his own life.'

One journalist called out, 'Prime Minister, are you responsible for his death: do you have his death on your hands?'

The room was then eerily quiet. The press corps waited for

174

a reply from a visibly shaken Proffitt. With an unaccustomed tremble, the words he uttered were, 'No, I had no knowledge that he might have taken his own life in this way. If I had, I would have ensured that some action was taken.' He then wanted to return to his pre-prepared speech, but the press had other ideas: 'Prime Minister,' interjected another journalist, 'we all saw how Dr Finch was treated by the government, and it appears that he faced carrying the can for the "dodgy dossier", any comment?'

'That is totally incorrect. Dr Finch was treated in line with the civil service code. As I have said, I regret what has happened and our thoughts must be with his family at this time.' Proffit looked at the sea of faces for a 'safety-net' to be thrown by one of the reporters who were sympathetic to the government.

'Are you going to continue with your meetings here in the Far East?' The reporter was in the front row.

'At this moment in time, that is what I plan to do. There is nothing I could do at home at this time that members of the cabinet cannot do. I am in constant contact and so I will continue to be updated on the incident.' Proffitt was relieved that a non-invasive question had been asked. Whilst in control he made an announcement: 'I can tell you that an enquiry is to be held into the death of Dr Finch, and an appropriate appointment is being made. The inquiry will begin as soon as possible, and it will hear all the evidence.'

'Is this an inquiry to get to the truth, or is it a cover-up?'

Proffitt did not like the question. 'It is a detailed inquiry into the death of Dr Finch.'

'Can I take that to mean a cover-up?'

'No, that is not what it is. It is to be an examination into the events that surround the death of Dr Finch.'

'If it is found that the inquiry is incomplete and is therefore a cover-up, will you resign?'

'No! Thank you for your time.' Proffitt left the room and the journalists, who would now speculate in line with their political point of view of events.

Away from the press corps, Proffitt was sweating. He wished, at that moment that he had Reilly with him. The media was baying for blood, his blood; and he had to carry on and ride out the storm.

* * * *

Proffitt arrived back in the UK where he convened an urgent meeting with Reilly. He had been kept informed of developments whilst out of the country, but he needed the full story, chapter and verse. He had already accepted that fingers were pointing at him, and it was unnerving. The media had a story and would not let go. They had already tracked down witnesses whose evidence would not be particularly helpful. There were a few who, if allowed to speak, would be downright dangerous. The implications were such that the story could evolve to a point where the government could be toppled. If that should happen, his credibility would be stripped away. It all rested on his small team of loyal supporters, who were doing stirling work and keeping one step ahead.

Reilly gave a detailed update about the death of Dr Finch, and the progress of the enquiry into his death. It was being managed, but he knew by the expression on Reilly's face that something else was coming, and that he was not going to like it.

'There is another problem,' declared Reilly. 'Following the incident with Finch, the body of John Pierce was found close to his home. He had been with friends at a local pub and was walking home. He was beaten to death.'

Proffitt, who sporting a tan, had gone pale. 'What

happened? Was it a mugging, an argument in the pub, what?' he enquired.

'Money and credit cards were stolen, but who ever did it put his wallet back in his jacket pocket with his driving licence still in it. There were no arguments or confrontations.' Reilly drew breath. 'The police say it was a professional job.'

Proffitt did not respond immediately. His mind raced. Pierce had been a thorn in his side for several years, and now he was dead, possibly killed by an assassin.

'Has there been any flack from family or friends?'

Reilly shrugged, 'Not really! The police say that in a statement from his wife, a big American visited the house the same day and threatened him. The police have drawn a blank on identifying the individual. Interestingly, the media do not seem to have linked his death with his campaign against you.'

Proffitt was not comforted by that because he knew that it only took one journalist to link the two incidents and create a conspiracy theory, and all hell would be let loose. He doubted that even the whizz-kid Reilly could keep the lid on that. 'OK, what do we do now?' he asked.

'Nothing, absolutely nothing,' answered Reilly. 'Nobody has made the connection, and so we keep our heads down and deal with the issue if we have to.'

Proffitt nodded his agreement.

21

Assistant Chief Constable Timothy Long was not a happy senior police officer. He had been drawn into the investigation of the death of Dr Finch, but had recognised, from the start that there were some powerful influences involved, particularly political ones. Senior appointments in the police were political; if he wanted to progress to Chief Constable he would have to walk a very thin line between fact and fiction. The complications began when he was presented with the statements from Sarah Hardy and Simon Roach, the civilian volunteer searchers who had found the body. He compared them to the report from Kate Hope and Eddy Sale, the paramedics who had attended the scene afterwards. The biggest problem was that those who found the body stated that there was no waxed jacket or indeed any jacket. To him, that was a fundamental observation. The searchers were trained to look and note what they saw. Similarly, the paramedics attended to Finch and they would have known whether he was wearing a jacket or not. Logic dictated that both pairs were correct, and that the jacket was put on Finch in the time gap between the two pairs being at the scene. Then there were the descriptions of the quantity of blood. The searchers had said that there was very little blood and that they had not seen a bottle of water, a knife, a cap or a wristwatch. Sarah Hardy, whose statement was the more detailed, had actually been close enough to check the body for any sign of life. The paramedics had also said that there was very little blood, and not enough to be consistent with the cutting of an artery in the wrist, which would have caused blood to spurt out under pressure. However, they had identified the other items as being at the scene. Then there was the post-mortem report, which described more blood being present than that identified by the four other witnesses. Of course, pressure could be put on the pathologist and the paramedics through their respective employing departments, but the civilians were not so easily manipulated.

He was still trying to get to the bottom of who DC Munroe was, and what he had been doing in the search area before the official search team had arrived. He had no contact with Clifton Vale police station, so how had he known about Dr Finch being missing? Why had he searched the woods in the area where the body had been located? He had been alone with the body for thirty minutes. There were discrepancies between what the searchers found and then what the paramedics found: had he played a part in these changes? Who were the others who had been with him when he met the searchers? Who authorised a helicopter to fly to the scene, collect Munroe and two other unidentified people, and fly away to an out-of-area airfield? Under normal circumstances, he would have had Munroe interviewed to obtain this vital information, but this case was certainly not normal. Long was told that Munroe and the others had been interviewed outside the area. When he requested copies of their statements, he received a curt, 'No'. The outcome was that this seemingly unauthorised intervention left more holes in the investigation than could be found in a sieve. Long was aware of the deep political situation; he decided that he would let the inquiry that had been set up, find the answers.

Then there was the telephone call from Dr Finch's dentist,

reporting that she had found an unlocked window at the surgery. A police officer had attended the incident, and had asked if anything was missing. Nothing seemed to have been disturbed. The police station had been awash with talk about Dr Finch, and so the police officer had asked if Dr Finch had been a patient. The dentist had confirmed that he was, and had gone to the filing cabinet to check his file. Looking through the filing cabinet, his file had been found to be missing. Nothing else was missing. A statement was made and it was now a police matter. Two days later, the dentist contacted the police to say that the records had reappeared back at the surgery. She did not know when or how they had got back, but they had. The police had taken the file as evidence, and had had it forensically examined. The tests had found fingerprints on the records and on the folder. Some could not be used for identification because they were of poor quality. Others were attributed to a staff member, and the remaining ones were unidentified. The unidentified ones were stored in police files after the tests. When Long briefed a senior officer out of his area, he was directed to take the line that there was 'no evidence' of any unidentified fingerprints being on Dr Finch's file.

There was also the official ambulance form that was completed and signed by paramedic Kate Hope when she attended the scene. She had submitted it to the control room when she arrived back at the base. It had disappeared. This form is required as part of the ambulance official close-out procedure. A record is started by the control room when the ambulance is directed to an incident, and then, to close the file, this form is obtained from the ambulance crew, checked and put with the file. The Ambulance Trust claimed that it had been handed to the police. The police at Clifton Vale police station claimed to have no record of it having been received. Long had ordered a search for the missing paperwork, but nothing had been found. He only had the statements from the two paramedics.

Long had also been provided with a statement from a man who had called in at the police station to express his concern. He had sighted, on the morning of the day of the incident, two individuals dressed in dark clothing near the scene where Dr John Finch's body had been found. He was well aware that Dr Finch had been found that morning. The complication was that there was not a single search officer on the scene at the time of the sighting. The only people in the area were Sarah Hardy and Simon Roach, the civilians who had found the body. Of course, what the man did not know was that two people had been at Bluebell Wood dressed in dark police-style clothing. Long knew that three men had been airlifted out of the area after the body had been discovered. One of those was DC Munroe. Long had arranged for a much larger police search contingent of about forty officers, but this force had not been assembled on the ground, so not a single regular police search officer was present near Bluebell Wood at that time. The first official police officers at the scene were PCs Devlin and Palmer.

Assistant Chief Constable Long was without doubt thankful that an inquiry into the death of Dr Finch had been established. It was not a judicial inquiry, but it meant that people would be called to give evidence and explain themselves. That took the pressure off him because he could defer any difficult questions as being a matter for the inquiry. The one thing that he was aware of was that in the inquiry's terms of reference, nobody could be forced to make a statement or give evidence.

One file that had landed on his desk gave him even more concern. It involved a Rosie Portray, a US intelligence operative who had been Dr Finch's interpreter in Maspamia. He noted her involvement with the intelligence services, and her long-term friendship with Finch. The ACC's superiors had determined that the woman had to be interviewed, to see what she was going to say about his death. If the contents of her statement were detrimental to the government and the Prime Minister's case, then it would be best if she said nothing, or at least they could stop her giving evidence. Two police detectives were selected and briefed before flying to the US. They spent a number of days questioning her. They eventually took a single statement, but maintained a record of the interviews. She said bluntly that she did not believe Dr Finch had committed suicide, and that he hated the prospect of taking all types of pills. She was at a loss as to how Dr Finch could have taken an overdose because he suffered from a disorder that made it difficult for him to swallow pills. Rosie also revealed that in the months leading up to his death, Dr Finch was unable to use his right hand for basic tasks requiring any strength, such as slicing food, because of a painful elbow injury. It would have been impossible for him to have killed himself by cutting his left wrist. Questioned further on this topic, Rosie did not alter her position, and was adamant that he could not have used his right hand. She explained, 'He even had difficulty cutting his own steak.' This cast serious doubt that he had swallowed a quantity of painkillers before slitting his left wrist. Her opinion that he did not commit suicide was firm. She was asked by the police officers if she would be willing to give evidence at an inquiry. She agreed, but requested that her evidence be given to the inquiry in private, or without her identity being disclosed. It was not unusual for security and intelligence people to do so in a court of law, and this inquiry had no such legal restrictions in any event. Most importantly, she was uniquely placed to offer insights into Dr Finch's personality and frame of mind with regard to WMDs, as well as his physical condition up to the time of his death. She had also spoken to him on the morning of the day he had disappeared. They had discussed their return to Maspamia to continue the search for WMDs. It was hardly the sort of discussion they would have had if he had been contemplating taking his own life. No, she was adamant that he had not killed himself but had been killed in, a botched fake suicide.

Long was tasked with managing such witnesses. Her statement was circulated to a number of departments, one in particular who were scrutinising the evidence and witnesses. He was directed to exclude Rosie Portray's evidence by not offering her anonymity. This was of concern to him because he knew that what she had to say was important, as being part of the overall process of getting to the truth. She could speak to the media, the evidence would then be in the public domain, and because she had not been called it would look like a cover-up. He followed the party line and directed that a communication be sent to her, stating that he regretted that there would be no anonymity. She replied, declining to attend, and so her vital evidence was buried. He was then ordered to record that her statement contained nothing of relevance, and so had not been entered into the inquiry evidence.

* * * *

Later that day, the situation for Long was made worse when he was informed that two men from London were in reception wanting to see him. He was busy with the case paperwork and a situation that was causing complications, so he delegated the task of talking to the visitors to an Inspector. Within minutes, the Inspector was at the door of his office. 'Sir, they won't speak to me, it's you they want to talk to.' He lowered his voice, 'I think they are secret service.'

Long looked up, 'I am really busy.'

'Sir, I don't think these people will take that as an answer.'

'OK, can you get them brought up?'

'Yes sir,' replied one very relieved Inspector.

A police constable was next to knock at the door, 'Your two visitors, sir.' He moved to one side to allow the two men to enter the office. The door was closed behind them. ACC Long faced two men who were dressed in expensive suits. 'Good morning, gentlemen, please understand my reluctance to see you: I do have a major incident to deal with.'

Neither man returned a compliment, but one stepped forward and showed his ID. Long looked at it. It showed a Mr John Smith from an intelligence department he had never heard of. He looked at the other man. He showed his ID. It showed a Mr Peter Brown, also an intelligence officer in the same department. The IDs and department meant nothing to Long, as he had never seen anything like them before. The first man, showing no emotion at all, told Long that if he wanted to verify their personae then he was to call the Cabinet Office. Mr Edward Reilly would confirm their credentials. 'Please sit down,' said Long, indicating the seats on the other side of his desk.

Long picked up the telephone and asked his secretary to put him through to somebody in the Cabinet Office who could verify who his visitors were. He looked at the men, 'I am sure you will understand that I have to check. This is a sensitive police investigation. Would you like something to drink?'

The men understood and declined the offer of a drink. The phone rang. Long picked it up and identified himself. He explained the situation and was advised that the men were under the orders of the Cabinet Office. He was told that he should assist them with their enquiries. He replaced the telephone. 'That's in order, now how can I help?'

'You are heading the investigation into the Finch case?' It was Smith who spoke.

'Yes,' replied Long.

'The government, and in particular the Prime Minister, find

themselves in an embarrassing situation. There are many people who, given the opportunity, can cause serious trouble for the government over the suicide of Dr Finch. Now you, being a senior police officer, will understand the situation and no doubt will want to do all you can to assist.'

Long felt the hairs on the back of his neck stand up, and he did not like the feeling. The pair who sat before him clearly wielded a lot of power, or at least they reported back to people who did.

'As you are well aware, Dr Finch committed suicide, which is most regrettable – but these things happen. People get the wrong idea and make accusations. For example, there are those who say that he was murdered. The situation has to be managed, and that is where you have an important role.'

Long looked at each man in turn. 'I am a police officer and I have a duty to uphold the law. There are rules that govern an investigation into a death, and I have to abide by those rules.'

'We understand that, but people die all of the time and many from suicide,' interrupted the man.

'Yes, I know that, but this case is not clear-cut.' Long felt better using the police code-book for investigating such incidents. 'I have witnesses and evidence to consider.'

The man grinned. 'It really is quite a straight-forward case. A scientist does something wrong at work that could affect his career and pension. He gets depressed. Then he goes for a walk, finds a nice quiet spot under a tree and takes his own life. What will your code book tell you about that?'

Long picked up a piece of paper. 'Well, the investigation so far has identified numerous irregularities. For example, there are no fingerprints found on the knife allegedly used by Dr Finch to cut his wrists. There was a lack of blood found at the scene, despite a report that he had cut open an artery. There are unexplained abrasions on Dr Finch's scalp. A very important point is the position of the body when it was discovered by the searchers, which differed markedly from how it was found by the paramedics and my police search team.' Long checked the list. 'Other examples include the waxed jacket and cap, bottle of water, knife and wristwatch that were located on or by the body when the paramedics attended as well as figuring in the observations of my search officers; but those items were not observed by the civilian searchers who actually discovered the body.'

Neither man responded.

Long continued, 'Then there were the events surrounding DC Munroe who was at the scene and alone for thirty minutes. During that time, Dr Finch went from wearing just a shirt to wearing a waxed jacket. How did that happen? Also, who were the other two seen with Munroe?' He paused, 'The list goes on.' He put the piece of paper down. 'Oh, and I have an American witness, an intelligence officer, who has worked with Finch for years and who has made a very critical statement. I have been told she will not be called as a witness, nor will her statement be used.'

Both men sat passively looking at Long.

'Then there is the situation at his dentist's where his file went missing, then was returned. We have unidentified fingerprints on the file. They are not to be pursued. The dentist's file is closed under the direction of a senior officer.'

'Well, that shows that none of what you have said has any relevance to the case,' added Smith.

Long ignored the remark. 'Then I have the helicopter that flies into the area of a crime scene and carries out three people, one of whom was alone with the body for thirty minutes. I am told that all these people have been interviewed outside of our area, but that I cannot have access to their statements.'

Smith responded again. 'This is a complex situation and involves national security. For example, you will know that eight computers were removed from Dr Finch's home by the security services, because they contained secret information and because the computers were the property of the government.'

'I know that, and it is not causing me any concern. This is an official police enquiry and all evidence, reports, statements and witnesses have to be recorded,' said Long, who was beginning to get a little impatient.

'Well, ACC Long, you are the person in charge of the case. You understand that this could all be a very real problem for the Prime Minister. I am sure he will be very grateful for your cooperation in this matter. The inquiry will be straightforward, without complications, and we need your assistance to make sure it is. We can't tell you what to do, but only offer you our best advice.'

Long then made an off-the-cuff remark, 'I suppose that if I don't accept the advice I will end up dead in the woods.'

Neither man made any expression or comment.

'That was a joke,' added Long.

'We don't do jokes,' said the man.

'No, don't expect you do,' replied Long.

'The bottom line is that you need to be selective with the information you pass to the inquiry, and who you propose as a witness. The chair of the inquiry will run the proceedings based upon a very detailed and narrow brief. But that is not your concern,' concluded Smith.

Both men stood. Smith spoke, 'I trust you fully understand the situation, and that the government can look to your cooperation.'

'I fully understand,' said Long as he showed them out of the door.

'We can find our own way out,' said Smith, the more communicative of the two men.

When they had gone, Long's secretary observed, 'They were a nice pair, security service!'

Long looked at her, 'You don't know the half of it, nor do you want to.' He went back to his desk, sat and stared at the pile of papers that comprised the key elements of the Finch investigation.

22

The events surrounding the death of Dr Finch were, for the most part, forgotten by the public. Assistant Chief Constable Timothy Long received a commendation for his work on the Dr Finch investigation and enquiry and was promoted to Chief Constable. The inquiry was very successful in that it was a whitewash and just held a place in the annals of history. The key players gave their evidence to the inquiry but nobody challenged them. There was no cross-examination of witnesses, and there was deemed to be a logical explanation for all events when it was blatantly obvious there was not. The volunteer searchers gave their evidence, as did the paramedics, and it differed greatly. That issue was not addressed: the truth was not investigated and neither pair were challenged. DC Munroe gave his version which differed from everybody else's. Again, there was no challenge to his account. Nobody asked who the other two people were who were seen with him. The landing of the unidentified helicopter was not raised. It was just accepted.

The pathologist packaged it all up in a neat suicide. To make sure, restricted access was ordered for the autopsy report, and the findings were to be held secret for thirty years. It was a big can of worms, and the inquiry neatly allowed the lid to be put on. It would now gather dust in an archive until it was retrieved by somebody who would allow justice to be served. Prime Minister Proffitt and his trusted advisor Edward Reilly survived the maelstrom, and continued to rule by dictate until they decided to stand down from office. Proffitt left the office of PM, but did not remain an MP as there were much bigger fish to fry. The biggest was to make money. The war gained him favours and now he could collect. The media alleged that millions of pounds awaited.

* * * *

Dan was at the Legion's base at Aubagne in southern France. He checked his immaculate, tailored uniform in a long mirror. It was, for him, a special day as he was departing the French Foreign Legion after more years service than he had ever planned. He would even get a small pension. He had done well and been promoted to Sergeant Chef in charge of the snipers in the elite 2ème Régiment Étranger de Parachutistes, the 2nd REP. During his time he had seen plenty of action and, for him, life had been good. Waiting to go on parade, he reflected on how he came to be in the Legion.

The UK had been dragged into two wars that it did not want. In the first Gulf War the US supported by the British and other countries, had attacked Maspamia to oust the regime of President Akrawi, but they had stopped before the decisive battle. British soldiers died and Dan's brother, serving with armoured infantry, had been killed by friendly fire. US aircraft had attacked British soldiers in their armoured vehicles and they had paid the ultimate price. Dan's father David had begun a campaign to get justice for the relatives of those who had died in service. He had written a succession of letters to the Prime Minister, to ask about the legality of the conflict and about support for the families where family members were being killed and wounded. He had received a reply from the Prime Minister's office, which had been a general letter to

190

confirm receipt of his and that a reply would follow. The reply had not been worth waiting for. Worthless drivel was how David had described it. Undaunted, David had written another letter to the Prime Minister, only to receive the same cold non-descript reply. He had written yet again, getting the same response. David had stepped up his campaign of demanding answers. The turning point for Dan had occurred whilst he was in the jungle of Guiana in South America. He had been told about the death of his father, but it had been far too late to attend the funeral. As soon as he could, he had had a long telephone conversation with his mother.

Dan reflected on how he had ended up in the Legion. He had been a member of the British Parachute Regiment when he had met up with some French Foreign Legion paratroopers. He had got the facts of what the Legion was about, and what it offered its men. He had also got chapter and verse about the bad bits, and it seemed that there were a lot. He had soldiered on in the Paras, but, had become despondent and had left. He had found his family hard to bear, as his father had been in a battle with the Government, and the action against the Prime Minister in particular had been consuming him. Dan had taken time to consider the choices open to him. The UK had been going down the toilet, there had been anger and frustration everywhere: it had been not a good place to be. It had not been surprising that he had made his way to Paris and the Legion.

He reflected on his journey to the Legion, from his knocking on the wooden door of the Fort de Nogent in Paris, then on to Aubagne, the HQ of the Legion. Having been accepted he had gone to Castlenaudary, the principal training facility, to begin the process of becoming a Legionnaire. It was during the initial training that he wore the White Kepi for the first time. He kept his head down, kept out of trouble and endured all that was thrown at him. He had done the same when joining the British Parachute Regiment years earlier. During his service with the British he had become a sniper, and that was to be his chosen speciality in the Legion. He had worn and kept the famous Kepi Blanc but today, as a senior non-commissioned officer, he wore the Legion's blue and red kepi. The parachute badge was pinned on his right breast, and his medals on his left.

Dan had said his farewells to friends and colleagues in Corsica, which had been his home base for the majority of his time in the Legion. His good friend Napoleon had been injured, and had eventually left the Legion. He kept in touch with Dan, and told him of his mercenary exploits. He had found a lack of bullshit and loads of money to his liking. He told Dan that the outside world would be his oyster; the good men got the good jobs. During the making-up-his-mind period, officers tried to get Dan to stay with offers of further promotion, courses and desired postings: in the end, he opted to leave. Their last word was that if things did not work out for him as a civilian, then he would be welcomed back. He only had to turn up at a Legion base or recruiting office, tell them who he was and to contact the 2nd REP, and they would do the rest. He was now back in what could be called the real world.

Those on the leaving parade were called to order, and marched at their slow pace onto the parade ground. Each man was in his dress uniform, which in every case was immaculate. The line began with the most junior rank, through to the most senior. Dan was at the end of the line as the most senior leaving on that day. They were turned to face the flags of France and the Legion. The Commandant of the Legion came to the front of the Legionnaires and looked along the line; he then marched across to the most junior rank and spoke to him. It would be the same for each man in turn, the Commandant referring to their personal dossier for information. He did not hurry, and he gave each man the chance of changing his mind and signing on for a further period. Once the man was committed, he handed over their Certificat des Services Militaires.

As the Commandant stopped in front of him, Dan drew his right hand up to salute and gave his name and rank. He then pulled his hand down to slap his thigh. The Commandant returned the salute. He studied Dan's file. He then said that with a record like his he should consider remaining in the Legion. They needed men like him. Dan, looking straight ahead, replied that he had given it a lot of thought and would like to leave and see what the outside world had to offer. The Commandant smiled. He told Dan that he had one year, and that if he returned, then he would go straight back to his Regiment at the same rank. It would be classed as extended leave. After a year he could still come back, but he might not get all the privileges. Dan thanked the Commandant and accepted his certificate: he was, in Legion terms, a free man.

23

Dan had been given a mobile phone number for contacting Napoleon, who was now a well-paid security/body-guard; being a more polite term for a mercenary. He telephoned him from Aubagne and they arranged to meet in Paris. Dan thought he was rather paranoid about being spied on, as evidenced by an obscure letter that had arrived, giving details of a meeting-place and a time. Having worked out the contents, Dan had left Aubagne and made his way to Paris by train. He found a suitable hotel, checked in and spent two days buying some clothes, a mobile phone and a new lap top computer. He was also a tourist in the big city. On the third day, Dan made his way to the meeting-place. He arrived at a busy Paris street café to meet Napoleon, but spotted him at an outside table talking to another male. He decided not to approach them, but sat at another table where he could observe them. If Napoleon wanted him in on the conversation then he would call him over; otherwise, he would stay out of it. Dan ordered a coffee and played with his new mobile phone. He had read the instruction book, which explained how to take photos; he continued experimenting. He aimed the phone at the street and pressed the button. The result was an image on the phone. He held up his newspaper and, having made a hole in it, lined up the phone with the hole and focused on Napoleon and the man. As he pressed the button the man turned and looked in his direction, but not directly at him. Dan looked at the phone to see that he had a frontal image of the man's face. He was pleased with the phone, a thing he had not really bothered about in the past. He lowered the paper and looked about him. People were reading newspapers, some just watching the world go by others were in deep conversation.

The man with Napoleon stood up. They did not shake hands on parting; the man just walked away. When he had gone, Dan remained sitting where he was, as did Napoleon. It was part of the meeting instructions that were provided in the letter. After about ten minutes Napoleon got up and walked over to Dan's table. There was no great reunion, only the ordering of more coffee. They brought each other up-to-date with what they had been doing. Then Napoleon said that the guy he was talking to was a mercenary called Cornell who worked for a US company and who was looking for people to hire. Leaning forward and speaking quietly, he gave Dan the story: 'I had been doing jobs all over the place, then, one day, I was between jobs when I was contacted by a woman. I was sitting right here in this café and she came over and spoke. Now, you won't believe this, but the woman was the one in Africa. You remember when I got hit and we covered her rescue. Her name is Rosie Portray.'

Dan nodded his understanding. 'Yes, I know who you mean.'

'I was introduced to an organisation she was connected to who sought out people like us to do jobs. They paid well, and I was asked to infiltrate the outfit that Cornell works for. Once in, I just had to provide information about them. You know: who's on the books, what jobs they've got, clients names, that sort of thing. They said that if it was discovered, what I was doing, I'd be taken out.' He grinned, 'Hey, that's what the job's about.'

'So, what's the score on that one?' asked Dan.

'That was my first meet. I have to go to the office this afternoon for a briefing by Cornell. He seems to be a key player.'

'So it will be beers on you afterwards,' added Dan.

'We can do that,' replied Napoleon, 'then I can update you on how it went.' 'Oh, one of the reasons for our meet this morning is that the organisation I work for wants to talk to you. If you're interested, I can let them know and they will arrange a meeting.'

'Sounds good,' replied Dan.

The two of them chatted for about an hour, then agreed to meet at a bar close by at seven o'clock. Napoleon departed down the street. Dan muttered when he discovered that he had been left both tables' bills to pay. He was about to stand up when a female voice asked if he had a light for her cigarette. He turned to face the woman, to explain that he did not smoke, only to discover that he recognised her face.

'Hello, Dan,' she said. 'It's been several years since we last spoke. I'm Rosie Portray, do you remember me?'

'Have you been sitting here all morning?' he enquired.

'Yes, I thought you would never stop talking; and they say women talk,' she chided.

Dan grinned. It was the eyes, once seen never forgotten.

'Unless you have something else to do, walk with me and we can get some lunch whilst I tell you about the organisation.' It was almost an instruction, but he had nothing else to do; and walking the streets of Paris with a beautiful woman was better than being in a bar in Corsica.

She explained that she was part of an organisation that tried to help people who were under threat from governments and unofficial government agencies. There were people all over the world who supported what they did either physically or financially. Many corrupt people had been brought to book, but it was no easy task and it was very dangerous. They stopped and soaked up the sun's warmth while looking into the river Seine. She explained that some people could be brought to justice through legal channels; others had to be dealt with in other ways. If he was interested, he would be of extreme value to the organisation. He needed no explanation. They were looking for a facilitator, a nice name for a mercenary who had specific skills, like a very professional sniper. They had reached a floating restaurant and Rosie led the way on board.

Neither had a big meal, and the conversation covered a wide range of topics and issues. Then she broached the subject of the death of Dan's father. The police had not found who killed him, so it was another case shoved on the shelf. He explained that he was going over to see his mother, whom he had not seen for some time. She was sympathetic, and added that the organisation might be able to help find the person or persons who had committed the crime. His immediate reaction was that being a "hit man" was a small price to pay for such information. She suggested that Dan go and consider if he wanted to move forward, and gave him a piece of paper with a mobile phone number and a series of words on it. She explained that by phoning the number and quoting the message to the person at the other end he would be contacted. He was about to ask how they would know where to find him when she told him the name of the hotel he was staying at. He was not surprised, just becoming more aware of the murky world he was entering.

Napoleon had arrived at the office at the appropriate time. He knocked but there was no reply. He tried the door and it opened. He entered and was about to call out when he heard a voice. It was that of Cornell the American. He stepped into the open-plan office which was deserted. Cornell was in a room at the back. The office had probably once been a shop and it was well-decorated, with pictures depicting words declaring the need to have good management. A desk, computer and filing cabinet filled the back area, leaving space to go through to the back room. Two sofas fronted by a coffee table completed the room. Management magazines adorned the table, giving the whole office an air of quiet efficiency. Clearly, the desk should be occupied; and he thought that the person who usually sat there was either with Cornell or out at present.

Napoleon realised that Cornell was talking to somebody on the phone, and so he moved closer to the desk, holding an envelope containing photocopies of documents he had been asked to bring. He moved so that he could hear the conversation and watch the door for anybody about to enter. Cornell was talking about a past operation. He had been tasked to go to the UK to kill a biological warfare scientist and make it look as if he had committed suicide. The guy had been a liability, stating that there were no WMDs, and he had had to cover the arses of the then President and UK Prime Minister. He was saying that at that time, the Prime Minister had been in the States and then, had gone to the Far East; but his right-hand man had been in on the deal and, as far as he knew had been giving the orders. They had had some security people on the ground, sorting things out. He considered it to have been a rush job with bad planning, but it had had to be done within a set time frame. It had been such a mess that the Brits had set up an enquiry to do a cover-up, and to take the heat off those involved. Then the press had got hold of the story, and had found out that things did not match up. He added that by that time he had been long gone. There was a pause; then he added that he had gone up the country to sort out a guy who was causing the Prime Minister some grief. That had been just a "quick beating", and then he had gone back to the States.

Napoleon moved quietly and effortlessly away from where he was standing to the furthest sofa, and sat down with a magazine open. He was just in time, because Cornell then entered the office. He looked at the empty chair, at the desk and then at Napoleon.

'Where is she?' asked Cornell, nodding to the empty chair.

Napoleon shrugged in good French style, the corners of his mouth drooping at the same time. 'I don't know, I just came to see you as arranged.'

'How long have you been here?' snapped Cornell.

'Just arrived: I knocked but nobody answered, so I came in and sat down to wait.'

Cornell stared at Napoleon, 'I was on the phone, could you hear what I was saying?'

'No,' he responded in defence.

'You sure about that?'

'Certain,' said Napoleon, 'I just came for the interview. I could hear that somebody was speaking but not what they were saying.'

Cornell glared at Napoleon for a good two minutes, then told him to come through to the back office. It was vastly different to that at the front. Here the magazines depicted guns. Books were about mercenary operations. Pictures were of soldiers in full special forces battle-kit. It was a 'boys' own' cavern of warfare. Cornell told him to sit, and indicated a wooden chair. Whilst Napoleon sat Cornell, having heard somebody enter the front office, went to the door to see who it was. It was obviously the missing female from the desk. Cornell shouted at her, asking where she had been and telling her that she was not to leave the office without telling him. His voice reverberated round the office. He thought she would be terrified and make good her escape, but she did not. Napoleon thought about the pictures on the wall describing good management. He had just heard a bawling-out that would have terrified a bunch of Marine recruits, as opposed to a woman manning a desk. When he had finished, he demanded two coffees. Napoleon was getting a coffee whether he wanted one or not.

Back in the room, Cornell sat at the table on a comfortable chair opposite him. The woman, probably in her thirties or early forties, and very good-looking, walked through the office to the small kitchen which was further through the building. When she came back with the coffee, he could see the effects of the shouting-match. She looked pale and had been crying. She placed the coffees on the table, and was told by Cornell to close the door on the way out. Napoleon thanked her for the coffee.

Cornell sipped his coffee. 'So, you say you did not hear what I was saying on the phone.'

'No, sir, I did not. What you say is not my business. I was on the seat near the door and could hear nothing.'

Cornell let it go and talked through Napoleon's career to date. He took the copies of various documents and checked his passport. He had a form and asked the questions: did he operate under any other name; did he have dual nationality; did he have any medical problems; where did he live, would he work anywhere? The questions continued, and Napoleon answered. Cornell made notes. He then came to his military records.

'So you served in the Legion,' declared Cornell.

'Yes, eight years.'

'Why did you leave?'

'The Legion has its own way of doing things, and I needed a change.'

'You were a para and a sniper?'

'Yes, one of the best.' Napoleon gave a slight smile.

Cornell caught the slight facial expression. 'Nothing to smile about: the Legion are a bunch of pussies.'

'Not in my opinion.'

'Well, your opinion don't count and they are all a bunch of pussies.'

Napoleon wanted to tell Cornell about the jungle assault

course in Guiana where Legionnaires complete the 'hell hole' course in twenty to thirty minutes. The US Marines had sent a selected group to test the course. They had set about the task and just managed it in two hours. However, he thought now was not the time to divulge those facts.

Cornell handed him a small file identifying some details they required, such as bank account, any dependants and contact details. On other pages there were addresses and telephone numbers for the company, Worldwide Executive Management Inc. Then the meeting was at an end. He could fill in the details and leave the forms with the woman, or drop them off at some other time. Once they had been processed he would be contacted. He would get small jobs and, if it worked, out he could progress to the serious stuff. Cornell stood, walked to the door and opened it. Napoleon walked through. There was no welcome to the company, not even a grunt of "goodbye thanks for coming". The door closed after he had passed through. He sat, eyed-up the secretary, and filled in the forms with the relevant details. He stood and walked to the desk to hand the forms to her. She took them and laid them on the desk. He just said 'thanks' and departed.

Napoleon checked his watch. He had time to go to his apartment, shower and change before meeting Dan. He took the precautionary measures of identifying if there were any followers, as he was very careful about anybody knowing where he lived. He had given the details with a map to Dan. Then he realised that he had put his address on the forms he had just completed. That was a bad move, especially after what he had heard. There was little point in avoiding anybody, he had bloody well told the world.

The apartment was on the third floor of a large house. The entrance had a flight of steps up to the communal front door. He stood down the street opposite the building and watched. There was nothing out of place, but he was dealing with professionals. He decided to go in and, crossing the road, he bounded up the steps, opened the door and entered. Inside, he closed the door. The hall-way and stair-well was in need of repairs and a paint job, but the apartment itself was in good order. It seemed to be a French thing. He moved up the stairs to the landing of the 3rd floor. His door was closed and when he put the key in the lock it was secure. He opened the door and slowly pushed it. Nothing happened so he entered. Nothing was disturbed. It was not a big apartment and so it took little checking. It was clear.

He put the kettle on to make coffee, and found a pad of paper and a pen to write the details of what he had discovered. He decided not to use his mobile phone to call Dan; he would tell him about it when he saw him later. Having finished the note, he carefully folded the paper and put it in a place where, if anything happened to him, Dan would find it. He drank the coffee and ate a baguette filled with cheese and tomato. He then showered and put on clean clothes. He grinned. He had to be reasonably smart to be out with a former sergeant chef of the Legion. A few beers and then the red light area, probably not the last item!

He checked that he had everything for the evening, and was preparing to leave when there was a knock at the door. He was not expecting anybody and nobody in the building knew him. He feared the worst. He went to a drawer near the bed and opened it. Under some clothing was an automatic handgun with a silencer fitted. He pulled it out and checked that it was ready to use. He crept to the door. There was another knock at the door. He ignored it. There was silence. He was on the inside, and whoever was banging was on the outside. The door between them offered little protection. He sat on the floor to gain a small profile and levelled the gun at the door. It was a stand-off. He decided to call Dan in case he did not get out.

Dan had made the bar and had ordered a drink when his phone rang. He could barely hear Napoleon who was speaking in a whisper. Dan went outside so that he could hear better. The situation sounded desperate. Dan told him to hang on, that he would be with him as quick as he could and that he was not to open the door. They were still on the phone when there was another knock and a woman's voice spoke. She sobbed the words, 'I was at the office today: I need to speak to you.'

Napoleon gathered his thoughts. 'Is anybody with you?' he enquired, an urgency in his voice.

There was silence. Then, after a pause, she answered, 'No'.

He was still not sure. She would know where he lived from the forms he had completed. He had seen the way she had been treated. Did she think that Cornell was coming to get him? Then, again, there was her strained voice, 'Please let me in.'

'OK, just a minute,' replied Napoleon. Dan had picked up what was being said. Napoleon confirmed it.

'It's the secretary from the office, she wants to talk: it's OK,' said Napoleon in a normal voice.

Dan was shouting down his phone, 'Don't open the door, don't open the door.' He did not wait for an answer but began to run as fast as he could towards Napoleon's apartment. The problem was that he did not know Paris, and so was not certain were the apartment was.

Napoleon moved quietly across the room and pulled the curtains to shut out some of the early-evening light. At the door he undid the lock and opened it. He saw and recognised the woman. The corridor seemed brighter than the room, but in that instant his brain expected to see just the woman; in the blink of an eye, his brain did not evaluate the full picture. It did not in that moment of time fully register the hand over her mouth, the tears running down her face or the gun being pointed at him. She was a human shield. There was not enough time for him to react. The picture in his brain went blank. The bullet from a silenced handgun had penetrated the front of his head and from that single shot he died instantly.

Cornell threw the woman into the room. He followed. She stumbled forward, falling over Napoleon's body. She turned to look up at Cornell who had pushed the door closed. He saw her pathetic body lying close to the target. She was a witness and of no value to him, so he shot her too. On the floor was Napoleon's mobile phone. He picked it up and checked to see if anybody was still at the other end. There was nothing. He checked to see the number of the last person called. He pressed the recall button. It rang but was not answered. He would deal with the phone call later. He moved quickly to the table where the remaining company papers lay, and picked them up. He had a look round for anything else that might be of interest, but there was nothing so he left the apartment, closing the door. He went down the stairs and out of the front door. He did not wait around but hurried along the street.

Dan was running as fast as he could. He was not armed and so he would have to take care. He stopped just long enough to check the directions and get his bearings. He listened to the phone. Napoleon was not talking or listening so he switched it off. Until he met up with Napoleon the phone was considered compromised. At the end of the street where Napoleon's apartment was situated he stopped. He needed to get his breath back and observe the area. He could not rush in. If he got shot then that would help no-one. He looked along the row of buildings but could not identify which was the one. His next action was to walk down the street at a fast pace glancing at the buildings to see the numbers. He also looked at the cars to see if any had people in them. He then thought he had reached the building, but he was on the opposite side of the street. He stopped, felt in his jacket pockets, then his trouser pockets, inside and back pockets. Doing so he looked across the road to see the number. He was not sure, but he remembered that Napoleon had told him about a sign outside. It was there. It was the fifth building along. Having thoroughly beaten his pockets without finding what he seemed to have lost, he turned and retraced his steps at a fast pace. He hoped that if anybody was waiting they would have thought he was just a passer-by who had lost or forgotten something and gone back for it. At the end of the street he crossed over, and hurried along a wider road.

He arrived at an alley that was wide enough for a vehicle, which provided access to the rear entrances to the apartments. He began the walk down it. If anybody was waiting for visitors it was a good trap. It was not a professional approach, but he was concerned that Napoleon might need help in a hurry. He peered over the walls to count out the buildings, and at the fifth he stopped at the gate. He tried the handle and gave it a push. It opened. There was no sound, so he went through into a small courtyard. Rubbish bins were the main occupants, along with a metal spiral stair that formed a fire-escape. It had seen better days. He moved carefully up the stairs to the third floor. This was the route that Napoleon had said would provide an escape-exit in an emergency. It was now proving to be an entry route in an emergency. At the third floor he could see that at what he thought were the windows of Napoleons apartment, the curtains were drawn. He tried the emergency door handle, and to his surprise it opened. That would be down to Napoleon. There would be no time to slide bolts or find a key if he had to move in a hurry. Inside the door he found himself in a corridor, and he could see the door to Napoleon's apartment. It was closed.

He crept along the short passage and listened at the door. Nothing. He had put gloves on before trying the door. It opened. He pushed it further, waiting for the thud of bullets to follow. Nothing happened. The room was dark with the curtains drawn. Crouching down, he moved into the room. He had done this a million times before, in numerous countries and numerous buildings, when looking for observation or sniper sites. His hand slid up the wall by the door and found the light switch. He clicked it on. His eyes scanned the room, then stopped at Napoleon. He pushed the door closed. A quick check revealed that Napoleon was dead. A single bullet wound to the front of his head, resulting in a messy outcome. He saw the woman and checked her. Although there was blood, she was alive. He pulled her to a sitting position and she groaned in pain. He checked for a wound and found a slight seepage of blood to the left side of her body. She was more in shock than at risk from the wound. He went to the bathroom and found a clean towel which he pressed over the wound. Looking about, he found an unused military field dressing laying on a desk beside a pile of books. He opened it and wound it round her to secure the towel. It seemed to do the job. He asked her if she was OK and whether she would be able to walk. She muttered something, and Dan took that as a 'yes'. She had a bag slung round her neck, and he realised that it had helped to deflect the bullet. She tugged at the bag. He pulled it so that she could open it. Inside was a packet of pain-killers. He got some out and then fetched a cup of water, and helped her to take some of the tablets. He went to another small pile of books and picked one of them, placing it in Napoleon's small rucksack. Napoleon's gun was also put into the bag. He checked the room one more time and then lifted the woman up. She winced with the pain, but with his help she made it to the door. He turned the light off and pulled the door closed. Half-carrying the woman, he walked to the emergency door and went out onto the staircase. It was a hard and painful journey down but the woman did not cry out with the pain, for which Dan was very thankful. They passed through the courtyard and out into the passageway. He retraced his route back to the road. Dan could hear sirens, and considered that whoever had taken out Napoleon may have tipped off the police, in the hope that the person on the end of the mobile phone was at the apartment.

On the streets of Paris with a wounded woman, Dan wondered what he had got himself into. They could not go to a hospital, and he had no contacts to call on to help. But perhaps there was one. One of the staff at the hotel had got into financial difficulties and had been desperate. Dan had broken every rule in the book and trusted the man. He had loaned him some money which had helped to avoid a very difficult situation. He had already, in just a few days, managed to pay some of the loan back. Dan had the man's mobile phone number and called him. He needed a favour big-time. Thankfully the man answered and, after a quick conversation and having given his location, he hoped that something would happen. They had not waited long, just long enough to be concerned about the noise of police cars in the street a block away, when a car approached, slowed down and pulled up alongside them. The driver looked at Dan, 'You from the Legion?'

Dan replied, 'Yes.'

'Papa sent me. Get in quick.'

Dan opened the door to the back seats and helped the woman get in. Once they were both in and the door was shut, the car pulled away. Dan looked back: it had come just in time, as the blue flashing lights heralded the arrival of a police car that seemed to be going to the alley at the back of the apartments. As they sped through the streets of Paris, Dan removed the simcard from his mobile and pushed it out of the window. The driver said nothing whilst he drove them to the back door of the hotel. Dan thanked the driver and gave him some money. The man at the hotel was waiting for them, along with a woman he had seen before but did not know. She turned out to be the man's sister. They made it to Dan's bedroom unseen, and then they got her into the bathroom. The man said he had a friend who was a doctor and who would be coming, unofficially of course. The doctor came and went: the woman, whose name was Marianne, had been very lucky. The bullet had been deflected by her leather bag and its contents, which had been slung over her shoulder and under her jacket. It had creased along her side, leaving a flesh-wound. It was now treated and bandaged, pain-killers provided relief and an anti tetanus jab had been given as a precaution. Dan paid the doctor, who was to return in two days. Marianne now lay asleep on the bed.

The man and woman fussed about, cleaning up and then getting them some food. Dan ate a little. It was getting late when he slumped into a chair. He had fallen asleep, and the next thing he knew was when he woke to a gentle tapping on the door. He opened to find the man with a breakfast tray. He put it on the desk, and told Dan that he had told the manager that his girlfriend had arrived and that they wanted breakfast in their room. He said that there had followed some comments about bedroom activities and they had all laughed; so there would be no problems. Marianne was still asleep, but as he sorted the food out she awoke. She felt better and had something to eat and drink. They went over the details of the previous day and it painted a very murky picture. She asked about Napoleon and Dan said that he was dead. She said that it was her fault, as she had got him to open the door. Dan told her that she had been placed in a very difficult position, and not to blame herself. It was Cornell who had done the deed and used her. She explained that she had joined a security company to do the administration. The boss of the office was away, and they had sent Cornell to look after the place, but that he had been very unhappy with that. He seemed to take his anger out on her and was verbally abusive but, apart from the apartment incident, he had never laid a finger on her. Her real boss was different, and she had decided to endure Cornell as her real boss was due back.

Dan was contemplating the loss of Napoleon. They had been through so much, and for him to die in that way did not seem right. He then remembered the book. Taking it from the rucksack, he looked at it. He explained to Marianne that, when a man left the Legion, his mates bought him a copy of *The Legion* and all in the company or section signed it. He opened the book and went to the back cover. Only just visible was a slit along the inside of the cover nearest to the spine. He used his leatherman knife to ease the paper apart and locate a small piece of paper. He gently pulled it out. He put the book down and opened the single page of paper. Napoleon had written the note after the meeting with Cornell. He explained how he had overheard the telephone conversation. He said that Cornell had killed a bio weapons scientist in the UK, linked to Maspamia. He had then gone up north, found somebody and beaten them to death because they were causing problems for the UK PM. It finished with the words: 'If you are reading, this then Cornell did the deed'. Dan was shocked. Not much shocked him, but this note did. Marianne asked if he was OK. He passed her the note. She read it then dropped it and made strange noises whilst sobbing.

'I have to go to the UK to see my mother,' said Dan. 'But the first priority is to get you to a safe place and medical care.'

Marianne looked at him, 'I can wait and go back when my boss returns.'

'Cornell is no ordinary security man: he is what is called an assassin. Because you were at the scene when Napoleon was killed and you survived, you are a target.' He paused to let the message sink in. 'Do you have anywhere where you can go: relations, friends? It needs to be well away from Paris.'

She thought about it, then said, 'I have a sister who lives in Switzerland; she is always saying I should go and see her.' She smiled, 'I can phone her and tell her I'm coming.'

'No.' said Dan in a firm voice. 'They will know your mobile number, so we need to get rid of your simcard.' Dan was annoyed that he had not thought about that when he dumped his.

She had already opened the phone and taken the card out. She gave it to him. 'I have to go to my apartment and get some of my things.'

'Too risky for you; we will sort that out later.' Dan thought, 'Do you have a passport?'

'Yes, in my bag, and my driving licence, all the things we have to carry.'

He looked around the room. 'That's good. OK, I will go and get the train times for Switzerland and a new simcard, and I'll get rid of your old one.'

'But I have an account.'

'You have to forget that for now: he can find you through things like that.'

She sat and looked out of the window.

'I won't be long,' he said, walking to the door.

* * * *

Dan arrived back at the hotel carrying a number of bags. He laid them on the bed. 'Thought you would need some other clothes.'

She smiled, 'How did you know my size?' she enquired.

'I didn't, but there was an assistant that looked about your size, and she helped me.'

She emptied the bags and admired the content. Then, selecting some of the clothes, she disappeared into the bathroom. When she emerged, she was transformed. Dan gave suitably positive comments. He had made some coffee from the ample supplies that had made their way to the room. He showed her the train times and the various stations. He gave her a new simcard which she installed, and she noted the number. Dan also noted the number. He reminded her that it was a pay-as-you-go, so to keep calls quick. He had also found out about flights to Manchester. Dan gathered his things together, and stuffed his life back into holdalls. He would carry one, and leave the rest at the hotel until he returned.

At reception they were sorry to see him leave, but he said he would be back; after all, he was leaving his bags in storage. He went and found the man who had helped them, and explained to him what was happening. He told him that the debt was written off and gave him some more money. The man asked about his girlfriend. They both grinned. He said that she was going to stay with friends, somewhere in the south of France. Dan had decided that should the heavy mob ever trace them to the hotel, information about their whereabouts, particularly hers, would cease. The man asked if the woman needed any of her things from her home. Dan had already asked her for a list, more to keep her occupied than with the prospect of getting it. The man explained that he knew people who owed him a favour, who could slip in and out with anything she required. It could be held at the hotel until Dan returned. That was one more problem solved. But it was costing him money, his Legion savings were under attack.

24

Arriving in the UK at Manchester airport, Dan found a long queue at passport control. He passed through without problem, and made his way to the car hire receptions. It was some time since he was last in the UK, and he found the airport very busy. He processed through the formalities, having to explain that he had a French driving licence because he lived and worked in France. He omitted to say that he was a former Legionnaire because that would have catagorised him as a risk-taker. Insurance companies did not like that. He was given the keys to a car and told where to locate it. Once he had found the car, he left the car park and, following the road signs, headed north. The roads were manic but, despite having to look for signs and avoid maniacs driving other cars, he made reasonable progress.

As he got closer to where he was born and grew up, he thought the houses looked closer together and smaller than he remembered: it was always the same at every visit, which was not very often. He found the road, turned in and drove slowly along to stop outside the house. To him as a child, the house had always been big; now it looked small. The garden was neat and tidy. He went to the front door and rang the bell. He heard it chime in the hallway. The front door opened, and he was face to face with his mother. It was the first time he had seen her following the murder of his father.

'You don't have to ring the door-bell: it's still your home, just come in.'

In the hallway she grabbed hold of him and hugged him for several minutes.

'Come on through to the kitchen,' she said, leading the way.

His first thoughts were that his mother had aged, but she seemed in reasonable spirits. He could tell that she certainly missed his father.

'So how is the Legion?' she asked.

'It was good, really good, but I am a civilian now.'

'What will you do with yourself?' she enquired, filling the kettle. Tea was at the forefront of every visit.

He could not tell her that he was a hit-man for the good guys, so he stuck with a half truth. 'I am joining an international security company.'

'Oh, that's nice,' she replied. 'Are you staying long?'

'Long enough to try and find out what happened to Dad.'

'That's easy: he upset that Proffitt person, and he had him bumped off. As Prime Minister he was a nasty person, along with that advisor of his. A real sour-face, that one. If you ask me, if you put the pair of them in a room full of poisonous snakes, the snakes would die, not them.'

Dan grinned, he had never heard his mother speak like that, especially when his father was alive. 'That bad?' His voice was questioning.

'Well,' she said, 'they had that dodgy dossier that took us into an illegal war. Trouble-makers, the whole lot of them. More families lost their relatives, and for what? So that lot could make more money out of misery. No good will come of it, you mark my words.'

They sat whilst they had a cup of tea and he had to have a slice of sponge cake, which she said used to be his favourite. 'Do you see any of dad's old friends?'

'Sometimes, although less these days. Sammy pops round to see if everything is OK and if I have heard anything officially from the police.'

'Speaking of the police, do they keep in contact?'

'Now and then. A nice police lady pops by to say the case is still open, but that they haven't found anybody.'

'Do you have her name?' Dan asked.

'Yes,' she got up and went to a drawer, opened it and took out a piece of paper. She gave it to Dan. 'She told me to call her if I needed anything.'

Dan made a note of the name and phone number.

'Does Sammy still live at the same house?'

'As far as I know he does, never thought to ask him.'

They spent the next few hours chatting and reliving the family events prior to the two disasters that had befallen them. Then she cooked a meal. It was the first proper meal she had prepared since her loss. Dan helped her clear up. It was then time for her to watch the soaps on television. Dan said that he would go and see if he could find Sammy and have a chat. In the car he made a call on his mobile phone to the number for the police officer. A female voice answered. Dan said who he was and asked if he could have a chat sometime. She was on duty the following morning, and would call at the house at ten-thirty if it was convenient. His mother went to a club at ten, so the timing was good for a private chat.

He drove the car to Sammy's house and knocked on the door. A woman's voice spoke from behind the closed door. 'Who is it?'

'My name is Dan Pierce; my father David was a friend of Sammy's. I just want to have a chat with him.'

'Hello Dan, he's gone to see a couple of mates at the pub. Do you know the one?'

'Yes, I will go and find him there. Sorry to have disturbed you.'

He went to the car, aware that she was watching him. Dan reflected on what sort of country Britain had become, when somebody would not open the front door to speak to you.

In the pub he ordered a pint. He spotted three men in conversation and went over. Dan looked at one of them; he had not seen him for years. 'Sammy?' he said, unsure that it was him.

'Yes,' was the reply, with a look of recognition but uncertainty.

'Dan Pierce,' offered Dan. The three men's faces lit up and they told him to join them. Dan sat down, and each of his dad's friends reiterated how sorry they were for what had happened.

'I am going to speak to the police about it.' He looked at the three faces. 'I've got a meet tomorrow morning. Mum's out, so I can push the issue of what has happened and what is happening.'

'I can answer that for you: nothing.' said Sammy, his voice lowered so as not to be overheard. 'They said it was a mugging, but from the inquest it was plain that he had been professionally beaten to death.' The other two men nodded their agreement.

Dan was about to ask if they had anybody in mind when Sammy continued, 'Your father was leading the challenge against Proffitt for the deaths of our troops in Maspamia and the illegal war; and he was asking about the rewards he has got since leaving office. Proffitt did not like it, nor did the other one, Reilly; he's worse than Proffitt.'

Dan had no idea just how much his father had been involved. 'What you're saying is that Proffitt and/or Reilly had my dad taken out.'

Sammy answered, 'That's just what we are saying. They didn't do it themselves, but they were implicated. We think the yanks also wanted him dealt with, so they probably did it.

215

He had the local police on his back over minor matters, and he had men in suits arrive to warn him off. That did not stop him: he wanted justice.'

'Is that what you all think?' asked Dan.

Each man agreed, and one went further, 'It's not just us, it's what most people think, although they may not go so far as to say so in public.'

Dan leaned back in his chair. He was lost for words. He was hearing that there was a link between the former Prime Minister, his advisor and the death of his father. 'That's quite a claim.'

'We sat through the inquest, and from what we heard and saw around here and having spoken to your father ourselves he was what you might call a pain in the arse for that lot. They needed him stopped and they would not have cared how. He told us on the very day he was murdered that a big yank had called at the house and threatened him. You know your father, he would not back down, so after he left us they did him.' There was anger in Sammy's voice as he spoke.

One of the other men added, 'We have yobs round here, and when they do a mugging they threaten with a knife or gun. If stuff gets handed over, they take it and clear off. Sometimes they stick a knife in if stuff doesn't get handed over. We've not had a shooting around here yet. They said your dad was mugged, and they took money and his credit card; but they left his wallet and driving licence. Muggers normally take those to sell on. No, it was no mugging.'

Dan decided to get back home. Whilst he was around there might be snoopers, looking to see what he was up to. He thanked the men and departed. At home, his mother was still watching television. He told her that he had met up with Sammy and a couple, of others but did not go into detail.

The doorbell chimed and Dan went to open the door. He glanced at a clock: it was dead on ten o'clock. On the doorstep he found a woman, probably in her mid-forties and dressed in conservative clothes. She held up her ID and identified herself as PC Dianne Reynolds. Dan invited her in, and they went into the kitchen where he made coffee. He thanked her for calling round at short notice, and explained that he wanted to talk whilst his mother was not present, as the subject of his father upset her.

Reynolds gave an overview of the case investigation to date. It amounted to not a lot. Dan asked about the attack. 'My father was threatened in this house by a big American on the morning he was murdered. What has happened about finding him?' Reynolds was about to reply when Dan continued. 'I am told the beating was a professional job, and that it was not a mugging as not everything was taken.'

'This case has played on my mind since I first became involved,' answered Reynolds. 'The police often get the dirty end of politics and this is one of them. This conversation never took place, and if you quote me I will deny all knowledge.'

'Fine,' replied Dan, 'I've not got any recording equipment on the go.'

'OK, the police got an emergency call that a male, your father, had been found beaten up. A patrol car and an ambulance were sent to the scene. Your father was declared dead at the hospital, although he was probably dead at the scene. Police officers came here and were told about the threats from the American. This was reported back to the station. All units were alerted and a call was made to airports and seaports. That is when people high up in London got involved and, it appears, put the brakes on. Police officers do a job and follow orders. Sometimes the orders are considered strange, but then the full picture may not be known. So we pulled back and looked locally for known trouble-makers. The problem was that the style of attack did not match any of those that we usually have to deal with. The coroner was concerned as the autopsy highlighted what was considered a professional assault. London ruled, and it became a mugging because we up here followed orders.'

Dan contemplated the information. 'What you are saying is that my father was murdered by some sort of professional hit man, an American, and that the hunt for that person was stopped by some suits in London.'

Reynolds looked at Dan. 'That, off the record, is what I am saying, and it is my opinion. Not just mine, by the way. Your father was fighting for justice for himself and for other families. It did not meet the political agenda so he was dealt with.' She paused, 'You know, it was just after a bio warfare scientist was supposed to have committed suicide down south. He was involved in Maspamia bio warfare weapons, and would not agree with a report which has been called a dodgy dossier. There are lots of loose ends, and they have made the coroner's report a secret so that nobody can have access to see what was found. Then your dad was murdered just after that.'

Dan thanked her for being straight with him. He realised that she had put her neck on the chopping-block, and that he could not use anything she had said. 'Is there anything about me floating about the police station?'

'No, they don't know who you are or even that you are here. So no, you have not shown up on the radar. My advice would be to keep it that way – or you could be found dead in the woods.

'Is the case still open?'

'Yes, but it's not going anywhere. I call round sometimes to see how your mother is but, as I say, it's not going anywhere.'

Dan avoided any mention of the Legion or his future plans. He had to get to grips with the information he had learnt since coming home. He thanked her again for being straight with him. She in turn said that he would need to be careful, and that revenge would be complicated and have an impact on his mother. He saw genuine concern.

His mother had a good morning at her club. He asked if she wanted to go shopping, but she didn't need anything. He suggested they should go out to eat, but she didn't want to. She was going to cook them their meals. For the next couple of days he did odd jobs about the house and some gardening, doing her neighbour three doors down the road out of a job. Still, it was only for a few more days; then Dan would be gone and the neighbour would be back on the duty roster of mending things when they broke.

Dan decided to take a big chance and show his mother a photograph of Cornell. He hoped that if his mother saw it she would react, and say that it was him who came to the house. The opportunity arose when they were chatting.

'I have a photograph I want to show you which may upset you, but I need to have an answer.' He had laid the photograph face-down on the table.'

'That sounds a bit ominous,' she replied, sitting down.

Dan turned the photograph over. She was in the process of putting her reading glasses on. Picking up the photograph, she looked at it. She then looked at Dan and demanded to know why he had the photo. She was physically shaken. He explained about Napoleon and what had happened to him. He asked her if this was the man who came to the house. She said that it was.

'They never found him, you know. A big chap with an American accent, and they could not find him.'

They sat for a while talking, and then she got up and said it was time to prepare a meal. Later he said he was sorry for upsetting her. She asked if he was going to find the man, and he confirmed that that was his plan. That man had a lot to answer for. She seemed comforted at that.

25

Dan returned to Paris and the hotel that he had made his base. He had negotiated a good rate, and it was cheaper than renting an apartment. The latter would also make him accessible to anybody searching for him. His new-found friend Papa was invaluable. He was the one who had helped him with Marianne after she was shot. He had managed to recover her valuables and place them in safe storage. It was Papa who asked Dan if they could meet at a café round the corner from the hotel. He had some information for him. Papa looked around to make sure nobody could overhear their conversation before speaking. 'I have been told that the police arrived at the apartment and found the body of your friend Napoleon. They checked the room and questioned a lot of people, but put it down to a robbery gone wrong or to the possibility that your friend was involved in some gang-related problem. They found some papers that showed him to be an ex-Legionnaire, so they contacted the organisation. It seems that they were not very helpful. Apparently many Legionnaires become mercenaries and end up suffering violent deaths. There was no known family or friends. The police closed the file, and the state was tasked with the burial. The funeral was the bare minimum, with just a few words spoken by a priest. An old man wearing a green beret stood by the grave and saluted at the appropriate time. When it was over, a detective spoke with the old man to find out what he knew about the deceased. He did not know him personally but had been a Legionnaire himself and had been contacted by the Legion and asked to attend on their behalf.' Papa took a piece of paper from a pocket and passed it to Dan. 'It's the details of Napoleon's grave. I have to say that it is not safe to visit; and the authorities have to report any visitors to the police. There are also other prying eyes.' Dan looked at Papa. 'How did you manage to get this information?' Papa grinned, 'We are nobodies: we do not count, so we move about and go places, as lowly workers, where others could not go.'

Two days after the meeting with Papa, Dan received a call from Rosie, saying that she needed him to attend a meeting in London. He had contemplated going to Switzerland to find out how Marianne was getting on, but realised that he had no idea where she was living. He had tried calling her on the new mobile number, but it was disconnected. That was now all on hold, as he flew from Paris Orly airport to London City airport. He then made his way to a hotel in central London where a room had been booked for him. He checked in as Mark Chester and elected to pay cash for any extras. He had been told that cash was the best option, as credit cards left a trail that could be traced. He checked in and took the lift to the second floor and room 2015. Opening the door, he entered the room and dropped his bag on the suitcase stand. The bathroom was a reasonable size and well-appointed. There was a double bed, a desk and chair. It was just a hotel room, and he had certainly been in a lot worse. He went to the window and pulled the net curtain back. Looking down on the Strand, he observed the melee of people and traffic. The mass rushing about seemed the norm. His watch showed five past five; that would explain the number of people. Like little ants all departing for their nests. He had been in some of the worst countries in the world and seen the effects of genocide; but here, in so-called civilisation, people were slaves to pay-day and organisations who demanded everything from those engaged. He let the curtain fall back, and the outside world was shut out. His watch now showed a quarter past five. He could expect a phone call at six o'clock, when he would be told about the next part of the journey. His first task was to leave the room and identify the main stairs that would take him up or down in the hotel. Emergency exits were checked. If there was a problem he would have exit options.

Rosie had contacted him and outlined a project but had given no details at all. She had made the arrangements and he expected to speak to her at six. In the forty-five minutes he had to wait, he showered, dressed in clean clothes, turned on the television, searched the channels and turned it off again. Then, at the prescribed time, the phone rang. He picked up the handset. 'Hello,' he said, keeping it short and to the point.

'Good evening, Mr Chester,' responded a soft female voice.

'At six sharp,' he said, then reflected that it sounded rather a strange thing to say.

There was no comment apart from, 'I am in the lobby downstairs, please join me.'

'On my way,' he replied, replacing the handset.

The lobby was busy with people coming and going. It was a popular hotel for tourists and those going to the theatres, as well as for the normal business clientele. He looked about but did not spot her and it was only when he walked past her, and she spoke that he recognised her. She had made a great effort to change her appearance, and it had worked. There were relaxed and informal greetings between them, but it was business. Rosie suggested a drink in the bar. Dan agreed, and in the bar he ordered drinks whilst Rosie found the quietest spot to sit. Aware that ears were listening close by, they chatted about things in general, but Rosie wanted to go beyond general chat. She wanted to explain the purpose of the meeting the next day.

'You need to be at the building tomorrow at ten o'clock. When you go inside, report to reception using the name Mark Chester. They will tell you which floor to go to. I will be there and will meet you at the lift. I will then take you to a small meeting-room. You will not meet any of the participants in the meeting, and they will not meet you or know what you look like. You will be able to see and hear everything that happens in the meeting on a large television.'

Dan's expression did not change, but he was listening.

'The only person in the building who will ever know who you are and what you look like is me.' She paused, looking at Dan. 'That maintains security, as you are a very valuable asset.'

'Will I be able to speak to the people in the meeting?' he enquired.

'No. Communications from you will only be switched on if we want you to ask or answer a question. If you do speak, your voice will be heard but it will be scrambled. You will hear normal speech from them. As I said, they will not see you.'

He nodded.

'What we are asking you to do is very serious, but security is very important. There are some very nasty people, some in high places whose actions cannot be tolerated. There is one such target who you will be told about, and a proposition will be made. You either accept or decline. If you decline then that will be the end of your participation in that meeting. It does not mean that we will never call on you again. There may be a very good reason why you do not or cannot accept the assignment. However, if you do accept, then what I can say is that the organisation will provide whatever support you require. But if you do not accept, it is not a problem.'

Dan asked how long the meeting would take.

'I don't know, but there will be refreshments in the room. You will be party to the wider picture, so you will see why the foundation has decided to take action. I know that is unusual, but it is how the foundation does its business. By doing this you will have a clear picture of those involved and the need for action.'

Dan was being paid, so it was a case of "go with the flow". The hustle and bustle in the bar began to subside as people moved on. Rosie then declared that she had a story to tell.

'You will know from your own experience that Maspamia caused many upsets, and I had one which I have not got over.' Her voice dropped to an even lower level, 'You will recall our first meeting in Africa where I was with intelligence and acting as an interpreter. Well, I did a number of jobs and was assigned to Maspamia to support weapons inspectors. They were looking for chemical and biological weapons. In fact I was assigned to one particular inspector, Dr John Finch.'

Dan stated that he had heard the name. 'Didn't he die in suspicious circumstances?' he enquired.

'He was the UK's leading scientist in biochem warfare. We spent months searching in Maspamia but found nothing. He had problems back here because the government and those in the US needed bio weapons to be found so that they could justify going to war. They put a lot of pressure on him and the rest of the inspectors, trying to get them to say that there were weapons when they had not found any. I was quizzed by my bosses in the States as to why John would not go along with what they wanted. The thing is, his life had been devoted to finding and removing such weapons, but he would not be manipulated by their power-struggle dealings. He was a scientist, and he told it how it was. He had many stories to tell about these weapons in a number of countries around the world and, most interestingly, about who supplied those countries. That was the reason he had decided that, when he retired, he would write a book and expose it all. But most of all he was considering moving to America. Even though he would be retired, there were other possible openings for him as a consultant or lecturer. He had talked to a publisher in the UK and was exploring options in the US. In fact, when he came to the US to do lectures or attend meetings, he would often stay a bit longer and fly over and stay at my place. I had this what they call a neat, suburban ranch-style red-brick bungalow, which was situated in a suburb area about a ten-minute drive from the air base where I worked. He used the address as a base where he could be contacted. Oh, we were not romantically involved, as many seemed to indicate. He was married, and had grown-up children. I've met the family at their home. I was 43 and he was 59 so there was also an age gap; and I suppose that I was trendy and he was the sober "nutty professor" type. In a strange way, workwise, we really did get on.'

'What happened to him?' enquired Dan.

'He was the ultimate professional, but he worked under some who were not. They were civil servants with no skills other than a job for life: you know the sort I mean, with their head up the boss's arse. John was not like that, he was straight and told it how it was. He was not given the proper grade that his position warranted; but he only had a year to go before he would retire, and he could hardly wait. But it was the fiasco about the chemical and biological weapons and the illegal war in Maspamia that caused him to become unhappy. The government said that there were weapons, and that they could be delivered onto a target in a short period of time. He said that there was no evidence, so he could not support them. The media found out and it looked bad on John. He was the fall guy and paid the price. The real bad people got away with it. It was a real mess, and so somebody had him killed to shut him up.'

Dan just sat and looked at Rosie ,who was visibly upset but added, 'What was worse was that they said he committed suicide.'

'How was he killed?' asked Dan.

'They said he took an overdose of pain killers and then slashed his wrist so that he bled to death in some woods. But it is simply not true. The evidence from those who found him and tried to treat him showed that the suicide option was not possible. I know that John could not have taken an overdose as he suffered from a disorder that made it difficult for him to swallow pills. As for cutting his wrist: well, he was unable to use his right hand for basic tasks requiring any strength, such as slicing food, because of a painful elbow injury. He would therefore have had to have been a contortionist to have killed himself by slashing his left wrist.' To emphasise the point, she added, 'In fact, when we had a meal together, he had difficulty cutting his own steak; he was too weak to cut his own wrist.'

'Was this information made public?'

'Oh, selected witnesses were called to an inquiry, but some key people were not called. I was told that when some people who were involved told lies, there was nobody to challenge them. The UK police found out about me, and detectives came to America. I was interviewed over a few days, and I told them what I have just told you, only in much more detail. I made and signed a statement. They asked if I would testify at an inquiry. I said yes, but I was not called. The excuse was that they would not allow me to testify in private. I was still undertaking military intelligence work. At the inquiry a senior police officer said that my statement contained nothing of relevance. That was pure bullshit. What I had to say was very relevant, but they wanted a cover-up.'

Dan was not surprised by her words. He had heard the same story from his father, following the killing of his brother.

Rosie then added, 'John's life had been threatened because he strived to do what was best for humanity. He deserved more from his country than a dodgy investigation over a dodgy dossier from a dodgy government.'

Dan contemplated what had been said, then realised that he might have a link. 'When I went to Napoleon's apartment in Paris after he was killed, I took his Legion book, it's a Legion thing. Inside was a note that said that the person he met, and went to get some work from that day in Paris, had been on the telephone, and he overheard him say that he had killed a bio scientist. He then killed my father to shut him up. He said his name was Cornell. I had a picture and my mother identified him as having visited the house and threaten my father. I reckon he killed him and that's why the police never found out who did it.' Dan thought about it, then added, 'OK, he's the operator, so who engaged him?'

'It's much bigger than just one person,' added Rosie. 'That's why you are invited to the meeting.'

Dan had one important question. 'Are you still with the military?'

'No. After John was murdered it became very difficult for me. I was in military intelligence and they were concerned about my connection with him. The media interest did not help, so I was reassigned and that helped. But because of what I had said in my statement I suppose they thought I was a security risk. We came to a mutual agreement and we parted company. I already knew about the Excalibur Foundation, so when I was approached I knew what I would be getting into. We are not connected to any military or security service organisations, we are independently funded and have a very diverse group of people. We are, as you will see, secretive and we need to keep it that way so as to keep our people safe.'

When they parted company, it was back to formality. Dan was a step closer to finding out about Cornell and Rosie had off-loaded her burden onto a kindred spirit. It may have been unfair, but the whole dirty business was unfair.

26

Dan walked into the building at 09.45 and reported to reception which was attended by a security man and woman, both in uniform. The woman asked his name, checked a computer, then issued a security pass under the name Mark Chester. Dan had died his hair almost black, had not shaved for two weeks and wore glasses with non-magnifying lenses. His jeans were clean on and he wore a new baggy zip-up jacket, underneath which he wore a good quality white T-shirt. He had checked himself out in the room's full-length mirror before leaving the hotel. He had walked to a tube station and begun to take a diversionary route to his destination. He had been told that the City was alive with CCTV cameras, and so his every move could be tracked if somebody wanted to. He had done nothing to alert the authorities, so he moved about with limited precautions.

The security man told Dan to go round to his right where he would find the lift. He needed to go to the fifth floor and, when out of the lift, wait for somebody to meet him. The security man emphasised that he should wait by the lift and not go wandering about. Following instructions to the letter, Dan entered the lift and got out at the fifth floor. There was a corridor to the left and right, and in front of him, a leather sofa. He walked to the sofa and sat down. There was no noise, no voices, nothing. He watched the lights showing the lift going up and down, but never stopping at the fifth floor.

He heard the footsteps coming from his right. It was a woman's footfall, with short steps and the noise of high heels. He fought the urge to look up to see who was approaching and stared at the lift. The walking noise stopped just to his right. 'Good morning, Mr Chester, would you follow me please.' Rosie had spoken. She smiled when he looked up at her. He stood and followed her down the corridor. No words passed between them: this was professional territory. Last night was personal. He could not spot any CCTV cameras, but presumed that they were all over the building. Rosie stopped at a door and opened it. She gestured for him to enter. Inside it was a medium sized office, with a conference table accommodating eight chairs. A sideboard was at one end, and it had refreshments on it. Rosie was the first to speak. 'Thank you for coming, Mark; the Excalibur Foundation welcomes you. You will be in this room and you can monitor events on this TV screen.' The picture showed another, larger meeting-room which had a number of people sitting at a large table. It all looked very informal. There was no sound on, so he could not hear what was being said. Rosie continued, 'Through the door at the end is a wash-room.' She smiled and her eyes twinkled. He thought of her and John together in the desert looking for nasty bugs and germs. 'I will come and check that you are OK as we progress, so please make yourself comfortable. Oh, I know you do not have a camera, but do you have a mobile phone? It's no pictures and no phone calls. Security is at its maximum.'

Dan muttered, 'Right, thank you,' and turned off his phone. Rosie opened the door, passed through and closed it behind her. He grabbed a cup of coffee and sat down opposite the screen. Using the remote, he pressed the button to increase the volume. He was eavesdropping on a conversation and he did not know what they were talking about. He counted eight people in the other room, five men and three women, one of whom was Rosie. She was clearly one of them, whoever 'they' were.

They had begun when a number of people from different countries had been concerned at the way that some governments acted when dealing with people who did not follow the party line. The concern was that governments were not averse to undertaking political assassinations. In fact, some countries had secret killer teams who were able to undertake such tasks. It was not just an issue which concerned dictatorships: it also involved many so-called first world countries.

The victims were not criminals or terrorists but generally people with high-profile jobs, as well as many undertaking secret government work. If those people disagreed with what a government was doing and it became public knowledge to some degree, or could influence the political standing of a member of a government, or expose a government's wrongdoing, then that person might be silenced. The killings would be contracted and the individual or individuals would be terminated in such a way that it looked like suicide or an accident. It was a tried and tested system. Those involved in raising the contract put in place elaborate and effective safeguards and covered their trails. Few would or could challenge the situation because they would then face the possibility of elimination themselves.

In a quiet hotel in Switzerland, with views over a lake and of the mountains, nine men and women had gathered with one aim. They wanted to see what could be done to counter the killer teams. Sitting round a table for the first time, each had looked at the others with some uneasiness and a little distrust. Some knew each other, whilst others did not. They all had one thing in common. They had raised concerns about political assassinations and the fact that they were covered up. An Englishman had spoken first. 'My name is Charles and I found you. I then sent you information and an outline proposal. I think we all have similar views. I know most of you do not want to be identified, and have already created a cover for your identity. That is fully acceptable. Of course we will have to carry out security screening, but as you can see that is feasible. Perhaps, if I may suggest it, we could progress through the proposal.'

Two days later, the nine men and women departed the hotel as founder members of the Excalibur Foundation.[3]

The public face of the organisation was to assist victims of political intimidation and possible killing. They would also assist the families of those victims. Charles had been voted to chair the Foundation and he accepted. He would establish a Foundation base and introduce a security system. Without doubt, those who made use of the killer teams would want to infiltrate the organisation. Substantial funding was available, as well as a long list of potential clients. A secondary objective of the organisation was highly secret, with only a minimum number of members involved. It would seek justice for those who had been killed for political reasons, with retribution as the only option. One woman who had been present at the meeting had been a member of a military intelligence organisation. She had become very disillusioned with its manipulation for political ends, and a growing number of political assassinations. People were being killed just to keep them quiet. She had left the intelligence community and been approached by the Excalibur organisation. Rosie Portray had first-hand experience of the killing business, and her skills, knowledge and contacts would be invaluable to the Foundation.

When the meeting in the other room started, Dan heard the man speak and realised that the words were directed at him.

[3] Excalibur is the legendary sword of King Arthur, the king who brought justice from the round table.

'For the benefit of a visitor who is not in the room, I would like to explain. First, we offer you a warm welcome to the Excalibur Foundation. You have been asked to join us because we have a very serious problem and we need specialist help to deal with it. What will happen is that some people, victims of political crimes, will join us so that you and the committee here can hear their evidence. Each case will be a summary, as they have already been interviewed in detail. Once we have evaluated the evidence, we can get down to business with you.' The speaker was a man in his mid-to late sixties; he sat in the middle of the group. He had a kindly, relaxed face that did not show the signs of stress that so many portrayed in modern times. He had a well- spoken English accent, and was dressed in an immaculate dark suit with a white shirt and blue tie. He wore glasses, but did not seem to be at home wearing them; and he was the only male who had not taken his jacket off. The same man leaned forward and addressed one of the other men, who stood and left the room. He returned a few moments later, accompanied by two women who were shown to seats opposite them. One of the women belonged to the Foundation and sat next to the other. The man in the middle smiled, and now spoke in a soft voice. 'Thank you very much for coming, I trust all of the arrangements were to your satisfaction.'

'Yes, thank you, sir,' she replied, her American accent unmistakable.

He smiled again. 'Good,' he continued, I know that what the meeting is about has been explained to you, that it is an informal one and that, because of the sensitivity of its subject matter, there will be no names used. If you have something to say, then we want to hear it. I propose we chat for a short while and then have a comfort break. Is that OK? And by the way there is no need to address me or any of my colleagues as sir, or madam in the case of the ladies.'

The woman took in all that was said. She had been flown

from her home in the USA to London with a friend. She had made use of the time and combined a short holiday with the meeting. They wanted to talk about her husband, who had been killed in a mugging several years before. The man then asked her if she would tell them in her own words what had happened.

The woman seemed to slump in her seat as she was reminded about her husband. She looked along the line of faces opposite her and then began. 'I had been married to my husband for thirty-eight years and we have four children. He, Charlie that is, was a scientist and worked in bio-chemical warfare. His job required him to go to other countries and look to see what weapons they had. Most of his work was secret and so he never spoke about it at home. He would go away in the cold of winter and come home brown from the sun, so I knew he had been overseas. As I say, he did not speak about it much. What he did say I didn't understand.'

'Have you heard of Maspamia?' asked the man.

'Of course,' replied the woman, 'Charlie spent a lot of time going out there. He did tell me they were looking for chemical and bio weapons. I knew that because it was on the news. The US was going to war because the President said that they had these weapons and were going to use them.'

'Did you ever meet any of the other scientists?'

'Yes, one time the wives were invited to a conference. We were looked after and spent the days sightseeing and we all met up for meals in the evening. It was real good.'

The question was rephrased. 'Do you remember any of the other scientists?'

'Of course, but I don't remember any of their names. There was one, he was English, a real gentleman, like your royal people.'

The man passed her a photograph.

'Does this man look familiar?'

233

The woman took her glasses out of her handbag, put them on and looked at the picture. 'Yes, that's the English scientist.'

'Thank you,' responded the man.

The woman then added, 'He died, and Charlie said he was killed. He was distraught about it. He kept saying, "they've killed him, they've actually killed him". He said the English scientist told others that he would be killed.'

'Do you know who "they" were, did Charlie ever say?'

'From the way he spoke I thought it was the Government, because it was all so secret. You read about such things, don't you?'

He gently asked her if she could say what happened to Charlie.

'We were home one day when somebody came to the front door. Charlie was out back. I shouted to him but he didn't come, so I went to see who was at the door. I was in the middle of baking. When I opened the door a large man, you know, body-builder type, stood there. There was something about him and it fair worried me. He asked if my husband was in and could he speak to him. I said I would go and find him and I shut the door. I found Charlie out back and told him. He went through to see who it was. I heard them speaking, then there was a raised voice, threatening. I picked up the telephone to call the police, but before I had called the number the front door slammed shut. I rushed through and found Charlie by the door. He was angry but said it was nothing to worry about. It was to do with work. I did worry but went back to my baking.'

She paused and again looked along the faces.

'It was about a couple of weeks later when we were having the family over for a BBQ. It must have been about six in the evening when Charlie received a telephone call. He said he had to go and get a package from somebody at the Riviera parking lot. He had done this before and so it was no big deal.

He would be half an hour tops. So when he had not returned in an hour we began to get worried. When it got to two hours we called the police. They came and took information and put out a call for officers to look for him. It was just after two in the morning when the police came. They had found a man who had been beaten up in a rough part of town. I had to go and see if it was Charlie.' The woman was sobbing and the woman next to her comforted her. The man asked her if she wanted to stop.

She looked at the faces again. 'No, sorry about that.' She wiped her face again. 'It was my Charlie, he had been beaten to death. The police said it was a mugging and they were looking for who did it.' She paused and looked up at some point in the room. 'It was about a month later when a policewoman called. She handed me Charlie's wallet which, when I looked, had his money, credit cards and driver's licence still in it. She said it was at the police station and, as the case had been put to one side, she thought that I should have it. She was aware that it still had the valuables in it. When she had queried it with her sergeant, she was told to keep her nose out. It had been gathering dust ever since.'

The man who had been taking notes looked at her. 'So, nothing was taken from the wallet, which means that it was not a robbery. In addition, are you saying that the police did not pursue the investigation?'

'That's right,' replied the woman.

The man asked, 'Are you allright to continue, or would you like a break?'

'I'm fine,' she replied, 'I'll carry on.' She paused to gather her thoughts. 'The family hired a private investigator, but after a week of digging he quit: he told us he had been threatened. That's how it's been the rest of the time.'

'I would like to show you some more photographs, and ask you if you would look at them and say if you recognise any of the people in them.' The man passed three different photographs of the same person to the woman. She put her glasses on and looked at the pictures. The reaction was instantaneous: she shook and began to cry. It took at least ten minutes for her to regain her composure.

'That's the man who came to our house and threatened Charlie.'

In the other room, Dan had been glued to the TV monitor and had already put the pieces of the jigsaw together, including the last piece, the face of Cornell. He could not see the photographs, but he did not need to because he knew who it was. The woman answered a few more questions and was then thanked for telling her story. She left the room with the woman who had sat next to her. She would look after her until she departed for her journey back to the US.

The big room was a buzz of talk but he could not ascertain what they were saying. He got another cup of coffee and took some biscuits. It was about twenty minutes before the next person entered the room. It was another woman employed by the foundation who accompanied another visitor. The process followed that of the first woman. She and her late husband came from Canada. He was a chemical and biological weapons inspector, and had also worked in Maspamia. She did not recognise the photographs of any of the other scientists she was shown, but she knew that her husband communicated regularly with a leading weapons inspector in the UK. She said he used to chuckle, after having made a call, about those listening having to decode some of the technical terms. He said it was a game, a deadly game. She said that a man had visited, a large man, an American who gave a warning and then made some threats. My husband did not take it too seriously: he said that it was normal in the job he did. She was asked if she had seen the man who had threatened her husband. She had, and she recognised him in the photograph. She told them that it was about a month after the visit that her husband had committed suicide.

The report said that an empty pill container was found close to his body, that he had taken dangerous pills and then had hung himself. She explained that he did not take pills and that they were not his. The knot in the rope was not one that was normally used. The family had a separate autopsy done. It found that only a small quantity of the pills were in the body, and nowhere near enough to kill him. They also found that the rope had been put around his neck and then pulled, to haul up the body and make it look as if he had done it himself. She passed over a brown envelope which contained a copy of the report. Almost as an afterthought, she told them that the matter had been raised with the authorities but, whilst at a lower level there had been interest in doing something to follow it up, it had been stopped at a higher level. She, along with the majority of those involved in the case, believed that he had been murdered.

The woman was thanked for sharing her information. A third woman joined them and shared hers. The couple were South African, and her husband had become a biological weapons inspector and consultant. She recognised Dr Finch in the photograph, as he had visited their home when in South Africa on business. Her husband had been visited by a well-built American. There had been harsh words and threats. She identified the man in the photographs. There had followed an unusual death. Again, no perpetrator had been found. Cornell had been a busy man.

When the woman had left, the man leading the meeting called a halt for lunch. Dan was joined by Rosie, who told him that it was lunch time and that he could leave the building, but that she would like him back in the room for two o'clock. He felt he needed the break, and he walked the streets window-shopping until he reached a sandwich bar. He purchased a sandwich and bottle of orange. Others making purchases rushed in and, their lunch bought, rushed out to get back to their offices. He wandered along the street and found a little garden, a sanctuary in the great metropolis. He sat, ate the sandwich and drank the drink. The walk back amidst the crowds of people walking fast, bumping and nudging as they went past, was part of being there. Strange lands, jungles, deserts and mountains seemed a preferable option at that moment in time. Back in the room, he noted that the refreshments had been changed and that the people were back in the other room. Rosie entered to check that he was back and that he had everything he needed. She explained that there were just two more people who were going to provide their stories, and that then they would talk to him. She then left him to rejoin the others. Once she was in the other room, all the participants took their seats. He looked at the screen and realised that not one person stood out from the others. Even Rosie seemed to have blended in and become a "plain Jane".

Retired civil servant William Pape was the next to enter the room. He sat down and faced the others across the table. The chair spoke. 'Thank you for agreeing to meet with us; we do understand how difficult this is for you.' The man's voice was sympathetic.

Pape smiled. 'It's not a problem. I hope I can help.'

The man began, 'You were a civil servant and worked with Dr John Finch.'

'That's correct.'

'We all know that he disagreed with some of the contents in the infamous "dodgy dossier", and that he was exposed as having spoken to the media about it.'

Pape looked at each face in turn. 'John would never have spoken to the media in the way that they said he had.'

Another member enquired, 'Did you know John very well?'

'We had worked together, on and off, for about fifteen years.'

The man nodded, then asked, 'How was he up until his death?'

'He had taken a pounding about his views, in particular from the head of personnel. He was being treated badly and he knew it. There were two things that kept him going: his work and his pending retirement.'

'Would you say he was depressed?' enquired the man.

'No, shell-shocked at his bad treatment, but not depressed. It was helpful that he worked from home and so was out of the way of the office politics. He was not depressed.' Pape was adamant in getting the point over. Pape smiled and added, 'He got a real buzz when they found the balloon trailers and told the world they had found WMDs.'

A member of the committee raised the point, 'Did he go and check them for himself once they had been found?'

'Oh yes, he was ordered to do so and, being under such scrutiny, he wanted to make sure he was not being set up. The political lot were not to be trusted.'

The committee member sat back and nodded. He could not tell Pape that his name was Danny Davis, and that at the time in question he had been an aide to President Franklin. Nor could he tell him that it was he himself who had phoned the President and given him the message about the trailers being part of a chemical weapons system. He could not tell him about the outrage it had caused on both sides of the pond. When Franklin left office, Davis had also left and joined the Excalibur Foundation.

'When was the last time you spoke or communicated with John?' enquired the man.

'There had been a constant flow of e-mails between us on

the day he left home for the last time. I spoke with him on the telephone three times.'

'How did he sound?'

'Fine, absolutely fine; I had sent him his travel details. He had requested some information and I had sent that. It was all very normal. My last telephone call to him was just before he left home. He said that some friends were coming over for a meal and he wanted to get his walk in before hand. The next thing I heard was the report of his death on the television.'

The man looked at Pape, 'There are many questions that we would like to ask, but you have dealt with those in your interview. I think, as far as this committee is concerned, we have covered the key issues and I would like to thank you again for coming.'

Pape stood, said goodbye and followed a woman out of the room.

There was a pause of several minutes before the door opened and two women entered. Although he could not see either of their faces, he could tell they were much younger. Once they were seated, another camera that was focused on them revealed their faces. Dan was looking at Marianne. She looked relaxed and stunning in her smart and probably expensive outfit. The last time he saw her was at a Paris railway station having been shot and on her way to safety in Switzerland. The same format was followed as with the other women. She gave her story. She explained about working for a security company, her boss going away and the American standing in. The visitor who was looking to be employed who then became a target. She recounted herself being taken at gunpoint to the apartment of the visitor, under threat of death being made to get him to open the door, the shooting of him and then of herself. She told of her rescue from the apartment and of the impromptu medical treatment. The photograph was shown, and she identified the person portrayed as being

240

Chuck Cornell who worked for a US security company. He did specialised jobs but she did not have any details. She left nobody in the room in any doubt that he was dangerous. When she had finished, she was thanked and left the room. Dan leapt up and went to the door. He opened it. He wanted to see her and speak to her, but the corridor was empty and silent. Nothing moved and there was no noise. He went back into the room. The people in the other room were standing in a huddle and talking. Then some departed and the room emptied, leaving the TV screen filled by the man who was chairing events and by Rosie. He looked at the camera and spoke to Dan.

'There are just the three of us now; you have been privy to a problem that we face and that has to be dealt with. The Excalibur Foundation is going to deal with the problem and we have a formal proposition for you. I will outline the proposal, and you have forty-eight hours to accept or to decline. The proposal, with its background information, is necessary. It will, for you, be lucrative; and total secrecy is assured.' He paused, 'If you accept the proposal and are successful, then there would be other employment in your speciality.'

The man began to outline the proposal.

27

The man leaned back in his chair. He now had a relaxed manner and when he spoke he addressed the camera. 'We thank you for your patience in this part of the process. I would point out that you can see us but we cannot see you. With that in mind, I hope you can hear me?'

Dan acknowledged that he could.

'Good. I am authorised on behalf of the Excalibur Foundation to put a proposal to you.' He paused. 'You will now be familiar with the man Chuck Cornell and his specific activities: indeed you have been affected by his actions personally. I have to say that your personal connection was a matter that gave us some concern, but Miss Portray has advised us that this would not have an impact on your judgement and professionalism. Cornell works for an organisation called Worldwide Executive Management, which is a large American company that undertakes work throughout the world. Some time ago, Cornell was recruited into a special secret part of the organisation, the "Black Eagles". They are the most ruthless operatives and undertake work such as assassinations. These are often carried out at the behest of governments who outsource such activities. Indeed, you have heard today of the sort of work the organisation does. You may ask why those who operate the company are not targeted; that would be a good point. They operate in great secrecy and, if anybody poses a threat to that secrecy, they are disposed of. They also hide behind a wall of respectability, so we need evidence. The higher up the command chain, the more difficult it is to obtain that evidence.

We continue to gather information but, as you have experienced, at the slightest suspicion that they have a leak, they take action to plug it.' He paused again and looked at some papers he held. 'The removal of people such as Cornell is a thrust into their inner sanctum, and they really do not like it. Even when the Cornells are identified, it is not easy to remove them. They only tend to show themselves when they are on an assignment and that means you have to know the target. What we do know is that after a special assignment, the operative generally gets a job guarding some VIP on holiday on a remote tropical island. It is a sort of paid holiday. They consider that the threat against a low level VIP is so small that they do not have a high regard for the safety of that VIP. Either way, the security team is minimal. Often, there is just the specialist and one other, who is not in the same league and who does the running around. Sometimes the VIPs take their own security, but that is for high profile potential targets. It is at this time that we can know where the target is, and take appropriate action. That is what we want to do in this situation. We find out when he has such a task and deploy you; that is, if you choose to join us. Our main priority is to safeguard you, as you are a very valuable asset, so we want a plan that is detailed enough to keep you a secret. You are at this time unknown in the security and mercenary world, and that is a major plus on both our parts.'

The man looked at his papers, then continued. 'The proposal is for you to remove Cornell. For that you will receive a fee of half a million pounds sterling paid into any account you name. In addition, we will provide you with intelligence and any direct support that you require, at our expense. We do expect such support to be reasonable and that it allows you to undertake the task. Providing the operation is a success, we would want to engage you and your services again. You would be rewarded well so that you do not go onto the mercenary market-place and become a known target. I must add that the support includes providing a suitable weapon. You tell us what you want, we will provide it and even remove it at the end of the operation. What we do not have is the skill that you do have, to get in and out of a location and use such a weapon.'

The man looked at Rosie then back to the camera. 'We would be able to identify a place where the target could be found, and we can help you get in and out if that is what you want.'

The man looked serious, then continued, 'We do not see ourselves as a bunch of gangsters who hire a hit man to do a job, we see ourselves as bringing justice where no formal justice applies. If people and governments want to rule by power, greed and violence then we respond appropriately. We would prefer to stop such injustice before it occurs, but that is not often possible.'

The man paused again, allowing Dan to absorb the information. He then added, 'What I suggest is that with this briefest of information, you take the time to digest the proposal and we can meet here as we are doing now in two days' time. Your hotel room is booked; we will cover your expenses and we will, of course, pay for your time. We trust that will be acceptable to you.'

Dan had already decided he would do the job but realised that there was a protocol that had to be followed, so he agreed to return in two days. The television screen went blank. The meeting was over.

Two days in a city with expenses paid would, for many, be a welcome break; but for Dan it was a painful drag. He thought he might have heard from Rosie but his mobile remained silent. On the second day he got up, showered but still did not shave, had breakfast and left the hotel. The journey to the office building was uneventful and he soon found himself in the room again with just the TV monitor for company. It was about ten-fifteen when the man and Rosie appeared on the screen. They exchanged pleasantries before the man asked Dan if he had made a decision. He said that he had and confirmed that he would undertake the proposal. Both the man and Rosie were pleased that he had decided to help them.

The man revealed that they had intelligence that Cornell was soon to be baby-sitting a "VIP" on an island in the Caribbean. 'It is a private island owned indirectly by a financial organisation but close enough to a larger holiday Island. I think that the larger island would be the base from which he would operate and we have people on the ground to support you. We would be able to provide a boat with a reliable captain to get you to and from the target island. Generally, security is minimal and, because it's a private island, there will not be any publicity as to who the VIP is that is visiting at the time.'

'Are those who offer support fully trustworthy?' asked Dan.

'Absolutely. We have an insider on the island who provides us with information.'

The man gave an overview of an outline plan. However, Dan was the operative and it would be a matter of how he wanted to proceed. It was thought that he should go to the main island as a tourist. He would then be able to use one of the island-hopping boats to do the job. The captain of one boat was associated with the Foundation, and using such a boat would provide a good cover as he regularly moved from island to Island. The captain also knew the islands. An added advantage was that the police force in the region, whilst good at policing the islands, did not have the ready resources to undertake a large manhunt; and, in any event, it was just a security guard who was the target.

Dan raised concerns about the number of people who knew what was happening or were directly involved. Was it a security risk? The man assured Dan that in fact just the three of them knew all the details. The others were part of the jigsaw but not the finished puzzle. He emphasised that, 'We can provide the boat and a reliable captain. You need to give us a list of the things you need that you would be unable to take with you on your holiday flight. For example, what rifle and sniper scope do you want? What about clothing when on the small island? Does it have to be camouflaged?'

Dan was already making notes; he had been doing so over the past two days, even though he had no idea where his target would be. They wanted details of a bank account. Half the money would be paid up front, the other half after successful completion of the operation. The frank exchange of information lasted about half an hour. Dan was given telephone numbers and security codes. If a meeting was required it could be arranged, but it was now a matter of waiting for the date and he should be ready to go at very short notice. It was at this point that the man added another factor. 'You will be based in a hotel on a holiday island and if you were absent for a longish period, even a day, it could raise suspicion when an investigation gets under way.' This had already crossed Dan's mind. The man told him that the younger woman who had been at the meeting two days before, who had been shot by Cornell and then rescued by Dan, wanted to help. She knew nothing of the actual operation and it would be a matter for Dan as to how much he told her. When he disappeared to do the job, then she would not ask questions but cover for him. If Dan agreed, she would accompany him to the main island so that they would be seen as a couple. Dan responded that it was a good idea. If nothing else, lying on a beach in the Caribbean with a beautiful woman was a bonus. The man finished by saying that there would be further communications through Rosie but, for now, he was booked on a flight back to Paris the following morning. He was to wait until called and that might be at short notice. The meeting ended and the screen went blank.

* * * *

Dan returned to Paris and the hotel he found when he first arrived in the city. He had already negotiated the rate down, and was now in receipt of a generous allowance from the organisation. He had not seen Marianne in London except on the television screen. Since the second meeting in London, his brain had moved into overdrive. He was going to undertake an operation with people he did not know; neither did he know their abilities. To gather his thoughts, he sat in the café where he had first met Napoleon with a coffee, and watched the people of Paris going about their business. He had spent some time in his hotel room preparing a list of what he required. It was specific and detailed. The rifle, scope, silencer and selected rounds were listed, along with an automatic handgun and silencer. Camouflaged clothing and lightweight boots. Camouflaged scrim net that would be worn over the head and shoulders to break up their outline. A small rucksack, water bottles, fighting knife, survival kit and a first aid kit, comprising bandages to deal with bullet wounds, antiseptic to stop infection rather than plasters, and ointment for insect bites. When he had finished, he reviewed the list to see if he could cut out anything that was not essential. He then made a list of everyday clothing to buy, as he was going to be a tourist. He knew he was not trendy and would select what suited him, rather than what was "in" at the moment. On his new laptop he adapted his list into the approved code words and, when done, sent the typed-up list through the hotel's wifi to the e-mail address he had been provided with. There were no messages for him.

For now, he finished his coffee and people-watching and took off to the shops. In his mind he pictured an island, the need for a boat that could get him to the island without raising suspicion. Locating the target and taking the shot was not a problem. The problems began when he had to get off the island. The options filed through his head, the "what if's". How reliable were the people who could get him in and get him out? Secrecy was one thing, but having virtually no information was another. In the Legion they generally had some intelligence and could develop a plan, but here it was very *ad hoc*. It was down to him.

Having completed the shopping trip, he returned to the hotel. He could not go far as he was waiting for the call, so he spent time doing exercise and then playing the part of a tourist. He noted that his luggage had increased since he first arrived in Paris. His sports kit and the clothes for his tropical venture had not helped. At the moment, the hotel suited him because he could move out and disappear; if he rented somewhere, it was a base and there were records of his existence. A permanent base would need to be discreet but could come after the planned operation.

A couple of days later he was at his favourite street café, a busy place with people coming and going all of the time. He could sit, eat and drink and occasionally chat or use his laptop without being disturbed. In fact, he even had his favourite table, which he thought was a bit worrying as he might soon become a creature of habit. He need not have been concerned because his mobile phone rang. He checked it. The text was to the point. He had to contact a number that he had been given as soon as possible, as the operation was on. He paid his bill and walked the streets until he found a seat away from flapping ears. He called the number. A female voice answered and she did a security check. He was then put through to Rosie. 'Hello Dan,' her voice matched her looks.

Dan answered. She continued, 'We received your list; all the goods are on their way to their destination.'

'OK, good,' he replied.

'We have good intelligence as to when the visitor will be at the location, and so we are sending you over a week earlier so that you can plan and prepare. If there are any problems you can let us know, which will give us time to take action.'

'Sounds good.'

Rosie informed him that, 'Marianne is being notified and will join you in Paris. We have made all of the travel plans, and a package will be delivered to your base. Please check the details to ensure that they are correct. Don't forget to take your passport. We have an emergency back-up plan which, in the event that anything goes wrong, we will activate. You will not have details so as to safeguard those on the ground. It's security for everybody. I will contact you in twenty-four hours to ensure that everything is in order.'

'OK, I've got all of that. Will await your call.' The phone went dead. He smiled: it was all formal now, no chit-chat.

He walked back to the hotel and collected his key from reception. The receptionist handed him an envelope which she said had been delivered about an hour ago. In his room he opened it, and found holiday documentation for a Mr and Mrs Mark Chester. He read through it and it all looked in order. Two weeks on the island of Guardinia in the Caribbean. He reflected on the hell-holes where operations in the Legion had taken him. This was certainly better. He had piles of clothes, those that he would take and those that he would leave at the hotel. His foreign bank account looked healthy, but for now he could live on the savings from the Legion.

The following morning he called into the café, and took his place at what had become "his table". The waiter did not ask what he wanted, but just brought what he had every time he visited. Indeed, he was becoming a creature of habit. The woman walked up to the table and, without speaking, sat down. 'Hello, Mark,' she said, smiling. He grinned and they exchanged the customary four kisses on the cheeks, a typical French greeting.

'Well, Mrs Chester, you are looking well.'

'So are you, Mr Chester,' she replied.

They both laughed.

Dan ordered her a coffee.

'I left my luggage in your room at the hotel. Then I came here as I thought you might be hanging about.'

Dan looked at her, serious for the moment. 'Are you sure you want to do this?' he asked.

'Certainly? Why do you have doubts?'

'None, but it could be very dangerous – and very costly if anything goes wrong,' he explained.

'I was asked to go, and that is what I shall do. I am getting a reward, for my part, so everything is fine.'

'Good,' answered Dan, 'we have the travel documents, so we are ready to go.'

'Do we know when that is?' she asked.

'Tomorrow evening.'

'Good job I arrived today,' she quipped.

They walked back to the hotel and sorted out the luggage. Marianne checked the travel information. All was in order.

28

Dan and Marianne exited the aircraft and were greeted by the warm sun and blue sky of the Caribbean. They had arrived on the holiday island of Guardinia which boasted hotels, clear blue sea, sun and miles of pure white sandy beaches. It had an airport and a small seaport. The hotels were generally created in low rise buildings, allowing the palm trees to almost hide their presence. All main roads were linked by a spider's web of minor roads and tracks, to provide communications for the locals and for visitors. Immigration and customs was a low-key affair: it was, after all, a holiday island. Outside the airport terminal, which comprised a neat single-storey building, they were met by the travel company representatives and directed to a mini-bus. It was a short walk to the appropriate bus where they found another couple were already aboard. With luggage stowed, the driver steered the vehicle away from the airport, in a sort of slow motion to join a road that formed a circle of the island and linked all of the hotels. Clearly, nobody on the island rushed about. During the journey the male passenger wanted to regale them with his life story, whilst his wife sat passively staring out of the window, completely bored. Dan wondered how often she had heard the story and reflected how many years she would have to endure hearing it again. Dan also looked out of the window; however, he was not looking at the scenery but at the island in general. He and

Marianne would point something out to each other, speaking in French, and still the man talked, still nobody listened. They passed through the outer limits of the capital of the island and continued towards the port. Whilst Marianne looked at the shops with displays of coloured cloth and clothes, Dan studied the port. There were a number of ships of varying size off-loading cargo, and he spotted a quay where a row of fast modern deep-sea fishing boats gleamed white in the sun. These were for the tourists and accommodated sea fishing, scuba diving or transport to other smaller islands. Further out, a cruise ship lay at anchor.

The mini bus arrived at the hotel and, as soon as the door was opened, the man climbed out leaving his wife behind. He went into the hotel lobby. Dan and Marianne let the other couple go ahead to check in as they wanted to avoid developing any sort of friendship as that could; jeopardise the plan. Checking-in was reasonably quick and efficient and the other couple departed for their room. The man grinned and waved to Dan and Marianne as they departed. The receptionist checked her list for Mr and Mrs Mark Chester. She inspected their passports and said they could collect them later. Details about the hotel, its facilities and meal times were outlined, and she told them that they had a beach villa and pointed it out on a plan of the hotel. Like most of the hotel rooms, it had some privacy on the beach side; that was what most visitors wanted. The communal areas of restaurant, bar and lounge were where people would meet others and have drinks and meals. There was a small library and an internet room. Other options available included private dining on the beach and a range of sporting and cultural activities. The large swimming pool combined as a lounging area to sun-bathe, sit in the shade or swim.

The room itself offered a spacious living area, with a large bed arranged so that you could lay in bed and look out through patio doors at the sea. There was a lounge area with sofas and a writing desk and chairs, as well as the obligatory satellite television and music centre. A separate toilet was next to a large bathroom with two washbasins and a shower room. It was all excellently appointed. The final touch was a veranda that looked out over the sea and gave access to a small private area of beach with two sun loungers.

They unpacked, put their documents in the room safe, and then Dan uncorked a bottle of wine. They went out and stood on the veranda, drinks in hand, and gazed out over the sea. 'What a beautiful place for a honeymoon', declared Marianne dreamily.

Dan murmured and added 'The island is out that way.' He pointed in the general direction of an unseen island.

Marianne was about to challenge him on talking about work, but realised that that was why they were there. Still, there was no harm in dreaming.

'More wine?' asked Dan.

'Please,' she responded.

Glasses topped up, Marianne proposed a toast; 'To the project coupled with some fun.' They sipped their drinks, after which she led Dan into the room and to the bed. It was three hours before the evening meal.

* * * *

The following morning Marianne awoke to find that Dan was not in the room. He was pounding the beach on an early-morning run. When he got back to their accommodation, he did not go into the room but into the sea. He did thirty minutes of hard swimming, getting used to the water and the fact that he might have a long swim after the operation. When he did get back to the room Marianne was up, showered and dressed. Dan followed suit and was soon ready for breakfast. The previous night they had gone to the restaurant and found a table well away from the man who was still talking and seemingly boring another couple. They checked to see where he was and went to the opposite end of the room. They enjoyed a relaxed breakfast. The hotel seemed quite full, and a number of languages could be heard. They noted that nobody spoke French, and so they continued to adopt it in order to put people off from trying to converse or listening in to a conversation. They enquired at reception about transport to and from the town and the port. The hotel had a mini-bus that ferried people to and from a central drop-off point which gave access to both. They could hire a car, or use one of the local taxis that frequented the hotel. Whilst waiting at the hotel entrance, the man, still talking, arrived with his wife; they were also set on going to town. He went up to Dan as if he was a long-lost friend and started talking. Marianne spoke to Dan in French. The man pondered the situation. 'Are you French?' he enquired in a way that answered the question. Before Dan could answer, the man turned away saying, 'I don't speak French.' Thankfully that seemed to end a budding friendship.

In town, the driver of the mini-bus stopped in a square surrounded by a number of touristy shops. He said that they picked up about every half hour, but that the bar-cum-café on the other side of the road was open, so they could always wait there, have a drink and chill out. Dan and Marianne headed towards the port, but stopped at some of the tourist and clothes shops on the way. They could see the port which comprised two distinct parts. One offered the commercial port, and the other area a quay with an array of expensive boats and some street-side cafes and bars. They walked down until they reached the quay and then ambled along as only tourists do. Dan was looking at the variety of boats that were moored. They varied in size, with some that were of a size to take a couple of fishermen out, whilst others could go further for deep-sea fishing or transfer to the other islands. Dan counted five boats that were of the larger type and would be used to shuttle people out to the various islands which had private accommodation. He was looking for one boat in particular, but he could not see it. Having walked around the private and charter boat area, they made their way to a bar and, sitting outside, ordered beers. They chatted and watched the world go by.

A large boat powered towards the quay and the mooring area. Dan assessed that it was one of the boats that provided transport to the islands. The captain had clearly done the manoeuvre many times before as he reduced the engine power to slow the boat down, then swung the craft round and gently came alongside the quay. The captain stayed on the open bridge whilst a crew member expertly dropped mooring ropes over the bollards and secured the boat. Dan watched every move and noted the name *MV Ocean Rover*.

With the boat secure, two couples left the boat. The crewman assisted them ashore and then transferred their luggage onto the quay. A mini-bus arrived and the people with their luggage were taken to their hotel. The captain came down from his place up at the controls and, after about five minutes, came out of the back cabin door and made his way up onto the quay. He checked the mooring ropes then wandered along the quay towards the bar. He was in no hurry and walked with a sway that was indicative of the peoples of the Caribbean. Entering the bar, he "high-fived" a number of customers and spoke to others. He looked at Dan and Marianne, flashed a grin of pure white teeth that stood out against his dark skin. 'Hi there, ow's you doin.'

'Real good,' replied Dan.

'Good,' and he walked on, talking to others.

About ten minutes passed and he came out and stopped at their table.

'Can I join you?' asked the captain, but it was more of a statement than a question.

'Sure.'

As the captain sat down he looked at them both. 'My name is George, and I'm the captain of the *Ocean Rover*, a fine boat.'

'Nice boat,' stated Dan, 'yours?'

'Nar, I just drive it.' George was still grinning. 'I do trips out to the other islands, some fishing and scuba diving. You interested and want to look over her?'

'Yes,' said Dan.

'OK man, I have to go someplace but you come back at four o'clock and I will show you the good lady.'

'Sounds good,' replied Dan.

George stood, 'OK man, four o'clock.' He then left the bar "high-fiving" others as he ambled down the road towards the town.

Marianne checked her watch. It was twelve-twenty, and she saw an opportunity to go into the town and do some shopping. Dan reluctantly tagged along; it did give him the opportunity to observe any police officers at work. He also found the local police station. Shopping was a limited experience, as it was a small town that mostly catered for the local population and those who migrated there for work. Some shops catered for tourists and, as they approached them, they were bombarded with demands to buy their wares. In their wandering they found a restaurant with a view over the quay. They found a quiet spot and had a very leisurely lunch. Marianne asked Dan if George was the contact. He was not sure but thought so. That was something he had to find out, but being asked to look over the boat was useful.

Standing on the quay alongside the *MV Ocean Rover*, Dan checked his watch. It was four o'clock exactly. He had not seen anybody, and when he called out nobody had answered. Then, as if by magic, a door opened and a face appeared. It was George. He opened the door fully and stepped outside. He continued doing up the buttons on his shirt. 'Hi man,' he said, greeting them. An attractive young woman followed him out of the door. She was dressed provocatively in a skimpy blouse and a very short skirt. She ignored them and tottered along the deck to climb onto the quay. Once ashore, she put on her high-heeled shoes and walked along the quay. George shouted 'Bye honey,' and she shouted back 'Bye honey.' George grinned, 'she's my book-keeper.' He then told them to come aboard. On the boat George led them into a large enclosed lounge area. He closed the patio-style doors, then turned and looked at them. The grin and the laid-back appearance was gone. He was serious.

He walked over to a drinks cabinet and stated what he had available. When the drinks were poured he indicated for them to sit. He then uttered one word. 'Excalibur.' Dan acknowledged that it was the sword pulled from a rock by King Arthur.

'Right on, man. Now, I don't want to be rude, but would missy go and get some rays while we do some talking?' He indicated to the after deck.

Dan was about to reply that Marianne should stay but she stood, smiled and with a 'No problem,' she walked to the patio style sliding doors.

'OK, my name really is George and I run this boat getting people to and from the islands. It's owned, through a number of companies, by the Excalibur Foundation. There is a lot of private property out there.' He indicated towards the open sea. 'I move a lot of them, so I know who stays where and when. The Foundation has some very interesting information about some very important people. We also see some very nasty people.' He took a mouthful of his drink. 'Many of those who stay are being rewarded for some dodgy deal. We get politicians, bankers, shady business people, murderers and others.'

'I get the picture,' said Dan.

'Now you have a job to do. I do not want to know any details, and it's best if I don't. My job is to take you covertly to Island Retreat and to bring you back. To do that you have to trust me and I have to trust you, that way we all get on and you do what you have to do.'

'That's just the way I want it,' responded Dan.

George pulled out a chart that showed signs that it was well used. He unrolled it and laid it on the low drinks table in front of them. Pointing to the chart he indicated, 'This is us on Guadinia, and the island you need to get to is here. It's called Retreat Island.' He pointed out a small island closer to Guardinia. 'This is Reef Island. Nobody lives there, it's just a big rocky hill with some sandy bays and it has an excellent reef. It's really good for scuba diving. It's also a good place for preparing your weapon and equipment. I can check to make sure nobody else is planning to be there diving when we want to do some shooting.' He looked at Dan to make sure he was paying attention. 'Just beyond your assignment destination is another island,' he pointed to it on the chart, 'it has a couple of smallish hotels.' That is important because when I have to take passengers there I pass Retreat Island. That will allow me to get you there and pick you up without generating any interest.' He took another mouthful of his drink. The whole area is under US surveillance by satellites and aircraft looking for drug-and-people smugglers. The US coastguard and navy ships would cause us real problems as they know how to search a boat.'

'Do you get stopped very often?'

'No,' replied George. 'They know who we are and what we are doing, so they leave us alone. But things change, best avoid any potential problems.'

Dan agreed.

George then produced some photographs of Retreat Island. They depicted a long island of rock with sandy beaches. Almost mid-point, the island rose up to form a pointed hill. The area was covered with trees and shrubs. The house was located at one end of the island; what appeared to be a track led down from the house to a jetty. George said that the jetty was large enough to take boats up to the size of his own. He pointed to photographs of an outcrop of rock that extended into the sea, separating two sandy beaches. It also lay below the point of the hill. There was one photograph that showed the house and the swimming pool that had been taken from the top of the hill. George explained that the organisation had got it, a few months previously, from a photographer that had been hired to take pictures of the island and the house. It was the only picture taken on the island that he had seen. Dan could identify that up on the hill he would have a good line of sight to the target area, as well as an escape route down to the sea. He noted that the rock face extended for some distance until there was access across sand and bush where he could hide the kayak. George told Dan that he could see, through his binoculars, tracks going from the beaches to the top of the hill. Dan explained that tracks meant people; the idea was to keep clear of tracks. George did not respond.

Dan was absorbing the information. 'Can I keep the photos.'

'Yes, they are for you, and you have a hand drawn map that shows you the island.' There was a pause. 'That's the best I can do.'

Dan grinned. 'It's fine, I've done bigger jobs with much less.'

George was happy about that. 'What I propose is that we get your equipment ready and then, when I have to go to the furthest island, I will take you. Just you! Missy will have to stay at the hotel. I will get as close to the target island as I can and we can launch a kayak. With your equipment you can paddle to the shore. I am told you are able to use a kayak.' Dan nodded. 'You must remember that when we are out there, the American's satellites and aircraft could pick us up when they are looking for drug smugglers. That means that they will know that my boat passed in both directions at the time of your project.' He contemplated this then added, 'Don't worry about the fine detail now, it's the overall plan that I need you to understand and be happy with.'

'How will I be able to be onboard if you have paying guests?' enquired Dan.

'That's not a problem. If we are carrying people then we have a hiding place for you. It will not be comfortable but it will be safe. By the time we have to drop you off, they will be drunk and asleep inside. Most will make use of the bunks.' George grinned for the first time since they had gone aboard the boat.

'Getting back?' enquired Dan.

'You will put all your kit in the waterproof bags provided. They can be carried in the kayak or towed. It's up to you. I have a neat radar on board that will pick up the reflector that you will carry and put up when you are out to sea. Once I have located you I will divert the boat to meet you. It is the only time I will stop and you have to get on the back platform as quickly as possible. We will tow the kayak and, once clear of the island, we will sink it along with all the kit, including the weapon. You will hide until I drop you off as close as I can get to your hotel. You have a beach room so you will have good access when you swim ashore. I will then continue back here and off-load my passengers.'

'Isn't using a reflector for location a bit old fashioned?'

George grinned, 'Yes, but if we use electronic communications equipment they can track us and they will know that I picked you up.'

'OK. Won't anybody question the fact that a canoe came and went?' asked Dan.

'The boat is just a form of transport and my passengers are either drinking, eating or screwing. A small kayak will not be seen or missed by anybody.' George paused, then added, 'I have the items you listed, and they are in a safe place.'

Dan became concerned. 'How many people know about this?'

'You, me and my deckman.' George spoke bluntly. 'Packages get delivered and nobody asks questions. We are fighting some real evil people here so questions can also get you dead!'

Nobody spoke for a few moments, 'You need not fear my deckman Johnny.' There was a pause, 'His wife was employed on Retreat cleaning and cooking at the house. She was a beautiful lady who worked hard. Her reward was to be attacked by a security man who raped her and, because she struggled hard, he killed her. Those houses on the islands are evil, and have evil people visiting them.'

Dan asked if the perpetrator was caught.

No, nothing happened: it was covered up. As far as Johnny is concerned, he lost everything. I picked up the pieces, so you have nothing to fear from him.'

Dan had more questions, but George called an end to the meeting.

'Don't want people to talk about visitors who spend too long a time chatting to the captain of a boat. So, tomorrow we go scuba diving at Reef Island and you can check your kit out. Be here at eight o'clock. We need to get away and onto the island to do your shooting before others arrive. We will go on my boat the *Blue Witch*. It's not as plush as this one but it will not draw attention and we can talk more. The *Ocean Rover* is having work done on her engine, so that's the best option.' He stood and led the way out on deck. His personality reversed, and now he was the laid-back local with the patter. He watched Dan and Marianne leave the boat and walk along the quay.

Marianne asked Dan if he was OK as he was very quiet.

'I'm OK, it's just that in the Legion you are part of a big team, a sort of family and you know where you stand. Here I am with a contract to take out an assassin and a lot of people know about it. Too many for my liking.'

'Well, everybody is on the same side; the job is here and you know who you are dealing with,' she countered.

'That's part of the problem: I don't know these people!'

'You trust me, don't you?' she enquired.

'Of course I do; after the events in Paris, you're as involved in this as I am.'

She smiled and the subject was dropped; after all, they were supposed to be on honeymoon.

After an early breakfast they travelled in a pre-ordered taxi to the quay. They walked along until they saw George securing scuba bottles on board a neat blue-and-white painted wooden boat. There was a kayak lying to one side of the large open deck. They climbed onboard and were greeted by George and Johnny. Once everything was secure Johnny cast off the ropes, whilst George in the small wheel-house manoeuvred the boat amongst other craft. Once clear, he opened up the engine and they were soon on their way to Reef Island. It was another clear blue sky and flat calm sea with the foamy white wake being left behind as they made progress. An awning had been rigged up over the back deck to provide shelter from the sun and from any prying eyes in the sky. The boat was alone as it plied its way. The sea had started light blue, but as the water got deeper the colour changed and it became darker. Dan was impressed with the speed of the boat and, much to her delight, Marianne was given full instructions on how to handle the craft at sea. She had already observed how to start the boat's engine and engage the clutch. The throttle was easier, you just pushed a lever forward to go faster or pulled it back to slow down.

Johnny pulled a holdall from its hiding-place and gave it to Dan. Inside was a long, sealed waterproof package. Dan carefully opened it. Inside was a plastic box in which was a Hecate II rifle. With it was a PGM sound silencer and telescopic sight. In a pouch were twenty-five specially prepared rounds. He took the rifle out and handled it with care. He fitted the stock, which was removable to reduce the overall length when not in use. Then he fitted the silencer and lastly the telescopic sight. He checked the weapon in the minutest detail and found no faults. He was in business again. As carefully as he had assembled the rifle, he disassembled it, putting it back in the carrying box and then in the waterproof bag.

Marianne called down to them when she spotted the island. George went up to have a look. It seemed a long time from seeing the island to getting to it. As they moved closer, George took the controls and Marianne was relegated to a spectator. She was absorbing the whole process of handling the boat. She had found the island by keeping to the pre-determined course. George had shown her how to plot the route on the chart. On arriving at the island, George moved round it to stop over the reef. Johnny scoured the island with the binoculars. When George was happy with the location he shouted to Johnny to drop the anchor. It splashed into the water, and was followed by a heavy-duty rope. When the anchor hit the bottom, the rope was pulled tight and the boat was then at rest.

'We need to get onto the island as quickly as possible so you can check your equipment,' stated George.

Dan scanned the surrounding sea to see that there were no other craft visible at the moment.

George told Johnny to get the inflatable ready. He then looked at Marianne. 'Missy, we need you to stay onboard and keep a lookout for other boats heading this way.'

'No problem,' replied Marianne, 'it's boys and their toys, so you are best left to it.'

'Right,' said George, 'if you see any other boats coming in this direction, get on the radio; it's short range but be careful what you say: the sky has ears.' They checked the radios. Marianne felt she was playing a valuable part in the operation, having been trusted to take the controls on the journey over and now being left in charge of the boat.

George pointed out to Dan a landing place under some trees alongside a sandy beach. George and Johnny would go in the inflatable boat whilst Dan took the kayak. He launched the kayak over the side and pulled it close to the boat. He climbed down the dive ladder and then put one leg into the cockpit. Turning and hanging on, he got the other leg in, holding his body weight with his arms. He began to lower himself down but the kayak was moving about. He used his legs to control the craft and, when the time was right, lowered himself in. The kayak they had selected had a broad beam and was reasonably stable in the water. He knew he had to get used to getting into the small craft from a larger one; on the operation there would be equipment as well, but he would have help. He knew he would only get one chance.

It was a short distance to paddle to the beach where palm trees sprayed their thick palms out over the sea. It gave good shelter. Dan beached the kayak and climbed out and pulled it up onto the beach. George and Johnny were already there and had carried the sealed waterproof bag away from the water. Dan looked around for a suitable firing position. Across the other side of the sandy beach were some more trees; that was where he would put the target. Whilst Dan prepared the weapon, Johnny walked along the beach to a tree that Dan had pointed out. He tied a red shirt to the trunk. Meantime, Dan carefully opened the waterproof bag. Inside was the plastic box where the Hecate II rifle was housed. He took it out and fitted the stock. He then fitted the PGM sound silencer and the telescopic sight. Removing the magazine, he fed five of the rounds into it and replaced it onto the rifle. When it was safe, Dan found a fire position and set up the rifle, making adjustments to the sight. He then peered through the scope. When he was satisfied he lifted the bolt, pulled it back then pushed it forward, collecting a round and pushing it into the breach. The bolt was pushed to its down position. He pulled the stock into his shoulder and aimed through the sight. He paused, then fired. He was at home with the rifle, its discharge noise and the recoil. Accuracy was what mattered. He made the weapon safe and jogged across the beach to the tree with the red shirt. The round had struck in the centre. He jogged back. He made a minor adjustment. Neither George nor Johnny said anything, because there was nothing to say to a professional. Dan repeated the exercise five times, and each time the rounds found their target. The rifle and ammunition were put away as carefully as they had been removed, and were again sealed in the waterproof bag. Dan was satisfied that the weapon was ready.

George and Johnny went back to the boat aboard the inflatable, leaving Dan to master the kayak. When he arrived at the boat it was evident that he was not going to get any assistance, so he grabbed hold of the dive ladder and pulled himself up and out of the kayak. He then hauled the kayak up onto the boat. George walked over. 'OK man, had to leave you with the kayak so you could see how it handles. At the island we plan to help you, but if we can't then you now know the problems. Onboard the boat Marianne had been busy preparing drinks and food. She had listened to the rounds being fired, and had noted the time gaps in between. After the fifth round the time gap was longer, and she had judged that they had finished and would be back shortly. They were just in time, as she had been watching out for other boats and was about to use the radio because two boats were on the horizon, seemingly heading towards the island. Johnny stowed the rifle away in a safe place. Whilst they relaxed and indulged in the food and drink, they watched the two other boats arrive in the area. Having allowed time for the food to digest they dived on the reef. Marianne, Dan and George swum around the beautiful coral and masses of brightly-coloured fish and sea life. When they had exhausted their scuba tanks of air, they surfaced and prepared for the journey back to Guardinia.

The quay was busy with boats and people. Some were in transit to or from other islands, some were just spectators. There were fishermen and scuba divers. George carefully moved the boat alongside the quay, close to a boat that was slightly larger than the one George was captain of. Alongside, Johnny leapt ashore and secured the mooring-ropes. He then got back onboard and prepared the scuba tanks for re-charging with compressed air. People were beside the larger boat and taking boxes from a mini-bus and putting them on the boat. Marianne heard the voice first, then turned to look up at a man on the quay. She gasped and trembled, not wanting to believe her own eyes. She was in sheer panic. She was looking at Cornell. Her hair was down and she wore large sunglasses which changed her appearance. Steadying herself on an awning support post, she turned to look at Dan. He did not need to be told that something was wrong, he knew. He walked over to her and managed to glance up. Cornell had not looked at her but was busy giving orders to one other man. Once the boxes were transferred, the two men boarded the boat which was cast off and moved seawards. Marianne went to the other side of the boat, leaned over and was physically sick.

'It's OK,' said Dan, 'he didn't see you, and if he had looked at you he would not have recognised you.'

'I know,' she replied, 'it was the shock of him being there. I was shaking and he would have seen that. I could have caused a problem for the operation.'

'Well, he is on the way to Retreat, so we can get back to the hotel. You OK to walk or do we need a taxi?'

'No, I'm fine, we'll walk, I will feel better then.'

'Right, George, we are going. Thanks for a good day and I await your call.' Then Dan added, 'Is Johnny OK?'

'Yeh, the bastard who gave Missy a fright is the same one who attacked his wife; I had to hold him back.'

'Shit! Does he know what's happening?'

'I haven't told him anything, but he obviously knows something is going down.'

'OK, look after him and see you soon.'

'Right on man, you both take care.'

29

George parked the pick-up truck outside the hotel and bounced across to the reception. He asked to speak to Mr Chester about a scuba diving trip planned for the following day. Whilst George chatted up the girl on reception, she sent somebody off to deliver the message. Dan and Marianne were on sun loungers outside their room. Dan was given the message. He put on shorts and a T-shirt before making his way to reception. When he arrived he found George in full flow with the receptionist, and it appeared that he had secured a date. George greeted Dan like a long-lost relative as they walked over to a quiet part of the lobby. George said that the operation was on. He had to do a boat run that would depart in the early hours of the morning. He needed Dan to come down to the boat to check his kit. Whilst Dan went to find Marianne, George chatted to his new-found friend. Marianne decided to relax in the sun. Dan joined George and they went down to the boat.

On the boat, Johnny was preparing for the trip to the islands later that day and Dan joined George in the large cabin. Dan sat down with the black holdall George had given him. 'Please check the contents,' said George, aware that this was also important equipment. Dan opened the holdall and pulled out the items. He was impressed that it contained all that he had requested. Lightweight combat jacket and trousers, green shirt, lightweight boots, fighting knife, a web belt with two water bottles in pouches, two other small pouches for equipment, a scrim net for his head and shoulders, binoculars and a lightweight range-finder. He checked the smaller items that completed the kit. He replaced all of the items in the holdall. George said he would take care of it until it was needed.

George suggested that Dan come down to the boat just after midnight. The plan would be to drop him off just before dawn; the boat would continue to the island. He would pick up his passengers and transfer them back to Guardinia in time to check in to a hotel and have an evening meal, as they would be flying out the following day. This meant that Dan would have to paddle out to meet the boat in the late afternoon, but it was a risk they had to take. Dan had to do the job and get back to the hotel in time for the evening meal. Marianne could cover for him during the day, but he might be missed if he was away any longer. Dan did not hide the fact that he was concerned about having to be exposed in daylight, paddling a kayak in a vast expanse of sea. They also knew that if the target was not seen and the operation not completed, then they would have to do the whole thing again. That would really expose them all to additional risk.

George had confirmed that there were only two security people on the island, one the target, the other new and probably not keen to expose himself to a sniper. He would call for help but, by the time they got organised, Dan would have paddled out and be aboard the *Ocean Rover*. He concluded that the police would tell those on the island to take cover in the house and keep out of sight. Anyway, they were not going to panic over the death of a security guard, even if he was a well-connected assassin. Their investigations would only become really serious if a VIP with connections was involved. Dan asked if George knew who the VIP was. If he knew, he did not say. George said that Johnny would pick Dan up at midnight. He would park on a track down the road from the hotel. It was a track that led down to a small bay. It was well-covered with palm trees and undergrowth, and anybody seeing George's pick-up would think that he was having his evil way with a woman. George said; there was one more thing he stood and, walking to the stern doors he opened them, stepped outside and closed them. Dan sat in silence. The door that led down to the cabins opened and, even with the blonde wig and large sunglasses, he recognised the woman who entered. He grinned and stood. 'Hello, Dan,' greeted Rosie.

'What's going on, what are you doing here? Checking up on me?' enquired Dan.

Rosie smiled, 'No!' We have had additional intelligence, and I have to pass it to you in person.' She opened an envelope and removed the contents, a note and a photograph. She handed them to Dan.

He looked at the photograph and then read the note. He handed them back, giving no emotional response. 'You have the main target and that is the priority; however, if the second target becomes an option, then you can take the appropriate action. Our position is that the safe extraction of yourself is more important, and it is only if an opportunity arises that you should act. Are you in agreement with the request?' asked Rosie.

'Yes.' He now had a potential second target. He handed the photograph and note back.

'Thank you, I will see you after the job.' She spoke as she walked out through the doors and then left the boat to walk to a waiting taxi. With business done, the two men had a drink, then George took Dan back to the hotel.

Back in their room, having had a relaxing meal, Dan prepared himself for a departure just after midnight. He did not tell Marianne about his meeting with Rosie on the boat, or about the additional assignment. They just sat out on the veranda, soaking up the tropical paradise. When it was time, he stood and walked over to Marianne. 'You going to be OK?' he enquired.

'Yes, I have to keep up the pretence that you are about the place, and that you plan to get back tomorrow evening.'
'That is if everything goes to plan.'

'If there is a problem with George, send me a text. I know how to handle George's boat and I will come and find you.'

Dan grinned, 'You would as well.'

She smiled, 'Yes, I could test my boat-handling skills!'

Dan was going to leave his mobile phone behind but decided to take it after all. He then got out the map of Retreat Island and showed it to her. 'I will land about here, and once I have completed the job, will paddle out to this area. There is a lot of sea so you would only have a slim chance of finding me. Also, the alarm would have been given and, when the police caught up with you, they would want to know what you were doing, alone in George's boat and close to the island. They would want to know where I was.'

She looked at him, 'It's a chance if things go wrong, and I'll take that chance.'

He grinned, 'Best you stay here and deny all knowledge.'

She kissed him. 'Be careful and good luck.'

'I've never had a send-off on an operation like that before.'

He walked onto the beach and disappeared into the night. He found Johnny in the pick-up and, once he'd got into the vehicle, they drove down to the quay. Dan sneaked aboard the *Ocean Rover*. When he was ready, Johnny cast off and they headed out to sea. Their departure would not arouse any suspicion because the few boats like the *Ocean Rover* were on call at all hours. George opened the throttle and the boat powered ahead, leaving a white wake shimmering in the moonlight. Up on the open bridge, Johnny showed Dan a locker located under a seat. It was cleverly designed so that, whilst it was a locker, it had a carefully concealed compartment which would not arouse interest in a search. In fact, once properly in place, even a close inspection would not reveal a hiding-place. He tested getting in and being secured inside. It was not a place he relished being locked into. But, if needs must, then it was a confined place of safety. There was another such place where his weapon and equipment were already stored.

George was absorbed with a chart and a watch. He was calculating how long the trip would take so that he could drop Dan off under the cover of darkness. Dan sat up on the open bridge with George. The sea was favourable and it was a calm trip, the only movement a slow swell. The pair went over the plan again and Dan examined the radar. It should pick up the reflector but, if George failed to find him, then he had a small beacon that would show his location; however, if he used it, his position would be open to anything watching from the sky. That said, spotting a small kayak in the open sea was no mean feat even if George got close, so a couple of small smoke canisters had been put in the kayak for emergencies. Both hoped they would not have to resort to their use.

Dan relieved George at the controls whilst he went to check the boat. When he returned, they chatted to help pass the time. Lights of fishing boats and other craft could be seen, but nothing was close to them. It was the time when those moving drugs were most active, and above them satellites and aircraft would be searching for them. To the men and women who manned the tracking facilities in some far-off location, his boat would be located but would not arouse suspicion, as they would have information from the port authority about vessel movements to and from Guardinia. George was confident that they would not warrant any surveillance. It was a clear night and the heavens were studied with stars. George scanned the horizon with binoculars and fixed on some lights. He took over the controls of the boat and handed the bino's to Dan. He pointed in the direction of the lights on the horizon where there were only a few specks.

It was not long before Johnny arrived on the bridge with two mugs of coffee. Dan was not sure how he managed to climb the ladder with two mugs and the boat moving about. Johnny said that he was going to get the kayak ready. Dan's holdall had been removed from its hiding-place and was now on the bridge. He sat down and began to change clothes. The sizes were almost perfect and the boots were soft, durable and comfortable. The boots would go into the rucksack and he would use the neoprene boots for the water activities. Once dressed, he felt like a soldier again. He reflected that this time he was not part of a unit, a team who he would be responsible for, a family of sorts. Apart from the three other people, he was on his own for this operation.

Time seemed to pass very slowly before Retreat Island became a reality. Three outdoor lights shone, indicating its presence, and George throttled the engines back. The large white wake that had streamed out behind them diminished, and he guided the craft as close to the shore as he dared. He was aware that rocks lurked below the waves, and he wanted to keep the noise of the engines as low as possible in order to reduce the risk of being heard by anybody onshore. The beach they had on the starboard side was a reasonable distance from the location of the house, so unless they had a patrol out looking for intruders then they should be allright. Whilst the boat wallowed in the long, slow, gentle swell, George scanned the beach with his latest toy: a night vision scope. He was looking for a rocky outcrop that spilled into the sea. It was a landmark and offered some protection from prying eyes for Dan landing on the beach. It also offered some protection if things went wrong and the shooting started. George was also looking for any signs of human life.

On deck, Dan and Johnny were close to the stern, where the dark blue-coloured kayak was laying. It had a wider beam than most kayaks as it was designed as a fun craft to be used by tourists, so in addition to offering greater stability it provided a little more room for storage. Dan removed the rifle from its carrying case and placed it in the sealed bag, along with the detached stock. The scope, silencer and rounds were put into the rucksack. The rifle went into the kayak and Johnny secured the safety cord from the bag to the kayak so that, if it turned over, the weapon would not be lost. Dan noted that because of the kayak's limited length and the length of the rifle, he would be sitting on part of it. He concluded that he certainly would have a sore arse and delicate balls by the time he was able to get out of the tiny craft. The kayak would be low in the water with the weight of Dan and the rifle and so Johnny gave him a cockpit skirt. The kayak would be susceptible to flooding from any water washed over it and the skirt would seal it. They had decided that the rucksack would be sealed in a separate waterproof bag and be towed ashore.

When the *Ocean Rover* had virtually stopped in the water, Dan went down onto the dive platform which was just above the water line at the stern. The boat was rolling gently, but Dan was having to hold on to the ladder with only one hand. Johnny manhandled the kayak down from the back deck onto the platform, where Dan guided it into the water. With the kayak in the water, Johnny lowered the rucksack in its bag. He then climbed down onto the platform. George arrived at the stern, looking down at them as Dan pulled the kayak to the platform. He sat down on the platform and, with his legs over the side, he pulled the Kayak closer and put his legs into it. Even in flat, calm water, with the added weight already in it, it moved about. Johnny held the bow rope and Dan moved himself round to put his legs further into the craft. He then found George had come down onto the platform and, using a powerful arm, he helped to lift Dan as he slewed round, pushed his legs into the craft and sat down. Dan winced as he sat on the rifle but was grateful that the kayak's cockpit was large. Whilst Johnny held the bow line, Dan fitted the spray hood. Once that was done, George passed him the paddle which he could now use to control the craft, combined with his body movement. Once Dan was settled George dropped the rucksack bag into the water. Dan checked everything and gave a "thumbs-up" signal. Johnny let the bow line go; and Dan was on his own. Whilst Johnny watched as the kayak moved about in the sea, George had rushed back to the bridge to take control of the boat. There were no goodbyes or other gestures. Dan disappeared into the darkness. George got his bearings and gently pushed the throttle forward, keeping noise to a minimum. He steered the boat slowly out to sea and then towards the next destination.

The kayak was sitting low in the water but Dan had it under control. The bag bobbed on the surface on the end of its short tow-rope. He could see the lights, and paddled keeping them on his left and towards the right of the outline of the island. He could not make out any rocks as it was too dark and he was too far out. The task was to make the beach before the sun rose and exposed him landing. Sitting on the rifle did not add to the delights of paddling the tiny craft. His next problem would be landing the kayak on the beach. He wanted to run in on the waves and beach it, but did not know how big the waves were, or even if there were any at all. Getting out would have to be done as quickly as possible, as he did not want to tip over or be dragged back out to sea. It took some time before he thought he could make out the rock outcrop to his left and he steered in that direction. Then, in the gathering lightening of the sky, with the dawn about to start a new day, he spotted the rocks and paddled hard in their direction. As he approached, he kept clear and paddled alongside them. He could hear the small waves breaking onto the beach. As the noise got louder, he did his best to paddle hard so as to drive the kayak up onto the beach. The rocky outcrop was on his left and he had kept as close as possible to it. With a small wave coming in, he paddled hard and rode it up onto the beach. As the sea drew back, the bow of the kayak was on sand. He undid the skirt and pushed down, raising his body up whilst his legs pushed back. He was up and out of the cockpit and standing on a sandy beach. Waves had followed him in and gone out but they had not affected the kayak. Crouching on the beach, he pulled the bag with his rucksack to him and placed it inside the kayak. He was looking at the rocks in front of him, but could not see a place to hide the craft. He had anticipated that this might be a problem and prepared to drag the kayak further down the beach.

It was the snort, cough and spit of phlegm that stopped him dead in his tracks. He knew what it was; he had heard it many times before. It was either a bored security man out on patrol, or somebody out taking exercise along the beach clearing their nose or tubes. Whoever it was they meant danger, and could compromise the whole operation. He could not make out exactly where the noise came from and he could not see the outline of a person. He worked on the presumption that if he could not see them, they could not see him. Keeping low and moving slowly, he gently pulled the kayak back into the sea. Hanging on he moved further out. The rocks would provide direct cover from one direction and background cover from the other. Whilst it was not yet light, he hoped that neither he nor the kayak would stand out. He moved further out until the water was up to the top of his shoulder. He stopped, his eyes straining to see any movement. Then he saw the light of a torch and an outline of a figure. It was like a black shadow that moved from the other side of the rocks to his side. Whoever it was, it was early morning and they had stopped at the rocks. Dan clinging onto the kayak could only wait. The ghostly figure shone the torch out along the rocky outcrop and Dan waited, exposed and anticipating being spotted. He was at a disadvantage being in the water. Then the figure moved, with the aid of light from the torch, back the way it had come, and disappeared from sight. As soon as he considered it safe, Dan moved closer to the beach and then away from the rock outcrop, through the water and parallel to the beach, dragging the kayak. Time was running out as the sky was becoming lighter with every minute. He could be left exposed to prying eyes. With difficulty, he travelled some distance, until he could make out what he thought was undergrowth beyond the sand line. He moved to the beach and dragged the kayak onto the sand. He then moved as fast as possible across the expanse of fine sand and into thick undergrowth. Happy that it would offer the cover he needed, he ran back to the water's edge. He had planned to take the rifle and rucksack up to the undergrowth, then return and drag the kayak up. But he decided to do it in one go. He grabbed the bow rope and put it over his shoulder. Using all his strength, he dragged the kayak with its precious load over the white sand and into the undergrowth. Once under cover and out of sight he felt more comfortable. A sniper spends his active life moving and hiding, making best use of cover. With the kayak secure in the thick brush, he ventured back to the beach. He carefully checked in both directions then, keeping low, moved back to the water line. Moving back towards the safety of the vegetation, he swept the soft white sand with a piece of palm tree, removing any traces of the kayak having been there. He sat down beside the kayak as the dawn became a reality. He was just in time, and now he had to make sure that the kayak was well hidden.

He was wet and sand had begun to find its way into his clothing. He had worn light neoprene boots and he could feel sand inside them, rubbing his feet and ankles and making it uncomfortable to walk. He was considering the surprise guest on the beach, and concluded that it was probably one of the security men; probably Cornell, out for some exercise before the sun came up and the person he was guarding made demands on him. He reflected that it was luck that he had not beached and dragged the kayak about at the time the individual came along. He undid the sealed bag that contained his rucksack and removed it. From inside he removed a pair of thin gloves which he put on. If he had to dump any kit, he did not want his fingerprints or DNA on it. He pulled out the web belt which he placed round his waist. He felt the comfort of having the kit to hand, in particular the fighting knife. In one of the pouches were some additional rounds for the rifle. In another pouch was a night scope; and there were two water bottles in pouches. In the sac he took out the scope and silencer. He removed the boots and; having removed the neoprene boots and cleaned his feet of sand, put his land boots on.

He then felt a few items of food and left them in the rucksack. He found the Glock automatic handgun and pulled it out. He checked it and the full clip of rounds. There was a full spare magazine. He cocked the gun ready for use. He pulled out a scrim net which was designed to be worn on the head so as to break up the outline of both the head and shoulders. He put it on. The next task was to remove the rifle from its sealed bag and check it. Rifles endured some rough handling in combat and were built for that purpose. The Hecate II rifle was proven in combat in all parts of the world and used by the Legion. It had been tested to the limits, he knew: he had done most of the testing. As it became lighter, he stripped the rifle down and checked each part. He then put it back together again and fitted the stock, along with the scope and silencer. Once he was happy that the weapon was ready he slid it back into the waterproof bag. He finally made time for himself and had a snack and some water, then secured all of the unwanted equipment in the kayak.

He crept back to the beach and checked for any movement. There was none. Fine sand and an inviting sea comprised a holiday ideal. The sun was on its way up and he could already feel the warmth. Moving through the undergrowth, he could see that the kayak was not on or close to any sort of path and was well hidden. He put on the rucksack containing the essentials and then slung the rifle over his right shoulder. Then, crouched over and with the knife drawn, he began to move carefully towards the hill. He had spent most of his life doing what he did now. The Legion excelled in finding hills and mountains and marching men up and down them. He had the knife and the hand-gun for defence, but knew that if he had to use either then the operation would be compromised. Moving amongst undergrowth was slow work. Noise had to be kept to a minimum. Intelligence had said that security was minimum, but intelligence was not always right; and that was from people he did know. In this case it had come from people he did not know.

30

Dan had been moving slowly for about an hour and the island was peacefully quiet. He had located the path that led to the top of the hill, so he chanced going up it. He had noted that it did not look well-worn, and that there was vegetation either side that he could melt into if he had to. Checking behind him, he needed to see if he was leaving any boot marks. It was clear, but he still kept to the sides of the track. There was no intelligence as to whether there were any electronic security devices. As he gained height, he looked close in front as well as further along the path. He was at home in the hostile environment, lightly equipped but weighed down by a powerful weapon that could kill at long range. He stopped when he noted what appeared to be a narrower track, leading off to the left and probably around the hill. That should give him a line of sight to the house. It would also avoid the need to go to the top of the hill. He diverted onto it, and followed as it traversed round and upwards. He found some spots where he could see the property, but that meant that someone might be able to see him, albeit they would have to use binoculars. He found a particularly good line of sight and moved off the track, climbing uphill through the undergrowth. His eyes, skilled at spotting a suitable location were hard at work. Then he found a potentially good spot. He carefully moved into it and weighed it up. He had full cover of vegetation from the top of the hill behind and an uninterrupted line of sight to the house and the grounds. He was well clear of any used tracks and he had a clear view of the house, swimming pool and the grounds. He rested the rifle against some heavy branches of a tree that had probably succumbed to a hurricane in the past. He removed the rucksack. He checked for routes out, so that in the event that his position became compromised he could leave the location and make good his escape.

When that was done he found a comfortable spot and, using his binoculars, observed the house and surrounding area. He sat on the ground to do this and was aware that his rear end was still painful from sitting on the rifle. He studied the grounds and house from left to right, some of it obscured by bushes. The house was bungalow-style, single story with a tall roof. In one part, to the right as he looked at it, there were rooms in the roof space with dormer windows. They were probably the staff quarters. To be sure, he checked the plan that had been provided: he could see the guest quarters in front of him and that the staff were located to the right. There was a satellite dish providing television and communications located to the rear. It was out of sight for the guests, but he had a clear view. Scanning back to the left he could see the swimming pool area, but the side closest to him was hidden by a row of low bushes. He then spotted somebody. It was the pool boy, a male probably in his thirties. He could see from his mid chest to the top of his head. It meant that the target area was restricted. The body trunk offered the best target, but the head was preferred. By comparison it was small, and that reduced the chances of a killing shot on the first round. But a good head-shot killed, a body-shot could wound. In this situation it was the head, and his first round had to hit the mark and kill. If he missed, the target would get down behind cover and the operation would be compromised.

Dan decided that the only place he had no knowledge of was the top of the hill. Leaving the heavier kit, he moved out of his hide and climbed upwards. He was now exposed to the hot tropical sun when not under the shade of trees and bushes. Nearing the top he moved with caution, keeping in cover and only moving when he was happy that there was no risk to his security. As he reached the top, he found that the undergrowth had been cleared away and that there were fabulous views all round the island. A small shelter had been built, and it had a seat so that an occupant could sit and look down towards the house. He looked down towards where his hide was, to find that it could not be seen. A path followed a route down towards the house, whilst another rarely-used path went in the opposite direction. He assessed that, if there was proper security, then the hill would be manned. They could see any boats close by and probably even his kayak. Satisfied that he had all of the information he required, he carefully retraced his route back to his hide. As the day progressed it got hotter, even though he was in the shade. He continued to observe the house and its surroundings, scanning the pool area and house. The pool boy had long since finished cleaning when Dan spotted the first person to walk into the pool area. He watched through the binoculars to note that it was a male, well-built and in casual clothes. When he stopped and turned around, Dan could see that it was Cornell. He watched as Cornell walked around the pool area checking it. When he stopped, he looked towards the house. Dan looked in that direction and saw another male coming to the pool. It looked like the second, younger security man. Even from that distance, Dan could see that he was not of the same calibre as Cornell. He thought that the man would hide and run rather than put his neck on the line for some overpaid and overrated VIP. He joined Cornell and they looked around them. Satisfied that all was well, Cornell went to the house and entered whilst the other man walked around checking the gardens. For Dan, the target of his contract had been spotted. He would wait as long as possible, take the shot and then get the hell out. He decided that if he needed to and the opportunity arose, he would take out the second guard. That would leave him a clear run to get away from the island.

Whilst the second security man was in the pool area, Dan used the range-finder. It was not a sophisticated device but gave him valuable information. Dan checked his shooting position so that it was comfortable and concealed. He checked the rifle, the scope and the range. He made some minor adjustments to the scope. He slid the rifle into position and let it rest, then pulled the stock into his shoulder. Looking through the scope, he let his eye adjust to the single picture. He focused on the second security man. The man was new and unsure as to what he should be doing, unlike Cornell who was very relaxed about the place. The final adjustments to the weapon were made and he was ready. He checked his watch.

Cornell reported to the guests that it was OK to go out to the pool area. The first of the VIPs to leave the house was a woman. He had no idea who she was, as she wore a large straw hat that either covered her face or cast a shadow over it. In any event he was not interested. Shortly afterwards a male left the house. He wore a hat and sunglasses, so again Dan could not determine who it was. He joined the woman. They were obviously going to spend some time sunbathing. Lunch came and went, and the VIPs went for a walk down onto the beach in front of the house. There was no sign of Cornell, but the other security man had been in evidence in the background. He reflected that these must be considered lower-level VIPs, because if they were really important there would be more security.

Now was the time when he needed the couple to come back, or at least for Cornell to show his face. It was the couple who he spotted first as they walked back to their sun loungers, and as they sat down they were soon out of sight. He then spotted Cornell, walking through the garden towards the pool. He had been keeping an eye on the pair whilst they were on the beach. Dan raised the rifle to his shoulder and aimed at the general pool area. He was in the shooting position. In a well-practiced motion he lifted the bolt and slid it back, leaving the breach open. The action of pushing the bolt forward would normally lift a round out of the magazine and push it into the chamber. But the magazine was empty; Dan took a round from the small pouch, checked it carefully and slid it into the open breach. He then pushed the bolt forward and down into the closed position. The rifle was loaded and ready. He was working on automatic now. There were more rounds ready, once he had fired the one in the weapon. The safety was on and, with the stock pulled back into his shoulder, he looked through the sight; moving slightly, he aimed at a number of objects to test the weapon's position.

Cornell entered the pool area without a care in the world. This was a rest rather than a job and he was making the most of it. He didn't even mind the obnoxious VIPs he was guarding. His instructions had been clear. The pair thought they were very important but the word from the top was that they did not warrant proper security. They were expensive and therefore expendable. In fact, had Cornell not been sent for a rest, it would have been two security guard rookies that would have been on the island. Dan moved the rifle slightly in order to follow him. He disappeared behind some shrubs, to reappear as he progressed to stop. He was looking at where the couple were, and began to speak. He then moved a little closer, nonetheless appearing to be fully aware of his place in the pecking order. His head was in the centre of the scope, the cross hairs confirming it. Dan had done this so many times before; and now he had the man who had killed Finch; his father; Napoleon; his best friend in the Legion; and who had almost killed the woman who was supporting him back on Guardinia. He felt no anger; in fact he was devoid of any emotion. The target, the centre of Cornell's face was in his sights. He clicked the safety catch off, breathed carefully and slowly, then just squeezed the trigger. The effect was instantaneous. The weapon's firing pin struck the base of the 12.7mm round, which fired the primer that ignited the powder in the casing, that pushed the bullet along and out of the barrel and to its target. The reduced noise of the round firing and leaving the gun through the silencer followed, and the recoil of the gun into Dan's shoulder followed that. In effect, to Dan it sounded and felt as if it had all happened at the same time.

Cornell didn't hear any noise of any sort, nor did he feel any pain. The power of the charge that pushed the bullet through the air was such that as it entered the skull at the bridge of the nose, it created a small hole. Once the bullet was inside the skull, it caused the contents to explode and spray out of the larger exit hole at the back of the skull. Dan did not see the bullet enter, but through the scope saw the spray of blood and brain matter when the body was lifted and flung backwards into the swimming pool. It was a perfect shot and the target was dead. Having fired the first round, it was Dan's automatic reaction to lift the bolt and pull it back. The spent round was pulled from the chamber and ejected. He slid the next round into the chamber and pushed the bolt forward and down. Dan's sniper's instinct was in full flow. With a round in the chamber, he gently moved the rifle so that through the scope he could scan the line of bushes shielding the pool. He was now looking for the second target identified by the Foundation. He was as always amazed at how often somebody would stick their head up to see if they could see who had done the shooting. For the two VIPs, it would probably be their rush to safety which might expose them. The other security man would be under cover and Dan doubted if he would show his face.

The VIPs were riveted to their sun loungers as they experienced their main security man's head seemingly disintegrate before them. His body fell back and floated on the surface of the pool, its colour turning red around the shattered remains of his head. What had happened suddenly registered, and they both rolled onto the ground and moved up behind the bushes that hid them but offered no protection. The man looked about for the other security man, but he could not be seen. He had, in fact, taken cover behind the wall of the building. He looked about but realised that he could be exposed if he chose to move. There was no way he was going to put his neck on the line for a "fat cat" and his rude wife. He thought he had better do something, so he shouted, 'Are you OK?' There was silence, so he shouted again. A male voice responded, 'Yes, but Mr Cornell has been shot.'

The guard grinned; so Mr Perfect is not so perfect after all. He shouted, 'Keep down and out of sight'.

The man shouted back, 'What are you going to do about the situation?'

'There's not a lot I can do; that's a professional bloody hit man out there, and if we show ourselves he can take us out.' He thought for a moment, and added, 'You are probably the target.'

Dan could not hear the conversation, but moved the rifle round to the satellite dish and identified a box just under it. A wire came out and went into the building and would provide the communications link to the outside world. He raised the stock to his shoulder and brought the scope to bear on the box. He fired. The round struck the box, but Dan reloaded and put another round into it. It was a better shot; he hoped that communications were now out of action. The security guard took a few moments to realise that the rounds were not coming in their direction but towards the building. He knew that the communications would be the target. The man and woman were still hiding in an unprotected position. The guard shouted, 'He is shooting at the satellite dish to take out our communications.'

A couple of minutes later when Dan, who had reloaded, was using the scope to scan the target area and was considering getting out, there was a movement. In the centre of his scope there was a face. He was, for a fraction of a second, mesmerised. Even at long range through the scope he recognised the face. It was only the head that was visible. Dan steadied the rifle and the cross hairs of the scope centred on the face. His mind was focused. There was no thought process, this was a trained sniper doing his job. He steadied the rifle, controlled his breathing and squeezed the trigger. He could see that the round struck the target exactly where the scope had indicated. It was a clean head-shot from which nobody could survive. He slowly drew the rifle back and picked up the spent cases. Easing back into the shadow of the undergrowth, he removed the stock from the rifle and put both into the bag. He scanned the area with his binoculars. One body floated in the swimming pool, the other was hidden from sight. Time was now against him and he carefully moved back out of his shooting position. He slung his rucksack and the rifle over his shoulder, and with the glock automatic in his right hand, he moved, keeping to the cover of the vegetation, round the hill and back down the track to the kayak.

The security guard could hear the woman screeching and calling for help. He assessed the distance from where he was hiding to the bushes where she was. They would hide his location, if not provide any real cover. His body seemed to react before his brain and he ran, zig-zagging as fast as he could go across the open ground, and flung himself onto the ground behind the bushes. Working on adrenalin, he then scrambled along to the woman who had left the cover of the bushes and was holding the body of her husband. She was covered in blood. 'Are you OK?' asked the guard. He knew it was a stupid question. 'Let's get you back to safety behind the bushes and I will get your husband.'

She pushed him away, 'Go and get the bastard who did this, do your job!' she screeched.

He knew his first priority was to his client, and that that should come before his own life. But his client was dead. The woman was gripping her husband and would not be moved. He crawled back to the bushes and then along them until he had the shortest distance to run to be in the shelter of the building. He prepared himself and then dashed, anticipating that at any moment his life would be snuffed out. But he crashed through the door and into the safety of the building.

At the kayak Dan removed his web belt and put it into the cockpit. He might well need the water later. The remainder of the equipment he jammed into the rucksack and then put into the waterproof bag. He kept his boots on and jammed the neoprene boots into the bag. He removed the silencer and scope from the rifle, placed them in the waterproof bag and slid it into the kayak. He positioned it better, so that he was not sitting on it. Once he was ready, he dragged the kayak to the edge of the undergrowth. The sun was still shining but it was on the wane. He checked the beach. Nothing moved and there was no sound other than the sea. He put on the spray skirt and then dragged the kayak over the beach to the water's edge. He returned up the beach to hastily remove the drag mark from the sand. He pushed the craft into the water, just clear of the surf but where he could get into it without too much trouble. Once in, he paddled to keep the craft stable and fitted the skirt. Then the long, hard paddle to his rendezvous began, the waterproof bag of equipment being towed behind.

He had left no trace of having been on the island and now, apart from the noise of the sea and some seabirds, there was no sound.

The guard quickly found that the satellite communications were down. The sniper had done a good job. They had no direct contact with the outside world. He could not find any of the staff, and realised that they would have taken shelter as soon as they knew what was happening. He had not been allowed to bring a mobile phone to the island for security reasons. The company phone was in Cornell's pocket, and he was floating in the swimming pool. He reasoned that the woman VIP must have a phone, but he was not going to risk the dash across open ground to find out. The plan was that the company made regular checks with the island when they had a client in residence. If no communication could be made then people would be sent from Guardinia, because to get no response from Cornell would spell trouble. So he could sit tight and wait for some outside action.

The VIPs wife walked into the room. Covered in blood and looking like hell, she had however, regained some composure and asked what was happening. The guard explained that the satellite system was down and that Cornell had the only mobile phone. She said that her husband had one and that she would go and get it. The guard argued against going outside, but she reasoned that if the assassin had wanted to kill all of them, he would have come and done it by now. No, he was in hiding and awaiting a boat to come and take him away. She left the room. When she had left, the guard sneered and muttered, 'Smart arse.'

Dan had paddled hard; he anticipated some indication that he had been spotted but none came. He had been very lucky, but that might not last. Thankfully, the sea was calm with only a very slight breeze; but he knew that could change at any time. He checked his watch and noted that he was making good time. A look back and he could see that the island had got a lot smaller. He slowed the pace. This was now the critical period: he hoped that George was on schedule and that he could locate him amongst the vast area of sea. Dan had kept the binoculars out and they hung round his neck. He stopped paddling and scanned the sea but saw nothing. He checked his watch and decided that it was time to put up the reflector. Johnny had fitted a bracket with a hole in it. He pulled out the two sections comprising a lightweight pole and joined them together. He then, with difficulty, pulled out the reflector. It came folded but opened up to provide a reasonable-sized target. He fitted it to the end of the pole, which he then lifted and fitted into the hole. The sun was on its way down as the kayak wallowed in the swell. He noted that it was a strange feeling, to be alone when only three people on the planet had any idea of where he was. He had kept some of the water for this part of the operation, and had a swig and a snack whilst he sat waiting.

Even with the binoculars it was just a blip on the horizon when he first saw it. He would wait and look again. Yes, it was something, but still a good way off. He had spent his life waiting and so this period was quite normal. He looked again and saw that the blip was getting bigger. When he next looked he could make out that it was a boat, and that it was coming from the right direction. He also knew that, in that expanse of sea, they could easily miss each other. What if the passengers had not succumbed to having a sleep and were wide awake? It seemed an age, for what was clearly a boat, waiting to make progress. It was another age, sitting in the gentle swell and watching the boat head straight towards him. Then he could see through the binoculars that it was the *Ocean Rover*; and then he could make out George on the bridge, with his raised position giving good all-round vision. It came closer and Dan knew he had been found. A true master of the boat's controls, a grinning George slowed the boat down and manoeuvred alongside the kayak. Dan was very impressed with how George handled the craft. As it inched past, Johnny was waiting on the dive platform. Dan paddled as hard as he could to close the gap and then threw the bow line. It arched up, but on its downward loop it missed. Johnny laid on the platform and, with Dan paddling as hard as he could, the bow of the kayak made it and Johnny found the line and pulled it in.

Dan dumped the reflector and pole over the side, then undid the skirt. Johnny pulled on the rope as the kayak came alongside. Johnny grabbed him and hauled, whilst Dan pushed up from the kayak and was up and onto the dive platform. It was not a graceful return to the boat. He removed the skirt and threw it into the cockpit. He then managed to get hold of the line which was attached to the rucksack bag, and pull it to the boat. He lifted it from the water and jammed it into the front of the kayak cockpit. Johnny told Dan to hold the bow line whilst he dropped three heavy weights into the cockpit. They caused the kayak to wallow very low in the water. Dan then paid out the line, allowing the craft to drift back. A pull on the line by both men made it dip down at the stern. Water flooded in and, combined with the weights, caused it to capsize. The trusty craft and the incriminating evidence sank to the seabed. The action had taken only a few minutes, but George was relieved when he could power up the engines as the two men climbed up onto the back deck.

Dan moved quickly up to the bridge, shook hands with George and opened the locker. It was all prepared and ready for him. George told him it was safe for the time being, as his passengers had been drinking all day and had only dropped off to sleep half an hour before the pick-up. George wanted to know what had happened; Dan explained that Cornell was dead and that he had taken out a second target prior to his escape. George did not want details. Cornell was dead and that was all that mattered. Johnny appeared, again carrying mugs of coffee. He was told the news and shook Dan's hand to such a degree that he began to spill his coffee. When he had finished his coffee George told him to throw the mug over the side. He did not want any evidence on his boat. Dan changed his clothes and Johnny put them in a bag along with a weight: they also went to the bottom of the sea. He was in swim shorts and a T-shirt.

They were making good progress when George spotted a boat heading in their direction. He picked up the binoculars and identified that it was one from the island. He turned to Dan, 'I am expecting that boat to be carrying police.'

'If it is the police, will they stop us and search us?' enquired Dan.

'Yes: we are coming from the direction of the island, and they will have been notified. That's where they are going. There are not many policemen or women on Guardinia; they have to get help from other islands, and that all takes time.'

With the two boats making a good closing speed, Johnny helped Dan get into the hiding-place and gave him a bottle of water. He grinned, 'Don't drink too much: you can't come out for a pee, and if you do it in there it will smell.' Once the panel was in place and secure, he replaced the life-jackets in the locker. Dan was not claustrophobic, but it was not the best place to be. He felt the engines throttle back and the boat slow down. He could only wait and remain quiet.

The voice on the end of the megaphone had summoned them to stop. George did as ordered and the *Ocean Rover* slowed to a stop, to move gently in the swell. As the other boat closed in, George waved to the captain of the boat who was a friend, one of those from the quay. Had George been at the quay, he might well have been hired by the police: it was luck of the draw. A small inflatable was launched and, with three policemen crammed aboard, the small outboard motor powered it to the stern of the *Ocean Rover*. Johnny took the rope and held it tight, and two of the policemen used him to help steady them as they made the transfer across. When two policemen were across, the third cut the engine and made the transfer. Johnny then let out the rope, allowing the inflatable to move away from the boat. Two of the policemen were from Guardinia and knew George, as he saw them most days. The third policeman was an inspector and was in charge. George did not know him. The inspector introduced himself and asked who was on board, where they had come from and at what time had they left. George answered with fact. He was then asked if he had been close to Retreat Island. He answered that they had passed the island, but not really close because of the rocks. George asked why they had been stopped. He was told it was just routine. In all the years he had been travelling between the islands, he had never been stopped; but he considered it best not to press the subject further. The inspector gave orders to the two policemen to search the boat. He said that he wanted to see the passengers. Johnny led the way down to the day lounge, where he left the inspector whilst he went below to the cabins to get the passengers.

A policeman who was chatting with George on the bridge looked around. He went to the locker with its seat cushion on top. He tugged at the top and it lifted. When it was opened he could see lifejackets. He removed a couple and lifted those below. He did not see the panel which blended in with the shape. Peering into the box, he was so close to Dan. On the other side of the panel, Dan could hear that somebody was rummaging about in the locker. Sweat poured from him as he lay hot and cramped in a space that was probably smaller than a coffin. The policeman, happy that nobody was hiding in the locker replaced, the lifejackets and closed the lid. Below, in the day cabin, the inspector confronted the four passengers. They were not happy at being dragged from their beds when they found that they had not yet arrived at Guardinia. The inspector did not get to exert his authority very often, so he was making the most of it. Realising that the inspector was not going to give way, they explained that they had been on the boat all day, and had partied until it was time to make the sea journey to Guardinia. Once underway, they had had more drinks, then gone below to lay down and sleep off the effects of a busy day and to pass the time of the sea journey, where there was nothing to look at. Passports were checked and notes taken of what they had to say. The inspector assessed those he faced: two overweight city types, each with a trophy wife; they were not capable of carrying out an operation that required them to go ashore and kill two people with a sniper rifle. The policemen, having searched the boat, did not find anybody else, nor any weapon or equipment. The inspector directed his policemen back to the inflatable boat. He told George that he might want to speak to him again, but that he could continue to deliver his passengers. Four annoyed passengers had already gone back to their cabins, and the policemen had returned to their larger boat. Once clear, George opened up the throttle and powered the *Ocean Rover* on its journey.

31

At the farm house in a remote part of America, Col Lee Chambers Jnr was wakened from sleep by the telephone ringing. It did not bother him: his whole life had been disrupted with moving from one place to another, and at all hours of the day and night. This was no different. He picked up the receiver and gave a clipped response. 'Yeh.' He heard the voice but did not recognise it. 'Who are you?' he demanded.

'I'm a company security guard on the island of Guardinia.'

Chambers knew immediately who he was, a new boy under the wing of one of his key men. He also knew that there was trouble, as Cornell would not have given out the telephone number. 'Tell me what's happening,' he demanded.

'Cornell's dead,' the security guard replied, awaiting a verbal tirade. But none came.

Instead, Chambers steady voice, hid his anger, 'How?'

'A sniper,' the guard paused, 'took the shot from the hill. It was a head shot and blew him into the swimming pool. It was in the open so I could not get to him, and I had to look after the VIPs.'

'OK, the VIPs are safe, that's one plus.' There was a long pause of quiet before Chambers spoke again, 'You still there?'

The guard replied, 'Yeh,' he then drew a breath, 'he got the male VIP as well.'

Chambers swung his legs out of the bed and sat up, 'Repeat that,' he demanded.

'He shot Cornell and then, when the male VIP put his head up to have a look, he was shot as well. The female VIP is safe.' Then, as a second thought, he added, 'He also shot out the communications system. I found this number in Chuck's stuff and I am using the female VIPs mobile phone.'

Chambers knew that the call was routed, and that it could never be traced back to the farm or to himself. 'What about the sniper?'

'Don't know, I had a VIP to look after and two dead bodies to deal with.'

'So a hired gun gets onto the island, takes out two people and then gets away; and you have no information as to how.'

'It must have been by boat.'

Chambers was slowly shaking his head. In all his years he had never lost a client or, for that matter, had one harmed. Now he had lost a client and a key member of his team. Then, on top of that, he had some idiot kid out on the island who had clearly panicked and failed to do his job. 'OK, who knows about this?'

'The police. We have them on the island. It's a big case for them, so I expect it will be in the news anytime.'

'You stay where you are, don't speak to the media and be very careful if you speak to the police. Destroy any reference to this phone number. If they need details, give them one of your cards and they can contact the organisation. I'm going to get some people out to you. He paused to let it sink in, then added, 'You got all that?'

'Yes, sir.' The phone went dead.

Chambers put the phone down and reflected on the conversation. He then walked along the passage to another room and went in. He shook the occupant out of a deep sleep. 'We've got trouble, need to get the comms up and running.'

From a deep sleep, the nerdy-looking man was up and out of bed. When Chambers used the word trouble, it was for real and you did not ask questions. The next call would be the most difficult. He pressed the buttons on the phone and listened to the ring tone. A crisp, wide-awake voice answered. Chambers identified himself and asked to be put forward to his boss. He waited until a gruff voice spoke at the end of the line. There were no introductions or pleasantries. 'Do you know what time it is? This better be good.' It was not good, and Chambers could sense the displeasure at the other end as he recounted events in detail. Heads were going to roll, and he himself might well be in the firing-line.

The boss gathered his thoughts before speaking. 'Get a clean-up team in asap.'

'We're doing that as we speak,' responded Chambers.

'Deal with the security individual: we don't want any loose ends, nobody mouthing off in some bar.' There was a moment's silence. 'Find out who wanted either the client or our man taken out. It may well be the client, as he was hated by so many; so that will be a long list.'

'Both have a track record to warrant a hit, but I agree that the client was probably the target and our man removed for safety. Whoever wanted the hit had good intel, and whoever did the hit was good. We are on the case. The man we lost was a real good man.' Chambers lacked any emotion as he spoke, but skilled operatives who could "do the job" were not easy to find.

'OK, get on with it and keep me informed. You know who I have to call now, and that ain't gonna be pleasant.'

The call was finished and Chambers was relieved. He could now concentrate on dealing with the problem. He wandered along to what was termed the comms centre. His one and only operative was up and hard at work contacting people. The coffee was on. Chambers poured himself some.

'I've activated Alpha Zulu and they are on their way to the island. They will give me an update as soon as they are in the air. The local police are on the ground and have requested back-up so, that will take some time. We have a local contact in the police, and I have requested a list of everybody staying on Guardinia and the other islands. That's gonna take time. I presume the VIP was the target, and that our man was silenced to allow whoever did the hit to get away.'

'OK, we need a list of countries, organisations and individuals who would want the VIP taken out,' added Chambers.

'His file noted him as a political project, although not now a high-risk one. I get the impression that he was a pain in the arse. You noted it as low-key and assigned Cornell to baby-sit for a couple of weeks. We even sent a rookie down for Cornell to assess.'

Chambers nodded his agreement. 'You need help here, son?'

'I've already called backup and they should be here any time.' He turned back to get on with the task that had been dumped on the organisation.

Chambers picked up the files on Cornell and the VIP and began to read the contents of both. Cornell could not easily be identified; the VIP was different: he had upset a mountain of people.

32

With the sun having gone down below the horizon, Marianne had showered and dressed for dinner. She poured out two drinks and waited for Dan to return. She had no idea how the operation had gone, and she knew that if any communication came it would mean really big trouble. Nothing had been heard so she assumed everything was going to plan. She had thought through what Dan may have encountered. Was the target still on the island? Had he been visible and still for long enough for Dan to get a crucial shot? She had been briefed on what to do if things had gone wrong and Dan was caught. She was aware that if he did not return to the hotel, they would soon be able to link her with him. It was all very well her saying she did not know what he was up to, but she could be implicated and the pressure would be on. She reflected that the company that employed Cornell would want revenge, and that they would send somebody, out of the Cornell mould, to find and kill her. It was what they did. She had managed the day well, from getting up and ordering breakfast for two in the room. When the breakfast was delivered, the young room-service waiter had entered the room and would have seen that two people had been in the bed: men's and women's clothes lay about, and somebody was in the shower which she had left running. She ate some of her breakfast, and put Dan's in a plastic bag and into her suitcase, to be disposed of later. The maid cleaned the room and, whilst she could not have seen Dan, she would have concluded that he was about. They did not always take lunch, so that was not a problem, and their little private beach area offered some privacy. But could she cope with more than one day? There were lots of "what if's and but's". She busied herself and laid out Dan's clothes, so that when he got back, if he got back, he could shower and change, and they could go out to dinner.

She was not expecting a knock on the door, and it was after the second knock that she walked over to open it. Dan would not have knocked. The events in Paris flashed through her mind as she reached for the door-handle. It was a hotel, a public place and there were people about, so she opened the door. She was face to face with a policewoman, dressed in a neat white uniform. She was a young woman and had probably not been in the job very long. Marianne fought to keep control as she stood waiting for bad news. The officer's face brightened, 'Excuse me, ma'am, but I need to check your passports. Can I come in?'

Marianne was relieved and opened the door, allowing the policewoman to enter. The room maid, who had been standing behind, followed the policewoman officer into the room. She was carrying what appeared to be a list of all the visitors in the hotel and the rooms they occupied. Marianne crossed the room to the built-in wardrobe, opened it and then opened the room safe. She withdrew two passports and handed them over. 'Is there anything wrong?' enquired Marianne.

'Just a routine check,' was the dry response.

The policewoman checked her passport and compared the photograph. She handed it back. She then opened Dan's passport. 'Where is Mr Chester?' She enquired looking towards the bathroom, which appeared to be empty.

'He's not here,' replied Marianne.

The police officer walked across to the bathroom and

looked in. 'I can see that, ma'am, do you know where he is?'

'He went for a run on the beach and a swim but he has not come back yet.'

'He went for a run and a swim! It's a bit late for that, isn't it? It's dark outside.'

'He does that sort of thing, but has been longer than I expected.'

The police officer was not happy. She turned to the maid, 'Have you seen Mr Chester today?'

The maid thought about it for a second and then answered, 'Yes, this morning.'

The policewoman stood looking at the maid. 'Are you sure?' The maid nodded in the affirmative. She looked back at Marianne. There was somebody missing and said to be out running and swimming when it was dark. Something was not right. She spoke in her best official voice. 'Mrs Chester, you are going to have to come with me whilst we look into your story.' She walked to the door, indicating that Marianne should join her. Marianne had no option. There was nowhere to run and hide, no safe place. They were on an island. If they searched her case they would find the remains of breakfast, and how would she explain that? They were about to leave the room when the doors to the veranda opened and Dan entered, dripping water onto the doormat. 'Hi darling, sorry I was so long,' he quipped. Then he looked at the policewoman. 'What's wrong?' he asked. 'Has something happened?'

Before Marianne could answer, the policewoman stepped forward. She checked his face against the photo in his passport. 'Everything is fine, sir. It is a routine passport check and you were not here. You are now, so all is accounted for.' She handed Dan's passport to Marianne and made for the door. She turned, 'Oh, sir, it's not advisable to go swimming when it gets dark. Good night.'

The door closed; Dan did not wait but dashed to the

bathroom. He relaxed under the shower, realising that he had made it back just in time. Marianne stood for several moments, rooted to the ground in shock. She then walked to the bed and slumped down, her brain whirling in overdrive with all sorts of thoughts. Did the policewoman see her panic, although at the time she felt as though she had maintained an outward appearance of control? Why were the police checking who was on the island? She realised that they would need to investigate a death, a killing, even though it was only a bodyguard. She heard the shower stop and Dan emerged from the bathroom. She leapt up and flung her arms round him. He was not used to such a reaction and did not really know how to deal with it. What he needed was a drink, then a meal; but Marianne needed reassurance that everything was OK. Dan dressed and they were soon at the restaurant, being guided to their preferred table. They acknowledged people as they went and could not miss the buzz of rumour and speculation about the police check. Nobody knew the truth as the police stuck to the story that it was a routine check, but even the staff had never known a check to be carried out before. Back in their room, Dan gave some of the details of the day's activities, but left out the important bits like the taking out of a second target. He did say that there was a bonus, but did not elaborate. Marianne had got over spending the day covering for him and then the passport check, so he was not going to rock the boat. The following morning might be a different matter.

As the sun rose to bring the dawn of another hot tropical day, Dan pounded the beach on his run. He did it every day and today would be no different. Marianne woke to find him gone but realised that he would be exercising. Today there was to be no dramatic action, so they could relax. In truth, Dan wanted to be off the island and back to the relative safety of Europe. The police would be checking those who left the island, and to go a few days early would, without a solid reason, raise suspicions. They decided that they would wait and see what was happening before making a decision. Having showered and dressed, they walked through the gardens to the restaurant to have breakfast. There was no hurry because on the island nobody hurried. Dan was expecting something to be said at breakfast, where developing news and subsequent rumours would emerge. As they approached the restaurant, looking to find a quiet table, there were other guests standing at the entrance looking at a notice-board. Once they had read the message they moved on so that, when Dan and Marrianne reached it, the message was clearly visible. Marianne read the words and immediately understood Dan's meaning of "got the job done with a bonus". The words in bold, black, hand-written letters said, 'The former British Prime Minister, Neil Proffitt, was killed yesterday, along with a security man, in a shooting incident on Retreat Island. Suspects have been arrested and the police are continuing to investigate.' Dan held Marianne's hand and guided her to their favoured table. His brain was already in escape and evasion mode.